Gratuity Not Included

—m—

Ricardo Estrada

To my brother, Daniel,
for the laughter we shared
during challenging times

I

Marcelo

Marcelo slammed the door of his Mustang convertible and booked across the sun-drenched parking lot. His flushed, sweaty face simmered from the heat radiating off the tarred lot. It had been a bummer of a day. The air conditioner in his ragtop had conked out that morning, and the mercury had shot into the nineties—not unusual for the thirteenth of May in St. Petersburg, Florida. Of all the days for the air to crash, it had to be on his twenty-first birthday. But if he bagged the promotion it would shoot the day to the max. He shoved open the double doors of the restaurant's rear entrance and marched in. Connie, the dining room manager, stood by the time clock.

"Hi, Connie, did I—"

"Sorry, you didn't get the job."

That couldn't be true. He was super ready to be assistant manager. "Are you jiving me?"

Her face told him it was no joke.

Marcelo groaned and stared at the freshly mopped red-tiled floor. Sweat bathed his face and his white shirt stuck to his spine. He swiped the perspiration off his face with his sleeve. They faced each other by the time clock while waiters and waitresses in black slacks and white shirts punched in for the Saturday night shift. Two of them must've read the frustration on his face and lingered with curious ears.

Why had he asked her in public? He could've avoided open humiliation. He'd wandered into that one like a deer into a gator's mouth at a watering hole.

"You could look a bit disappointed," he said. "Unless you had another pony in the race."

He could've waited until tomorrow for the news bulletin instead of having his birthday balloons popped with pointed reality. Connie touched his arm and gazed into his eyes.

"I think you'd do a nifty job," she said.

In the last year he'd filled in in every department: taking drink and food orders and serving customers in the dining room, mixing cocktails and pouring beer and wine behind the bar in the lounge, and grilling steaks and broiling fish in the kitchen. He could run the place from opening to closing.

The ticking of the time clock grew louder.

"I don't know why you didn't get it." Connie shrugged. "All I know is that Carmine said you didn't, and he said not to talk to Sergio because both of them agreed."

Once Carmine and Sergio made a decision, they never went back on it. If they fired someone, that poor soul went into the history books. So Marcelo didn't expect them to reverse a decision for him. And he'd rather take a stroll through the depths of hell than beg Carmine. But Carmine wouldn't be getting off too easy: he'd have to tell Marcelo the reason to his face.

"You mess with a white shark and you get the teeth." Marcelo abruptly darted off.

"Don't have a cow over it. Anyway, he won't be in for a couple of hours."

Connie's words tripped him up in midstep. He stopped and leaned back on the wall, not caring whether his white shirt got soiled. He hung his thumbs from the pockets of his black slacks and lowered his gaze to the drying tiled floor. That was not what he wanted to hear. After a couple of hours fuming, he'd be ready to unleash Hurricane Marcelo on Carmine, and he'd be justified. He had to keep it real, so he pushed off the wall and punched in. "What's my station?"

"It's C, and I'm sorry," Connie replied with an apologetic tilt of her head.

He took his black vest and bow tie from his locker in the employee restroom and headed to the lobby. Crossing the deserted kitchen, Marcelo passed pots, pans, and ladles of various sizes hanging above shiny stainless steel tables. As he slid on his vest and tie, he caught sight of Tyrone, the kitchen manager, in the back.

"Carmine doesn't know it yet, but I'm going to have a word with him," Tyrone shouted. "Can you dig it?"

Privacy didn't exist in the place. News and rumors spread fast as a summer virus and without discrimination.

"He can't screw my man Marcelo like that. You'll get the low-down when I talk to him."

With a terse nod, Marcelo crossed the cushioned, red-and-black carpet of the dining room, where eighty tables draped in white linen spread from corner to corner and booths lined the walls. They were set with polished silverware, china bread plates, and sparkling wine glasses. Candle flames in clear holders swayed to the air-conditioning current. A circular salad bar sat in the center of the room.

Jim, one of the busboys, placed linen napkins folded like two-sided pyramids on the table settings. When he noticed Marcelo, he scooped up the gray bus pan overflowing with napkins and caught up with him. Grease spots decorated the bottom half of Jim's white shirt and his gray pants were soiled on the sides where he'd wiped his hands on them. Jim didn't have a red apron on yet, which would hide most of the mess.

"Haven't you heard of a washing machine?" Marcelo asked.

Jim's hairless teenage face stretched into a goofy smile. Red blood vessels fragmented the whites of his eyes like lightning rods.

"I've got some fine smoke, Gainesville Green," he whispered, looking around. "I've got a doobie if you want to try it out. It's primo stuff."

"You've got me confused with somebody else." Marcelo hadn't smoked weed in six months, but Jim never failed to mention his inventory, even though Marcelo's response never varied. "And drop me from your customer list." He headed into the lobby.

"You used to be so hip, man." Jim shook his head and returned to his napkins.

At the cashier's counter, Jackie leaned back on a stool and filed her glossy, red fingernails. She glanced at Marcelo over her wire-rimmed glasses and then stopped filing to check out her nails. "What's the buzz?" she asked. "Why didn't you get the job?"

"Doesn't anybody say hello anymore?"

Her eyes widened. "Did you talk to Connie?"

"Yeah, she didn't say hello, either." He took a stack of checks labeled "C" and put them in his black check holder.

"I thought you'd get it. You've never missed a day of work."

Not missing one day was cool city in his book, and that made him super proud. Even the sun in the Sunshine City wasn't as reliable. The *Evening Independent* newspaper gave away its next edition when the sun failed to shine in St. Petersburg in any twenty-four-hour period. He'd completed twelve months without missing a single day and by beating Mother Nature. Not even Sergio or Carmine could boast that, and they owned the place.

"I'd love for you to be my boss." Jackie winked. "That'd be radical, even if you're a bit younger than me."

"You know I'm not in my thirties, right?" He flashed a smirk. "Let me know when Carmine gets here." He returned to the carpeted dining room.

When the Vineyard Restaurant kicked off its grand opening fifteen months ago, in early 1977, Marcelo hadn't paid much attention. Since he'd begun as a busboy at fifteen at the Owl Restaurant, he'd seen dozens of places open with a big bang, only to close with a fizzle. And because he worked in the business, he usually waited six months to see how a restaurant turned out before he applied there. But the Vineyard had made him stop and take notice weeks after it opened. It had quickly become known for first-rate seafood and steaks and for having the city's best salad bar.

Marcelo refilled the glass salt and pepper shakers in his section. Four tables, all four-tops, with a seating capacity of sixteen made up station C. If he averaged twelve people a seating, he'd roll in the dough and have a decent night. The calculator in his mind estimated his desired earnings when Jackie appeared. She blinked behind her glasses.

"Carmine's not coming in tonight." She winced. "But Sergio is."

"Doesn't anybody have good news around here?"

"If you need to talk to somebody, you've got to talk to Sergio. Sorry." She left saying something about how it wasn't her fault.

Marcelo sighed and retreated.

In the service area behind the dining room, waiters and waitresses prepared for the dinner shift: making coffee, stocking up on water glasses, and filling bread warmers. They moved in and out of the bustling kitchen with supplies in hand. The scent of fresh lemons hung in the air. Barry, in his waiter uniform, sliced lemons for seafood and iced tea on a wooden cutting board—his sidework and contribution in preparing the place to open. A half-full aluminum bowl next to the board held the cut citrus.

"What's shaking?" Marcelo asked.

"Man, that Carmine's bogus," Barry said. "You should've gotten that gig. That Sergio and Carmine have it in for both of us."

"I wouldn't go that far."

Barry's round face showed his discontent while his stocky body, in the shrunken shirt that squeezed his neck and biceps, continued on task. A calloused ear gave a window into his time on the Pinellas High Devils wrestling team.

"Man, if you want to split and go party for your birthday, I'm there," Barry said. "You know they're just using us as long as they can."

"I'll live," Marcelo said.

"Remember that wussie manager the time we walked out at the Lamp Post restaurant?"

"How can I? You won't let me forget." Marcelo poured a glass of iced tea.

"That pompous guy was riding my butt all night. Then he told me off because I wouldn't pick up an extra four-top on the other side of the room. Man, I lost it. The wuss wouldn't go outside and settle it like a man, but I didn't care. I was ready to let fists fly in the middle of the crowded dining room. The customers would've gotten a better show than at the Showboat Dinner Theatre." Barry snorted and tossed a handful of lemon wedges he'd sliced into the bowl. "You quit and walked out with me that night, remember?"

"That restaurant was going downhill anyway."

When they got jobs at the Vineyard, they'd made a pact to take care of business, hoping to someday cut the opening ribbon on their own place. Nothing fancy, just a breakfast-and-lunch counter downtown. In time, their partnership would flourish into a fine-dining eatery with a late-night liquor lounge and live entertainment. Marcelo wouldn't ask a friend to walk out anymore and hoped Barry felt the same way. They had plans.

"Thank you, and come back soon." Marcelo laid the check on a tip tray on the linen-covered four-top. He glanced up and spotted Sergio at the cash register, greeting waiting customers and talking to Jackie and Connie.

Barry approached Marcelo, arms hugging a round hand tray. "Need me to tag along?"

Marcelo shook his head and made his way to the front. His palms sweated, his breathing deepened. He had to be firm—dig his heels in and hold his ground. Sergio glanced up from the cash register. He wore his usual blue pinstripe suit and had dark hair to his shoulders.

"Come with me," Marcelo told the shorter guy and cringed at his cheap cologne.

They stepped outside in front of the busy 34th Street traffic. Marcelo led the way. The hot, humid weather embraced him as the orange sun dipped into the Gulf of Mexico.

Marcelo's heart thumped. He turned and faced his boss underneath the marquee sign. On it, a giant neon lobster opened and clamped its claws at drivers on the road. Marcelo narrowed his eyes. A rattled Sergio stepped back. Barry stood outside the front door, out of Sergio's view.

"Why didn't I get the job?" Marcelo could hardly suck air into his lungs in the humidity.

"We...we haven't made a decision yet. What are you talking about?"

The response disarmed him. "You haven't decided?"

"Who said you didn't get it?" Sergio asked.

"Carmine. That's what Connie told me."

"I don't know anything about that." Sergio raised an eyebrow. "But you best get to work before you lose the job you've got. Let me check this out."

They returned to work.

Marcelo removed salad bowls from a family of four. The toddler in the high chair had crushed soda crackers and knocked the crumbs off his tray all over the carpeting, kicking his legs and slamming his fists. His parents were the only ones amused at the Kodak moment.

"Come to the office when you can," Sergio said as he passed by.

They walked to the back of the kitchen. A desk lamp illuminated the desktop covered with invoices and catalogues. Unopened boxes of dishes, glasses, and silverware crammed the back wall to the ceiling. Two barstools with broken limbs, one inverted on the other, awaited their unknown fates in a corner. The radio was on; "Staying Alive" by the Bee Gees was playing. The song had been all over the airwaves for months. Sergio shut it off and sat behind the desk with a blank expression. He pointed for Marcelo to take a seat. Marcelo hesitated and sat on the edge.

"Carmine says you're too wet behind the ears for the job, that you're buddies with everybody, and that they'd step all over you. Still, he should've talked to me before jumping the gun. I'm sorry."

"He doesn't know me." Marcelo felt as if he'd failed an important school test. "What does the other brother think?"

"I...I believe you'd do a decent job, but Carmine's my brother and a manager, and we got to agree." Sergio leaned back in the high-back chair. "You're the best worker we've got. Listen, I got him to agree that we don't need to hire until the fall. It might turn out after all."

A smile emerged on Marcelo's face for the first time since he got to work, but then evaporated.

"I wanted to tell my dad I had this job so he'd get off my back for quitting college and having no future like he says."

"You've got a future here. Listen, I have a great management plan, and I want to make this the best restaurant in town. When people come to Saint Pete, I want them to say, 'We've got to eat at the Vineyard.' Don't be in such a rush, OK?" Sergio stood and met his eyes. "Get to work, it's Saturday night!"

Marcelo returned to the dining room to see it filled to capacity. It pleased him to see people talking, laughing, toasting. Across the way, Barry served surf-and-turfs to a teenage couple, both in awe of the Florida lobster tails and filet mignons on their plates. An eager crowd had gathered in the lobby, and Sergio offered glasses of wine to people waiting to dine. Connie took names from people surrounding the podium. She caught Marcelo's eye, smiled, and then resumed her work.

Barry strolled up to him and pulled off his bow tie. "You ready to rock and roll?"

"No, I'm parking it here a while longer," Marcelo said.

"Cool. I've got to make up the dough I just paid Jim for this bag of Gainesville Green." He patted the side pocket of his vest.

Marcelo frowned. "How about saving for our place?"

"Yeah...that comes off the top first." Barry elbowed him. "Check out the new waitress Connie hired. Hubba hubba."

"Oh, yes." Marcelo nodded. "I've noticed her already. Nice."

Marcelo noticed number 4 light up on the server board in the dining room. One of his orders waited for pickup in the kitchen. He headed for the linoleum-floored service area, threading through waiters and waitresses crossing one another, avoiding collision, carrying cocktails and covered dinners on hand and shoulder trays. With red cheeks, Jim huffed and puffed, his skinny arms carrying a loaded bus pan into the kitchen. Marcelo followed him in.

"I'll let Carmine know he shouldn't have done you that way." Tyrone wore a white kitchen uniform and a hairnet over his Afro. He turned steaks with a pair of tongs. "I'd like to pound his face like a cube steak for my own satisfaction."

"Pop a Quaalude and mellow out. You might have to wait till the fall for that, if I don't get the job then." Marcelo garnished his plates with endives, covered them, and shouldered the tray. "But thanks for the moral support."

By his table in the dining room, he eased the tray onto a stand. Joyful faces sprouted around the four-top when the cargo landed. Marcelo remembered what kept him going: bringing pleasure to those he served, which made his job worthwhile. Going through the ritual, he served a sturdy, graying guy and his guests.

"Astronomical. You've done a superb job," the man said, and others nodded cheerfully.

Did he have a prayer of getting the job in the fall? The promotion would've been the best birthday present ever. Instead, he waited on tables, just as he had the first day he'd wandered into the Vineyard twelve months ago. No, he wasn't going to kid himself. Something had to change, and it had to change fast.

II

Barry

At his station, Barry dug in his pocket and pulled out a handful. His shirt collar choked him when he counted four crumpled dollar bills. Man, he had to get cranking to make enough green to pay his moron landlord for the overdue rent. And if the bastard came knocking on his love shack again at the crack of dawn interrupting his love life, he'd cure him of that—in a New York minute!

He'd been certain it had been a sign from above when he turned on the tube and saw Alydar. That monster stallion was the favorite, and he'd bet May's rent on him, but Affirmed came from third place and galloped away with the Kentucky Derby Crown! Luckily, it was Saturday night, and the place was going to rock. No matter how much cash he raked in that night, he'd join Marcelo and slam down as many shots as it took to celebrate his birthday.

"What happened to you last night?" Angie asked.

She was fuming and buttoning the black vest hanging loosely on her lanky body. Man, he'd seen those angry eyes before. He'd stood her up! He'd packed the last bud of Panama Red into the bong yesterday and lost touch with reality. Hell, everyone and their uncle knew his mind was a slippery slope when high; he'd forget to sweat if he didn't live in the Sunshine State.

"A Mack truck knocked down a telephone pole on my street," he said. "We had no phone for hours. When it came back on, it was too late to call you. Sorry."

"Up your nose with a rubber hose," Angie said, straightening the silverware on her table.

He could've told her the truth. It didn't cost jack squat. But he'd served up bowls of excuses so many times that he didn't know when to tell the truth. It was for the best. Relationships shackled him to a life of responsibility and destined him to failure.

His eyes zeroed in on the shapely new waitress with auburn hair across the room. Maybe she was the one for him. A beautiful chick like that could break his heart as easily as a No. 2 pencil. But then, when did he know what was good for him?

Barry watched her take the order from a three-top of guys with no chance in heaven or hell of ever getting it on with her. The chick narrowed her eyes and then peeked in the burgundy menu before answering a question from a guy with Elvis Presley sideburns. And when she took the order, she walked around the table instead of staying put in one spot.

Yep, he could teach her right if he got the chance. Everyone knew he was the best waiter in St. Pete, and those who didn't, didn't know squat. Man, he should go over and introduce himself. How could he score a home run if he didn't swing the bat?

"Who's the new chick?" he asked Angie, who was filling the sugar packets at her table.

She flipped him the finger and strolled away.

"Listen, I forgot about last night," he said as she kept on her way. "I'm sorry."

He sighed and dropped his shoulders. Marcelo joined him, and he perked up.

"Smart move not going around with her," Marcelo said. "But you could've called her."

"I hear you," Barry said. "Still, it's for the best."

Later that evening, Connie sat deuces on three of Barry's tables: three parties of two on four-tops. Was she giving him only couples on purpose? He was sure Sergio had told her to do that to punish him. The night before, a party of four, two couples, had complained that he'd forgotten to bring their second round of cocktails after he delivered their dinners. By the time he returned to the table, they'd almost finished eating and didn't want the drinks. He'd told Sergio he never heard the order. Sergio apologized and bought them after-dinner drinks. To be honest, he did forget the order, but he'd never forgotten orders like that before. Still, he wasn't going to need a wheelbarrow to haul his green to his car if those deuces kept up.

On his first table, two starry-eyed lovebirds sipped margaritas before ordering; on the second, two grandmas crunched on salads; and on the third, two uniformed coppers cut into their rare prime rib. Jim, in a red apron, cleared the dishes off his fourth one. It gave Barry a chance to check on the others before jumping into action with the next one. And it'd better be a four-top.

In the lobby, starving faces waited to scarf down something no longer alive. He could hear their growling stomachs from thirty feet away. They sounded like that humongous brown-and-gold lion he'd seen at Busch Gardens while riding the monorail—spaced out of his mind—over the Dark Continent. The giant cat's growl had traveled across that park, out to the parking lot, and had died out somewhere down Busch Boulevard.

"What are you daydreaming about?" Connie sat two teenage girls at his four-top.

Another freaking deuce brought him back to the world like a slap to the face. That party confirmed the suspicion of his punishment. Would it last all night?

"I'm really going to make beaucoup bucks that way." He wrinkled his face at her.

"Don't be such a spaz," Connie said.

Maybe she wasn't giving him lousy parties on purpose. Sometimes that was the way the football bounced, being lopsided and all. But those girls were going to waste his time. They were going to order the cheapest items on the menu: cheeseburgers, fries, and iced teas. Then they'd run him ragged, asking for this and that when he got busier than a two-headed woodpecker. And they'd leave him 10 percent tip if he was lucky. He should just put a tin cup on the table.

"Bring us two 7-Ups while we decide," the girl with chrome braces told him. Her grill reminded him of his first car, a '63 Chevy Bel Air. That car coughed up black smoke out the tailpipe every time he stepped on the gas, and it drank a quart of motor oil a day.

At the service bar he got in line behind Curtis and his graying hippie 'fro. The scrawny mushroom would topple over with half a push. Curtis grabbed a couple of cocktail napkins while Sherry mixed his drinks. Barry could see the lounge was packed and energized; the horseshoe bar didn't have an empty seat, and diners, not dancers, sat at tables in front of the dance floor, sipping their favorite drink and killing time, waiting to be called to the dining room. The three-piece John Copper Band hadn't gotten there yet; beige tarps still protected the drum set and the giant speakers. They would start booming out Top 40 hits and Elvis tunes later, at 9:00 p.m.

"Put more scotch in the glass." Curtis pouted when Sherry finished pouring and went to wait on a customer at the lounge bar. "You'd think it came out of her pocket the way she pours."

"She doesn't pour heavy." Barry raised his eyebrows. "But take a look at that rump. USDA Choice."

Curtis puckered his brow. "She's married, you idiot. How'd you like somebody talking about your wife that way someday? What's wrong with you?"

Barry tapped him on the chest. "What's your problem?"

Curtis's jaw quivered, but he took off. Sherry came back, poured his 7-Ups, and dropped a cherry in each. When he served the girls their drinks, they ordered two shrimp cocktails.

"And we want two prime ribs medium, queen cut," the chrome girl said. "We want them with the bone. My German shepherd loves prime rib bones."

He wrote the order and held out his hand for the menus.

That was going to be a good party after all. It wasn't the first time he'd been wrong about customers. He needed to relax, but the walls had eyes and ears, and that made it hard.

Dogs always brought a smile to his face. When he was in grade school, he'd bring stray dog after stray dog home to feed and care for them. But his mother always took him and the dogs to the pound. He'd cry on the way, knowing what was to become of the defenseless animals. As a kid, he could never understand: Why was it OK for his mother to have five cats lounging all over the house, but he couldn't have one pup of his own to care for?

He served the girls their appetizers.

"Are you daydreaming again, Mister Space Cadet?" Connie asked Barry.

He'd been resting his back against the wall, staring into the service area. That pretty, auburn-haired waitress he'd spotted earlier stood beside Connie. She looked great in that stupid uniform. He pushed off the wall, pronto.

"I was daydreaming about you," Barry said. "Want the details?"

"Spare me, and I'm a bit too old for you." Connie grabbed two water glasses and went on her way. "You have a single guy on ten. Sorry, but he asked to sit there."

She parked one dude on a four-top! That was no coincidence.

Connie turned. "Barry, this is Emily."

His disgust evaporated. The shapely siren he'd seen from afar had tons more to admire up close. The ocean had washed her ashore at his feet. It had to be fate.

"Please show Emily the service area and kitchen quickly," Connie said. "She's working on the floor tonight and needs to know the layout. I'll water the single guy, and you can pick your station for next Saturday night." She slid off another glass of iced water from the counter.

"You know I'm always here to help," Barry said.

Soft eyes batted full eyelashes at him. Wavy auburn hair down to her shoulders teased him. Yep, he could get lost in her hair, and it probably smelled of spring flowers, like Herbal Essence Shampoo. He took her on the guided tour.

Behind the dining room, the service area ran the width of the restaurant between the dining room and the kitchen. Coffee and tea machines, creamers and sliced lemons, hot rolls and butter, all kinds of condiments, along with racks of glasses and cups, saucers, plates, and silverware stocked up the area, all on shiny stainless steel tables and shelves. A humongous ice machine and the service bar, where they ordered their cocktails, stood on opposite ends.

"Check this out. We've got a microwave oven." Barry pointed out the enormous metal box with two round dials before going in the bustling kitchen. "Here, Tyrone's king."

Tyrone chewed on a toothpick and turned steaks on the grill.

"Tyrone's the grill cook, food expediter, and kitchen manager. Turn your food order in this aluminum bowl, and he'll call it out to the other cooks. To pick up food, get in line, and then call out your table number when it's your turn. Your food will go under the heat lamps. Then you garnish and cover them, load the tray, and go. And when your server number lights up in the dining room, you need to pick up. Yeah, watch out what you do around here because Tyrone's writing a novel about this place, and he might put you in it in a negative light if you don't kiss his sweaty butt."

"Delightful," Emily said.

"If you're done showing her," Tyrone said, "get the hell out of my kitchen."

"Come on, now." Barry rubbed the back of his head. "She doesn't know you're joking."

From the dishwasher at the other end, Harry carried a stack of clean plates, his skinny arms held the bottom of them. Stringy damp hair hung in front of narrow shoulders. Black rubber boots, shiny wet with water, squished with every step.

"Make room for progress." Harry set the plates behind the line for Tyrone. "I'm Harry, dish room engineer," he told Emily.

His eyes were glassy and red, and he reeked of pot. Barry explained that Harry and the busboy Jim were twins, but although there was a resemblance, they weren't identical.

"Must be fraternal twins," Emily giggled, "but they do have identical red-colored eyes."

"If you need weed, they're your guys," Barry said. "I get all my stuff from them now."

"I believe I'll be fine in that department," Emily said.

"You burnouts going to pick up or make drug deals?" Tyrone wiped the sweat off his forehead. "Pick up or get the hell out of my kitchen."

"Pick up eight," Barry called out. "Tyrone's really my friend."

Tyrone gave him a hard-core stare and scanned the orders hanging in front of him. Then he looked on the floor. "I don't have a table eight for you or anyone to pick up," he said.

"Sure you do, two prime rib medium." Barry looked among his checks. "Here it is, sorry." Man, how can he forget to turn in an order? "Can I have them now?"

"You're lucky they're already cooked, burnout." Tyrone sliced the primes for the teen girls and put them under the heat lamps. "You better lay off those drugs."

Why was Tyrone busting his chops in front of this chick? Behind the cooks in white, gas broilers, oil deep fryers, and flat grills shot the muggy kitchen's temperature to the roof.

"Want a Coke or iced tea?" Barry asked Tyrone, but he shook his head. "It gets beaucoup hot behind that line," Barry said to Emily. "The cooks have the hardest job in the whole place. It's nice to offer them a drink once in a while."

"This is very similar to my last job in Miami Beach," Emily said. "I've worked at the Mountain Blue and other really nice places. I'm from Ft. Lauderdale."

"Ha!" Barry said. "My last trip to Miami Beach was a real disaster."

He told her about the last time he'd gone to soak in the blue-green waters of South Beach. The first night there, he got in a private poker game with a couple of pigeons he'd met in the hotel lounge. He got suckered and lost three hundred bucks that night.

His only option was to drive home the next day, barely able to afford a tank of gas and a hot meal.

"You know how sometimes you feel that you just can't lose?" Barry asked.

"She doesn't want to hear your sorry tales." Tyrone grabbed a new order. "One stuffed flounder and a fried shrimp dinner," he called out, "and one New York strip for me." From the stainless steel refrigerator beside him, Tyrone took a strip and slapped it on the grill.

Barry told her a better story. On Halloween the waiters and waitresses dressed up in costumes and waited on people. Last year's theme was *Planet of the Apes*. It'd been a blast seeing everybody wearing rubber gorilla masks and waiting on freaked-out customers.

"Barry, are you going to let those prime ribs get cold?" Tyrone asked.

"Pick up forty-six," Curtis said, next in line.

"This is Curtis. The hippie with the gray 'fro," Barry said. "He says he's an actor, but nobody here's seen him play the role of anything but a middle-aged waiter. This is Emily."

"Nice meeting you." Curtis glared at him. "Middle-aged? I'm thirty-eight years old!"

"Oh, I know." Barry loaded the meals on his hand tray. "That's why I said it."

Emily coughed. "Is that the end of the tour? I've got to get to my section."

"I guess so…" Barry said. "Anything you need, I'm here for you."

He stopped at the microwave oven and heated the primes before delivering them. He didn't need any complaints, and he didn't want to give anyone watching ammunition to fire him.

"Out of sight," the girl with the braces said. "Can we have the check now?"

He totaled it and laid it on a check tray. "I'll take that up for you when you're ready."

Barry's single customer, a muscle-bound guy, called him and ordered another martini. The poor sap had plenty of brawn but no date on a Saturday night. He knew that feeling.

With a full house, the conversation swelled and washed over him like a Cocoa Beach surfing wave. On the floor, twenty waiters and waitresses took drink and food orders, served meals, and helped busboys clear and set tables. From behind the cash register, Sergio looked his way, and he stepped back into the service area. Connie led a party of two, moving too fast for the old folks. They wore denim shorts and T-shirts decorated with pelicans. The old timer's dried-out arms swung at his sides. They took their seats at his station and picked up the menus.

"I'll give you the next four-top." Connie returned to the front.

"I'm hip to what's going on." He went to his party and introduced himself.

Wrinkled faces emerged from behind burgundy menus. Thin hair and milky skin greeted him. As vampires, the poor couple couldn't enjoy a sunny day at the beach; their frail skin was too sensitive. The walk from the lobby had taken the steam out of the senior citizens.

"Hello, young man." The old lady's glasses blew up her eyeballs like the Fly. "Your prices are so expensive."

All of St. Pete knew they weren't.

The old guy had caught his breath. "What are your specials, and what comes with them?"

After answering a hundred and one questions, he took the order. What a waste. They loved well-done sirloins; might as well scarf down shoe leather. Barry crossed Jim, who carried two buckets of ice to refill the salad bar. At the coffee machine, Marcelo filled a pot. The coffee aroma was fresh and strong.

"Everybody's going to the Quarterdeck to celebrate my birthday," Marcelo said.

"I'm buying the first round," Barry told him as Angie rushed past writing on a check.

That was the least he could do for his best friend on his day. At the kitchen entrance, Emily turned left, then right, then left again, more confused than a bull on Astroturf before she followed him in. He used to get frantic, too, when he was a rookie to the waiting game.

He turned in the shoe-leather order. "Pick up twelve."

"No can do," Tyrone said. "Angie took your stuffed flounders." He dished out a side of string beans for another order. "It was payback for standing her up last night."

"That's not what happened." Barry gave Emily half a smile.

"Angie forgot to turn in her order," Tyrone said. "She couldn't wait for her own flounders because people had to catch a movie. I just put two in for you."

Why did Tyrone screw him over? Stuffed flounders took fifteen minutes to broil, and his couple was more than ready to eat. Man, that was a recipe to kill a tip. Everyone in the business knew the unwritten law that said nobody ever took somebody else's food.

"Couldn't you stop her?" Barry threw up his arms.

"Hold your horses," Tyrone said. "I didn't let her take them." He put up the stuffed fish under the heat lamps. "You know I look out for you."

"Man, I owe a solid." Barry said.

"Who's Angie, your girlfriend?" Emily watched him garnish his fish.

Was she interested in him? "She's not my girlfriend...I'm available."

When Barry returned with the tray and food covers after serving his people, Emily strained to lift and shoulder a tray with four meals, but she had no balance. That food was going to hit the floor before she got it to the dining room.

"Take two dinners on your hand tray, and I'll follow with the others," Barry said.

"I've got to do this," she said. "I want Connie to see me shoulder trays."

"Didn't they show you how at the Mountain Blue?" Tyrone asked, but she ignored him.

"Then I'll follow right behind you and keep an eye on the tray," Barry said.

He shadowed her and the wobbly tray to her station near the front. From the podium, Connie watched her serve the family of four. Yep, the walls had eyes and ears in that place. When he returned to the kitchen, he brought back her large tray and food covers.

"Forget about her." Tyrone slapped a porterhouse steak on the grill. "It won't happen."

"You don't know shit from Shinola," Barry said. "Give me a few prime rib bones. It's for a customer's dog. Make sure they got some meat on them."

"We're saving them for Sunday's BBQ ribs special."

"Just bag them before I slap you into next week."

"Watch it, youngblood." Tyrone bagged the bones.

Barry would take the risk to hook up with a classy chick like Emily. Then, maybe he wouldn't hit the bars or Derby Lanes dog track—no more betting on greyhounds or horses and throwing away his money. Man, he had to shape up quick, or Marcelo would forget about him as a business partner.

Barry presented the bag of meaty bones to the girls. He could see the appreciation on their faces, and that made his night. No thanks were needed. Whatever he could do for an animal he would. They never disappointed people…like people always disappointed people.

A familiar figure in the lobby blew his nose on a handkerchief fit for a bullfighter. The rail-thin guy went out the front door. It was his landlord! Barry rushed to the front, through the crowd, and out the door. The weasel had disappeared. Was that really his landlord?

Later, he didn't see a tip on the check tray from the teen girls. And they were long gone.

"They paid cash, so there's no credit card tip," Jackie told him at the register.

Those chicks had stiffed him! What else could he expect on a lousy night? His last parties had better not be deuces or the whole night would be a major bummer. But he wasn't going to make a stink over the seating and draw attention to himself. After work, come flood or fire, he had to join Marcelo for a few boilermakers to celebrate his birthday. His buddy didn't need to know about his cash flow problem.

III

Emily

Emily glanced away and batted her eyes while Connie explained she'd been forced to triple seat her: she had the only vacant tables, and irritated customers had been waiting in the foyer. Emily swept her eyes across her section to see her unattended people turn their heads looking for her. She ignored Connie as if she were part of the furniture. Emily's number lit up. She was being called to pick up. Her mind shifted to the two broiled snappers waiting for her and drying out under the searing heat lamps—in a kitchen steamy as a terrarium.

"I've got to roll," she said. "Next time people get done, I'll tell them they can't leave."

"You could do that," Connie said, "or you could stagger them."

"I would if I sat them myself." She waved her off and headed to the stifling kitchen.

Connie followed her. "By stagger I mean delay one table and rush another. So you don't have two leave at once, or worse, three. You know what I'm talking about, right?"

"Yes…of course."

Once Connie explained stagger, Emily understood the concept, but a lot of good that did her then. By the time she served the snappers, the three new parties would be ready to order. And the interrogation would begin: they'd have questions about the specials, and they'd have questions about the preparation. The going back and forth to find answers to the inquiries posed to her got her behind in the first place—and that was when her parties arrived minutes apart!

At the pickup line she stood behind a young guy with a head of dark hair and an athletic build who was talking to Barry. He was slim, yet strong as a double martini. Earlier, she'd seen him across the room. As he turned to her, her eyes gleamed with curiosity and adventure.

"I'm Marcelo. What brings you to the Vineyard?"

"I needed a summer job." Even so, she had every intention of having fun before heading back to college, and the guy in front of her seemed promising. "I'm Emily."

"Oh, yeah," Barry said. "This is my buddy Marcelo. He's one of the good guys."

Ahead of them, a lanky waitress grunted and heaved a loaded tray.

"A summer job?" Marcelo said. "You must go to college, then."

"I'm a senior at Miami State," Emily said. "I mean, when school starts in the fall."

"Stellar," Marcelo said. "I wanted to go to State, but I have a year at junior college."

She brushed against him, and he moved up. The gangly waitress had left the line.

"JC?" she said. "Good for you."

She wasn't looking for an Einstein. Her summer plans didn't include meeting a brain to help her split the atom, only to help her let it all hang out once in a while.

"What are you doing after work tonight?" Marcelo asked. "Some of us are going out for a drink later. Why don't you come along?"

She'd definitely be there. "I'll have to see."

Two women made cold appetizers and salads at one end. One peeled boiled shrimp while the other shucked fresh oysters. A heavy glove protected the hand holding the mollusk. A young waiter with a crew cut joined the line. He was red faced, fuming, en route to a coronary. He slammed dollar bills on the counter.

"I got a three-dollar tip from six people!" He took a deep breath. A pencil-thin mustache lined his upper lip. "That's fifty cents a head, what a rip-off!"

"Roger here goes to college." Marcelo introduced her to Red Face. "He studies finance and accounting. This is our newest employee, Emily. She goes to State."

Barry stepped in. "Roger thinks he's going to get a job on Wall Street, but that's a heck of a stretch from Tampa College. That's the biggest laugh I've had in the time I've been here."

Roger frowned but ignored him. He brightened up when Emily came into his radar.

"A new recruit for the Vineyard brigade," Roger said. "We've got to grab a drink soon."

The lousy tip apparently a memory, his heart attack was averted. He kissed her hand.

"Did anyone tell you today that you have beautiful eyes?" Roger asked. "If the answer is no, I just did."

Gag her with a spoon! The clown needed to find his way back to the Big Top. "I have to pick up." She turned away. It was Marcelo's attention she wanted, but he had vanished into the Twilight Zone. No need for her to fret. The restaurant was only so big, and she was sure she'd have an opportunity to casually run into him before her shift ended.

"If you go out tonight," Barry said. "I'll buy you a drink...if you want."

She had no interest in the man-child. "That would be nice."

Emily loaded a large oval tray with four meals and scanned the landscape for Connie. She had to deliver it to the tray stand by her party or she might not survive the night. Earlier, Connie had told her she had misrepresented herself when she applied for the job, saying she had experience working at well-known Miami restaurants. It was an assault on her credibility.

"When I saw you carry a dinner tray at your waist instead of shouldering it, I knew," Connie had told her. "I'd ask you to leave, but we'll see how you do tonight."

Emily had been less than truthful about her experience, but she couldn't admit it, afraid she'd be let go for her deception. When she applied, she didn't imagine waiting required any skill—just writing down what people ordered and bringing it to them. How difficult could that be? It wasn't rocket science, but she was lost, maneuvering unfamiliar terrain without a chart or compass. But if she planned to spend her summer vacation in St. Pete of all places, she was going to earn money.

She lifted the tray and attempted to balance it, but it tilted back and the dinners slid. "Help!" she said.

Barry reached and grabbed the tray, but it was too late. The meals fell and crashed on the floor. Everyone clapped and cheered like a bunch of juveniles, including the salad ladies.

Tyrone came from behind the line. "If you rejects want to celebrate, get the hell out of my kitchen!" The food was sprawled at his feet. "Filet mignons are good, but we'll need two broiled snappers."

Connie walked in. The destroyed fish filets remained on the floor. "What happened?"

"She slipped on the greasy floor," Barry blurted out.

"We got it under control," Tyrone said from behind the line.

Connie glanced at Barry, then Emily, and returned to her duties.

"Thanks for doing that," Emily said.

"I know what it's like being under the microscope," Barry said.

Harry's thin frame made wet tracks from the dishwasher. He held a dustpan and a broom. "Make room for progress." Harry swept up the broken fish fillets.

"Come back in ten minutes for your food," Tyrone told her.

Later, Emily served the rehabilitated filet mignons and broiled snappers. What was she doing in St. Pete anyway? She'd planned to spend the summer at her college roommate's home in Aspen, going summer skiing and breathing in Rocky Mountain air before beginning her senior year of school. Before she had to face the realities of life and embark on a career. But her mother had had a different idea. She'd insisted that Emily spend the summer with Grandma in St. Pete before she finished college and got too busy with her life. The die had been cast. It was her sentence to endure.

"What a royal pain these people are, asking for separate checks." Emily rushed through the service area. "Can't they divide? It's one of the four basic mathematical operations." She studied the checks in her hand, spread out like playing cards. "Where is it?" She found the one. She had to pick up table 28. She wasn't going back to the dining room empty-handed.

"Don't come back out without our food," the paramedics at her deuce had told her.

The delay was her slipup. She'd overlooked turning in their king crab legs order on time, and the tickets had stacked up.

The overburdened kitchen had ground to a halt: food took forever to cook. She could only blame the delay on the innocent kitchen for so long before she lost any hope of a decent tip. And she'd just gotten double seated! She continued eyeing her checks.

"Whoa!" Emily heard and stopped abruptly, her hand to her heart. In front of her, the gangly waitress balanced a cocktail tray in one hand, with colorful swaying drinks in tall and short glasses. Inches from her face, the gangly girl's bony hand stretched out for protection.

Others rushed around them. "You've got to look where you're going, sweetie. I'm Angie."

"I'm sorry." She sighed and regained her composure. "I'm Emily."

"They didn't teach you to keep your eyes up at the famous Mountain Blue, either?"

How did she know about her work history? Confidentiality didn't call the Vineyard home: the parrots repeated whatever they heard without consideration for impact or repercussion, but she needed help. "Can you take a deuce for me? I can't get to them."

"You've got to stagger your people." Angie giggled. "What else you got waiting?"

"A four-top just sat down."

"I'll take the four-top. Thanks." Angie moved away.

"I can get to that one. It's the deuce that I need help with."

Angie turned to her. "When you're in the weeds, you take what you get. It's got to be worth my while, coming from the other side of the room." Angie's figure blended into the collage of the dining room.

"Fine!" Maybe she should search for another job.

Emily stood in the pickup line, closed her eyes, and rubbed her temples. A light tap on the shoulder made her open her eyes. It was Connie!

"Everything copacetic?" Connie asked.

"All's peachy keen."

Soon after, Angie appeared. "I picked up the deuce you wanted me to, and I got the cocktail order for your four-top. I'll get their drinks if you give me a check."

Surprised but relieved, she gave her one from her check holder. "You're a lifesaver."

"I'll leave the check at the table so you can take the food order."

When she called for her order, the king crab legs weren't ready, so she called for another. What else could she do? Under the heat lamps, she received a porterhouse steak topped off with a pile of mushrooms, and a prime rib king cut. She placed lemon wedges on her tray and looked for her Catch of the Day among the school of orders waiting for pickup.

"Tyrone, is that my grouper?" She pointed to a broiled filet of fish.

"No, grouper's eighty-six: we're out. Where you been?"

"Where do you think?" She looked at her wristwatch. "How can we be out at nine?"

"Grouper's eighty-six. It doesn't matter why we're out, we're out." He paused, but then laughed. "Take that fish. It's sea bass."

"Won't they know the difference?"

"It's the same family. That's what we've been selling for grouper the last two nights because we couldn't get any." He cracked up again.

"Why do you waste my time?" The plate she brought down was extremely hot.

"Maybe it's because we're not fancy like the Mountain Blue."
He laughed heartily.

As the night was coming to an end, Emily had settled down,
but the threat from Connie still loomed over her. The dining
room had thinned out, and she noticed that late parties drank and
ate slower because they'd already been somewhere, if anywhere
at all. Earlier ones were in a rush to make a commitment. She
totaled the check and spoke with the two students from State
before they left. They were vacationing in Clearwater Beach for
a week before they headed to Daytona Beach. She wished she
could join them.

"See me before you leave tonight." Connie brought her
another party.

Connie disrupted the temporary peace and placed her on high
alert.

Two women in the autumn of their lives strained to read the
menu, huddled toward the center of the table, close to the glowing
candle holder. They were no longer concerned with exposing their
gray hair or the wrinkles on their unpowdered faces.

"Good evening," Emily said. "What are you ladies doing out
so late?" One wore a fur shawl and long gloves; her companion, a
sequined dress, a pearl necklace, and a kind smile.

"It was too crowded to come here earlier." She slid her gloves
off. "We take an evening nap and go out later."

She could see the slack skin on her cheeks droop, the bliss of
time long departed.

"You have a system. Smart," Emily said. "Would you care for
a drink or glass of wine?"

"We'd like martinis. What do you have in imported vodka?"
The lady in fur smiled and covered her mouth in a girlish gesture.

Emily had no clue. She didn't drink vodka or much of anything.

"Oh, make it the usual: two Absolut martinis, very dry, of course," said her companion, and they burst into a series of high-pitched, spastic giggles.

Marcelo loaded two tall, fruity drinks onto his tray at the service bar. She knew she'd run into him in the immediate future. She leaned into him before he stepped away.

"I'm sorry," she said, and gave her order to Sherry behind the bar.

She struggled to remember what decoration went with dry Martinis: olives or lemon twists? It didn't matter if she knew; she'd already been unmasked. And Connie had already sealed her fate. Sherry topped off her drinks with lemon twists. Emily delivered them and strolled through the service area.

"Emily?" Connie said. "I need to talk to you."

"I've got to pick up now." She sought refuge in the kitchen.

"Wait," Connie said. "Can you work tomorrow? I'm down three people."

Emily stopped. Although relieved, she didn't show it. "I guess I can't really say no."

"Not this time. You're a sweetie." Connie sighed. "You did a decent job for being inexperienced. You'll be in next week's schedule." She flashed a smile. "I've got to set up this schedule so I can take off Sunday to celebrate my second anniversary." Connie moved on. "Barry, can you work Sunday?"

"Sure, I have to." He grumbled. "Thanks to those out-of-sight parties you gave me all night."

At night's end, Emily gloated, content with the tips she'd received and with the hard-fought victory she'd secured. If Margaret A. Brewer could become the first female brigadier general in the US Marine Corps, Emily could learn to wait on tables. She could do anything. Besides, customers who understood didn't mind that it was her first night on the job and instead appreciated her honesty and genuine efforts. The fact that she was working for the summer to return to college in the fall didn't hurt her in their eyes, either. Rather, it worked to her advantage, perhaps tugging at emotional strings, opening their hearts and wallets, especially from the State alumni.

Emily remembered she'd told her grandma she'd call her to say good night, but it was too late for that. Had she waited for her call? With the job secured, she could focus her attention on Grandma. Maybe she could get to bed early and go with Grandma to church the next morning.

"You wanna join us for a drink to celebrate Marcelo's birthday, college girl?" Angie took off her bow tie and unbuttoned her vest.

She had almost forgotten about him. "Sure, I don't have anything to do tomorrow. I'm on vacation."

IV

Marcelo

Marcelo was setting up his Pioneer receiver on top of the oak dresser. It was in the same bedroom he'd shared with Carlos for ten years, one with hardwood floors and a ceiling fan whirling at low speed. It was their parents' house. Marcelo had moved out last year, and he'd moved back in two days ago to keep his younger brother company—and to save for the business. He wasn't about to let his dreams float away like feathers in the wind. The feeling he got from making the move confirmed he'd made the right decision.

Carlos carried the wooden stereo speakers in.

"Just set them down anywhere," Marcelo said.

On the floor, the silent speakers faced each other. Their unattached wires and plugs waited to be connected to the receiver and the current of life. Marcelo placed the turntable and plastic lid on top of the receiver on the dresser.

"Feels funny without Mom and Dad here," Marcelo said. "Never imagined I'd be back."

The house was a two-bedroom bungalow. Carlos had decided to stay in St. Pete when his dad got a job in Miami. Their parents had moved south weeks before, and Carlos had taken the master bedroom.

"These are the house rules," Carlos said. "No partying on weekdays."

Carlos was eighteen years old and had graduated from Pinellas High School early, last December. Even though Carlos was a legal adult, Marcelo offered to move back in the house and keep an eye on his younger brother to reassure their parents.

"Sergio told me you start as a waiter next week," Marcelo said in Spanish, and connected one of the speaker wires to the back of the receiver.

"What took him so long?"

Carlos had worked as a busboy at the Vineyard for the last six months, often waiting on a couple of tables a night when they were short staffed and Marcelo or Barry got in the weeds. He'd often bailed them out, and his dedication had catapulted him into the waiter ranks.

"Don't forget the deal with Mom and Dad," Marcelo said.

"How can I? You won't let me," Carlos said in Spanish.

Carlos had promised his parents he'd enroll at Pinellas Junior College, JC, in the fall.

When Marcelo and Carlos spoke, they spoke English or Spanish. Often, Marcelo switched back and forth in the same conversation—he lived in two dimensions, two universes, shifting from one to the other, sometimes purposely, sometimes unconsciously. Marcelo had turned ten and Carlos seven before they arrived to the United States and St. Petersburg with their parents in 1967. In those days, when they went to Williams Park to feed the pigeons or went shopping at Montgomery Wards in Central Plaza and they spoke Spanish, people would turn around to see who was speaking that strange language. That hadn't changed much by 1978.

"Did you tell Dad about…you know…not getting the promotion?" Carlos connected the other speaker wire to the back of the set.

Marcelo's shoulders sank as if carrying a heavy backpack on the sandy Florida Trail.

"Thanks for reminding me. I'm trying to forget that conversation. Dad said I should go to Vo-Tech and learn a trade if I'm not going to college…and to think of the future. I always think of the future."

"State wasn't in the cards for me either, but we're lucky to have JC here."

Marcelo had always wanted to attend Miami State, but it was too expensive. He had enrolled at JC after high school, but with work and all, it hadn't been easy, and he dropped out after completing thirty semester hours. Marcelo knew the sacrifice his father had made for them by coming to the United States and trading in his profession for a low-paying job. He didn't know how he'd repay that debt.

"Barry and I've got to open that place soon," Marcelo said. "I'm done playing around."

"Then get serious and do it."

Carlos pushed both speakers against the wall, one on each side of the dresser.

"I've got six hundred bucks left after fixing the AC. With us splitting the utilities, I can save nine hundred dollars in six months. All we need for our place is fifteen hundred each."

With three thousand bucks, they could open the breakfast-and-lunch counter he and Barry had in mind. They'd done the math. Still, he was afraid to ask Barry how much he'd put away.

"What if the three of us go into business?" Carlos asked.

Marcelo threw a pillow at him. "You worry about college."

He believed Carlos would do better in school than he had. Carlos didn't have distractions yet, and Marcelo was going to make sure it stayed that way, and he was going to make sure Carlos honored the contract with their parents, no matter what. He was at peace with that.

"I know the deal," Carlos said. "Hey, we can watch football this fall like before."

"We'll get Barry and make it the three of us again."

Their passion had been and still was the Miami State Dolphins. It was Barry who'd explained the rules of the game to them the first time they'd watched a game on their Zenith color TV. Back then, Marcelo couldn't believe that after a player received the ball, carried it for seconds, and got tackled, the referee stopped the game and the players huddled together on opposite sides of the ball for about a minute. They stood around more than they played! It was odd at first, but Marcelo and Carlos, with Barry's help, figured out the game and watched the Dolphins win game after game each season. It seemed they were invincible. The three of them had imagined themselves in the excited crowd of students someday, cheering them on to victory.

"All Barry and I've done since high school is drop out of JC," Marcelo said.

"You tried," Carlos said. "And now you're both going into business."

Marcelo couldn't blame his friend for quitting college. Barry had been an average student in high school, but he wasn't ready for one of the top junior colleges in the nation. Barry hadn't known how to organize his study time, hadn't completed assignments on time, and had lost interest. Marcelo had dropped out for another reason: his fire for school had gone out. "I only enrolled at JC because you did," Barry had told him after dropping out.

"Barry will come through," Carlos said. "He always does."

Marcelo turned on the boob tube in the living room and took the recliner. Carlos settled in on the couch with his feet up on the coffee table. An evening breeze rattled the bougainvillea bush outside the window, one with red flowers atop thorny vines, and made the blades of the fan sitting in the window swirl.

The Incredible Hulk started on the TV in front of the fireplace. It was Marcelo's favorite show. When Bruce Banner got picked on by thugs, he always said, don't make me angry; you wouldn't like me when I'm angry. But the punks wouldn't listen, and they'd keep bullying him. Then they crossed the line, and Banner's eyes went crazy. He got enormous, turned green, and became the Hulk. And those guys got a butt whipping like never before. They ended up in the hospital in a heap of hurt, wrapped up like mummies. It served them right.

"How much was it to fix your AC?" Carlos didn't take his eyes off the set.

"Three hundred bills for a new compressor. Want to pitch in?"

He could've found a cheaper one at the Twenty-Eighth Street junkyard, but he didn't want to buy a crummy one and have to replace it in six months. Why would he put any used part in his '67 Mustang? His car was the ultimate.

"You've put a lot of money in that car."

True. But he didn't regret the black ragtop or the navy-blue paint job he got months earlier.

On the tube, the Hulk dashed into the woods after trashing a shack and the poor fools in it who refused to listen and leave him alone. The show went into commercials. Anita Bryant pitched orange juice from "the Florida Sunshine Tree."

Carlos turned to him. "I'm glad I stayed in Saint Pete."

"Where else would you go? This is home."

Marcelo hadn't told anyone, but leaving St. Pete and moving someplace else had entered his mind before his parents left. Maybe a fresh start in a different city was all that was called for. But he wasn't about to leave Carlos in St. Pete to end up as he did down the road, wearing out shoe leather in kitchens and dining rooms across town. It was sufficient reason to stay put.

"You can put your wrestling trophies on the mantle," Carlos said.

"I wish Barry would take our business plan as seriously as he took wrestling."

After high school, Barry got it into his head to try out for the 1976 Olympics. He'd gotten to the Florida State High School Finals, but the Olympic team?

"I don't know what came over him then," Marcelo said.

Barry had trained hard, had bused tables to save money for wrestling camp, and had entered Amateur Athletic Union tournaments, where he won two and placed in two others. But his skill wasn't Olympic team quality. Still, he'd been convinced that if he trained hard, he could make the team. After his failed attempts at qualifying, he'd confided in Marcelo.

"He told me he could've won the gold medal if he'd made the team," Marcelo said.

"That's a serious fantasy-reality disconnect," Carlos said.

"You would've lived in fantasy, too, if your life had been no picnic."

When Barry was thirteen, his father went to work one day and never came home. Barry missed a week of school going to the construction site hoping to see his dad sawing and hammering roof trusses, but his old man never showed. Before that, his mother had surrendered her life to alcohol to quiet her demons. Barry and his older brother, Mike, had been thrown overboard without a life jacket early in life. That didn't matter anymore. They'd have their business soon enough.

V

Barry

Barry got his station ready for the supper rush. His black vest hung on the back of one of his chairs. He wiped the water spots off the silverware with a damp napkin. Where did spots go after they rubbed off? He cracked a smile. Man, he was more than ready to cast his net and catch himself that beautiful mermaid called Emily. No, he wouldn't have to go to Weeki Wachee Springs to net himself a siren. The air was thick with anticipation.

"I have a feeling I'm going to be that chick's boyfriend," he said.

Marcelo filled the salt and pepper shakers on his tables. "Somebody better tell her because I don't suppose she knows."

Barry dragged the chairs away from his table and ran the sweeper under it—he shouldn't have to do that. That pothead Jim had missed breadcrumbs and those plastic cracker wrappers with the vacuum cleaner.

"I think Emily knows it, too," he said.

Marcelo turned to him. "Is that who you're talking about, Emily?"

"Why? You interested?"

Marcelo shook his head and got back to his chores.

It'd been quite a while since he'd gone out with a classy chick, and a girl like Emily fit the bill. The last one he'd gone out with—Angie—didn't come close. She always had a cigarette in her mouth and blew out smoke like a worn-out engine with bad piston rings. He was lonely; that was why he'd gone out with her. From across the room, Angie gave him the hairy eyeball. Could Angie tell he was thinking about her? Man, Emily was different. She could make him go out and howl at the moon after making passionate love. How could he win her over?

"When we open our business, we'll throw the biggest party this town has ever seen," he said. "We'll invite everyone we ever worked with."

"You got enough coin to rent out the Bayfront Center?" Marcelo asked. "We'll need a gigantic place like that to fit all the people when you figure the dozen places we've worked in."

"We might have to wait until we open our hundredth place to do that, then." Barry had to haul in a giant chunk of change that night and fill up that Folgers Coffee can under his bed. Paying his late rent had left him broke again. "Oh, we'll do it. I can feel it in my bones. We'll be the kings of the restaurant business, with two in each state and a chick on each arm."

"That's a lot of trouble to go through to get a couple of chicks." Marcelo lit the candle holders in his station.

Barry told Marcelo that, eager to write up their menu, he'd gone to Haslam's Book Store that morning to buy an Italian cookbook and look up pesto sauce. Man, he could find any book in that giant store. He never imagined he'd be in a bookstore after dropping out of college. How was history, algebra, or biology going to help him make a living in the world, anyway? College didn't offer him jack squat, but the business would. After they opened their place, there'd be no more employers using and throwing him away like a take-out container.

"There are many benefits to a college education, too," Marcelo responded.

Marcelo's mom had made spaghetti with pesto sauce on more than one occasion, and Barry had loved it. The first time Marcelo told him he ate green spaghetti Barry thought it was gross. He liked the sound of it: *pesto*. The recipe said fresh spinach could be used instead of fresh basil. He would make it one day—but with basil—and surprise Marcelo.

"I've never seen fresh basil sold around here," Barry said.

"Go to Tampa to get it. Cuban and Italian people there use it. That's where we got ours."

"If there's no fresh basil, we won't have it that day. We're not going to use spinach."

"Whatever you say, but don't forget to call me when you make it."

Barry got a kick out of cooking all kinds of dishes and making them even better. And he always invited Marcelo and others from work. He also made his homemade sangria. An excellent time was always had by all. He liked everyone to know he had no beef with anybody.

Barry found his favorite hand tray where he'd hidden it, underneath the seat cushion in a booth. He'd always remember if he put it in the same place. Lately, he'd forget his head if the neck bone wasn't attached to the head bone. What helped him was that he'd been working in the business since he was fifteen, and he knew the drill better than anything else in life.

"Hey, Barry." Curtis picked and puffed-out his hair. "You know, if I were a betting man, I'd put a bodacious chunk of change on Affirmed for the Preakness. That horse is a freak."

"Barry's not a betting man." Marcelo stared at Barry. "So he wouldn't do that."

"I work too hard to throw my money away like that," Barry said.

It was the duel: Alydar vs. Affirmed again, and this time Alydar would win. Affirmed couldn't beat him twice in a row, and Barry knew it. But he had no cash to play with. Luckily, Curtis moved on to cause trouble someplace else. Jackie headed his way.

"You've got six checks missing from last night." Jackie pushed the wireframe glasses up the bridge of her nose. "All in numerical order. Did you have any left that you forgot to turn in?"

"This is a freaking witch hunt." Barry cocked his head. "What are you accusing me of?"

"I don't have time for this," Jackie said. "You can deal with Sergio when he comes in."

"Answer her, Barry," Marcelo said. "She's only doing her job."

"I don't have them." He grabbed his check holder and opened it. "See?"

There were the checks, all in numerical order. Jackie rolled her eyes and took them.

"You're too uptight and spaced out," Marcelo said. "You've got to lay off the weed."

He noticed Emily in the dining room and forgot his worries. There wasn't much of a smile on that pretty face. Man, he'd love the chance to tattoo a permanent one on her. If only she'd get to know him, she'd fall for him; he'd make sure of that. He could see himself with her on his arm, walking into the Vineyard Christmas party.

"Emily's here," he said to Marcelo. "Remember, I saw her first."

Marcelo wiped the fingerprints off the wine list on his tables. "I saw her too, you know."

He stared at Marcelo. "Well, I *said* it first."

They'd had a deal ever since junior high. When one of them said, "I saw her first," the chick was off limits to the other guy; until the off limits was called off by the guy who'd called it in the first place. That agreement, sealed with a guy's handshake, had lasted through the ages.

"We could have fun this summer, me and that girl," Barry said.

"Tell her," Marcelo said. "Why are you telling me? Anyway, how is she going to be having fun with you when she'll be with me?"

"In your wet dreams."

Water spots on a wine glass caught his eye, and he wiped it crystal clear. He raised his sight, and Emily came into view in the cross hairs. Her station was in the center of the room. She pointed to tables and talked to herself, as if trying to figure out her station.

"Hey, sunshine!" he called out.

"Hi, there." His siren swam through the maze of furniture toward him.

He didn't even have to flex his biceps to get her over, and she was swimming directly into his net. Then she stopped at Marcelo's table, and Barry had to step in the picture.

"How do you like the Vineyard, the reason we get up in the morning?" he asked.

Man, what a doofus! Sure, it was his reason to get up, but he didn't have to sound as if he had nothing going on. That wasn't going to fly with a college girl.

"I like it here." She searched for Marcelo's eyes. "Everyone's so nice."

"Hey," Barry said. "You go to State, right? You've been to their football games?"

"Sure, plenty of them," she said. "I love football."

Marcelo's face lit up. "State's my favorite team. I've watched them forever."

Booh-yah! Barry found a subject in common with her, and now he wouldn't have to sweat trying to start a conversation. He could yak football all day long if he had to.

"We've seen them play on the tube," Barry said. "That's better than season tickets. You get to watch the game from every angle, and you got replays; can't beat that."

"I guess looking at it like that," she said, "TV watching is better than season tickets."

That was what he'd said to Marcelo since high school: they had the best seats in the house, watching the games with other waiters at the Bull Pen, drinking pitchers of beer and taking shots, and then waiting on State students during summer vacation and holiday breaks.

She turned to Marcelo. "Have you been on campus?"

What was going on? She was only interested in talking to Marcelo. Had he disappeared? Had he been teleported to another planet like Captain Kirk in *Star Trek*?

"I've never been on campus." Marcelo leaned on a chair.

"You never wanted to go." Barry frowned.

A couple of times, buddies from high school had invited him and Marcelo to campus. The friends had gone there the fall after graduation. He was willing to go, but Marcelo would have no part of it. Marcelo could be a drag sometimes...and he was stealing his girl!

"We were going to JC," Barry said. "But now we're opening a chain of restaurants from the Atlantic to Pacific." He stretched out his arms. "We'll be the kings of the hospitality business with a chick on each arm."

"Barry, close the shades," Marcelo said.

Marcelo was right; sometimes he talked too much. Even he could admit to that.

"How come you quit school?" she asked Marcelo.

"I quit too, you know," Barry said. Was he the freaking Invisible Man?

"I wasn't into school." Marcelo brightened up. "First we'll open a breakfast-and-lunch place downtown, weekdays from 7:30 to 3:00 p.m. After that we'll—"

"But you're going back to college, right?" she asked.

The smile dropped off Marcelo's face and broke to pieces at his feet. "I've got to eat before getting on the floor." He took off.

"Don't mention college to him," Barry said. "That's a closed book."

Why did some people think that the only road to the future went through a college campus? Millions of people had done fine without it. He pulled the fishing net back into the boat. His romantic fishing trip had been a flop. His mermaid wasn't taking the bait.

VI

Emily

Emily watched Marcelo march off, uptight as a West Point cadet, and disappear into the service area. What an abrupt departure! Was her question offensive in any way? It wasn't: he was either returning to college or he wasn't. She was only trying to get to know the guy. It was plain to see, she had to get to know all the players in that dramatic tragedy before she carved out her role.

"Is he always that touchy?" she asked Barry.

"Don't worry so much about him." He buttoned his vest.

She cleared her throat. "Would you check my section to see if it's ready?"

"Me? Sure. Be glad to," Barry said. "That's what I do."

He followed her to the center of the room, and she showed him her tables, two four-tops and two deuces. He pushed a couple of chairs all the way under the table.

"Settings are neat and in order, looks good," he said. "You can make bucks galore, but you've got to turn over those deuces. Don't let them park their cans for long and you'll cash in."

Emily took breath mints wrapped in cellophane out of her pocket and dropped them in her ashtrays, one for each chair. It was a tactic to differentiate her from the others.

"Nice touch," he said.

"I got the mints from Jackie, the cashier." She gave him a handful. "She's an angel."

"I've known her for a while," he said, "and she's no angel."

Connie walked by on her way up front. "You both about ready?"

"Ready when you are," Emily said. "By the way, how did your anniversary go Sunday?"

Connie turned. "He didn't even call. I finally called him at nine that night. He'd just gotten home from having a few drinks with friends. He had no idea what day it was."

"Sounds like an oversight," Emily said. "It happens."

Connie returned to the lobby, and Barry approached Emily.

"You don't know that guy," he said. "It was their second anniversary dating."

It wasn't Connie's boyfriend she was interested in. Barry seemed more approachable than Marcelo, but he seemed the type who would be happy with daily nourishment and shelter from the elements. God, she prayed Marcelo possessed more substance and maturity.

"I heard you guys go to the Bull Pen." Emily said. "Maybe I'll join you sometime."

He gave her a double look. "Sure. It's our party house. We—"

"How long have you and Marcelo known each other?"

"We've been best friends since the fifth grade." He sighed. "We've got to fold a bundle of napkins each."

Barry brought two bundles and slid into a booth where she joined him. They began to crease and fold. The conversation had been getting interesting, but she didn't want to be obvious.

"I can't believe all these wildfires we're having. Thousands of acres are burning throughout the state. I hope we're safe."

He stopped folding. "The rain better come soon, or we'll all burn sooner than expected."

Known as one of the driest months of the year, May had brought sudden fires across the state. The dead brush and dry grass had ignited into raging infernos with just a spark because of the scorching sun and scarce humidity. One flicked cigarette butt could set the state ablaze.

"Pray for rain if you believe in prayer," he said. "Because once the rainy season starts, it doesn't let up."

A blonde of diminutive stature made her way to their booth.

"Monica is nice people, but she's not into guys." Barry gestured toward the blonde. "She studies nursing at JC."

"Hey, you must be Emily. I'm Monica." She chuckled. "We're working next to each other tonight. It'll be fun."

Monica's smile oozed of pure youthful innocence. People either helped or hindered Emily from reaching her calculated goals, and she was quick to find out. It seemed Monica wouldn't be interested in Marcelo. Still, she possessed a knack for inopportune timing.

"We'll talk later, then." Emily lowered her sight to the napkins.

"Oh, sure…OK, then." Monica returned to her affairs.

Curtis, the senior member of the Waiter's Club, came toward them. His blond 'fro was symmetrical, but the bow tie tilted to one side. He was the poster boy for Woodstock 1969.

"You got a strategically located station, Emily," Curtis said.

"Yes, it's close to the service area and kitchen. Not much walking." She returned to folding. "And no, I don't want to trade."

He laughed. "I'm happy with mine. Right on, though; all that running around kills you on a busy—"

"Aren't you working the other side of the room?" Barry angled his eyebrows.

Curtis's jaw tightened and his face reddened, but he retreated.

On the floor, waitresses and waiters put the finishing touches on their tables before the dinner crowd. They lit clear candle holders and straightened settings. Angie and Monica leveled each other's bow ties. Across the room, Roger brushed a hand over his slender mustache and engaged in dialogue with Carmine, who wore a beige leisure suit and platform shoes. Two ladies in kitchen whites filled bowls at the salad bar with red beans and sliced carrots. In the foyer, Connie inserted the Tonight's Specials flyers into the cumbersome menus. Across the table from Emily, Barry continued folding.

"Did you ever wonder," he said, "if you sat down all the people you ever waited on, how many parties that would be and how long it would take you to wait on all of them?"

"No, but it wouldn't be many." She cleared her throat. "Do you guys have girlfriends?"

He sprouted half a smile. "No girlfriend here."

The poor guy was still trying, and she didn't know how to let him down easy. He didn't know it'd been point, game, set, and match for him two minutes into their initial conversation. Angie popped her head into the booth. She reeked of Jean Naté.

"Emily, you want to hit the Gallery Lounge in Pasadena after work and get down tonight? There's lots of real men there, not like here." She sized him up and down.

He raised an eyebrow. "We're busy here, as you can see."

"What's the buzz?" Emily asked him. "You and Marcelo going out?"

"Marcelo doesn't go out like he used to…but I'm free."

"You're free 'cause nobody's buying." Angie forced a laugh. "It's ladies' night at the Gallery. Be there or be square." Angie's slender frame gyrated to an imaginary rhythm. "I've got to dance and keep my girlish figure to become a stewardess. Rome, Paris—I'm flying far away from here."

"Travelling's the max," Emily said. "Can I let you know about the Gallery later?"

"OK, but don't waste your time on him." She moved on.

Barry said Marcelo doesn't go out like he used to. But what did that mean? All the guys she'd ever known always made time to go out with a woman. They could be failing out of college or unemployed, but they always made the time. They could be starting a job or getting over a breakup, but that never prevented them. Only one reason would prevent a single guy from making time for an attractive woman, and that didn't fit Marcelo.

"You could've listened to Marcelo's business plan," Barry said. "That wasn't cool."

That was why he had run away from her as if she were a burning building—major mistake. She didn't mean to be insensitive. But what kind of a future was there in a breakfast-and-lunch counter? In contrast, her expectations consisted of timely graduations, career promotions, and a resumé punctuated with professional achievements. But then, she wasn't marrying the man.

"Watch out for this guy." Barry got up. "I got to split and finish my sidework. Peace."

Carmine stood in front of her. His half-unbuttoned shirt revealed his hairless chest. A chain and crucifix hung from his neck. He placed a hand on the table and the other one on his hip. She had to get along with everyone in that place.

"You've got to be Emily." He took her hand with both of his. "I'm Carmine."

"I know about you." She took her hand back. "And I've met your brother Sergio."

"Anything you need, you come see old Carmine, and you've got it." He winked.

"I was told to go to Connie," she said. "I'd rather not circumvent the chain of command."

"But I *am* the chain of command." He flashed a smile and excused himself.

That was downright creepy.

Jackie rushed over to her, leaving the cash register unattended. A glare of contempt consumed her face. She was almost cross–eyed.

"I saw you with Carmine." Jackie folded her arms. "What can I help you with?"

"Nothing," she said. "He came over to introduce himself."

"You need anything, you ask Connie." She stormed away with a gaze full of indifference and contempt, and then turned around. "And don't you forget it."

That jelly-brain was wrapped tighter than a 7-11 sandwich.

At 5:00 p.m. the double doors of the Vineyard opened, and the restaurant came alive with the dinner crowd. Waiters and waitresses circulated the arteries connecting the dining room, lounge, and kitchen, carrying food and drink to their customers.

The Vineyard had introduced Emily to a cast of characters, to say the least, a couple of which she didn't care much about. Maybe the best she could do in St. Pete would be to work, save her money, and keep Grandma company. Then again, that wouldn't be much fun. It seemed Marcelo didn't have what it would take to make her summer worthwhile.

VII

Barry

In the men's restroom, Barry scrubbed his hands red but they still didn't feel clean. Emily didn't like him at all—something she had in common with a lot of decent girls he'd known. Even Stevie Wonder could see from an airplane that she liked Marcelo. Why couldn't he get a decent chick? Was he a leper? In the sink under running water, flesh rotted and fell off his fingers. He yanked his hands from the water and looked at them! *What the hell?* They were normal, and he could breathe again. What had Jim and Harry laced his smoke with that was making him see things? From the paper towel dispenser on the wall he pulled a sheet and dried his hands. The rough towel stung his raw flesh. He tossed the balled-up paper in the trash and looked in the mirror. His callous ear from wrestling didn't help him any with the ladies either. POW! He caved in the towel dispenser with his fist and rushed out of the restroom.

His first party of the evening was a guy and his preschool daughter. The dad looked at the right side of the menu and shook his head, then peeked into his wallet and bit his lower lip.

"I guess we'll have two salad bars," he said, "and water to drink."

"Can I have apple pie for dessert, Dad, please?" the girl asked.

"Not tonight," he said. "I'm a little short this week."

Oh, well. That party wasn't going to make his night, but it wasn't the girl's fault. He had another table to serve, and he crossed the service area into the kitchen.

"You ever ate pelican for Thanksgiving 'stead of turkey?" Tyrone asked Marcelo when Barry strolled in. Others waited behind Marcelo to pick up. "Indians ate them around here before the Europeans came. You can't tell the difference." Tyrone wiped the sweat off his face.

"You're a jive turkey," Barry blurted out. "There wasn't any Thanksgiving before the Europeans came."

"I didn't say they ate them for Thanksgiving, I said they ate pelicans before the Europeans came."

"Tyrone's right on." Marcelo nodded. "He didn't say what you think he said."

"He doesn't know what he's babbling about," Barry said. "Hitting the bottle again?"

"Don't joke about that," Marcelo said. "It's not cool."

"I haven't had a drink in four months," Tyrone said. "Scout's honor."

Tyrone put the plug in the jug after Sergio and Carmine put him on probation for coming in soused and overcooking steaks and messing up orders. The poor sap didn't even smoke weed anymore. How could anyone go through life straight, living in reality twenty-four hours a day?

"You pout like a snot-nosed kid that lost his tricycle," Tyrone said to Barry and put up Marcelo's order.

"Sit on it." Barry rubbed his throbbing knuckles.

Tyrone returned to his steaks and Marcelo was garnishing his meals when Carmine came into the kitchen jingling a huge ring with a hundred keys. That guy was asking for someone to knock his lights out, and Barry was blessed with the upper cut to do it. After all his buddy had done for the Vineyard, the bastard had thrown him under the train.

"Carmine!" Jackie stormed into the kitchen. "Some jerk bashed in the towel dispenser in the men's room." She held up a hand. "Connie's got the register."

"You seen who done it?" Carmine put the key in the office door.

"No. A customer told me about it, then I saw the damage."

"Don't ask me," Barry said. "I only saw Mister Whipple squeezing the Charmin." That was the stupidest commercial he'd ever seen.

Carmine glared at him. Then he told Jackie to come in the office and locked the door behind them. Marcelo arranged his meals on a large oval tray.

Even Carmine had more luck with the ladies than he did. That idiot took to pretty waitresses like a duck to a June bug. Actually, they didn't even have to be pretty—just young, the younger and dumber the better. The fool thought he was a smooth operator. He'd buy them jewelry and take them out to supper and around town in his Continental. A handful of airheads had tumbled into his trap. Jackie was the latest. She didn't know it, but her prince charming would trade her in for any younger princess who'd have him—in a New York minute.

"His old lady better not catch him messing around," Tyrone said.

"That guy is discreet as a neon sign," Marcelo said.

"Carmine looks like that punk I had to wrestle when we wrestled Gulfport High," Barry said to Marcelo. "The one who said he was going to beat me because he was from Ohio and they knew how to wrestle there, remember?"

"I don't know what you're talking about," Tyrone said. "But I'm sure you'll tell me."

They had traveled to Gulfport that night to wrestle against the Buccaneers, and he couldn't wait to tear into the guy. During the ride there, he paced up and down the aisle of the school bus hitting his fist. The pressure cooker was ready to blow its top. When the referee blew the whistle to begin the match, he could've swept the leg and taken him down, but instead he picked him up, slammed him on the mat, and knocked the air out of him when he landed on top.

"It's a wonder he didn't crap his shorts," Barry snorted.

Since high school, he'd been wrestling with his demons and was ready to grapple with the devil himself…and win. Barry imagined his arms up in divine victory.

"Want me to rub Carmine's ugly mug into the parking lot?" Barry cracked his knuckles.

"It's not your battle." Marcelo shouldered his tray.

"But you can make it yours and lose your job over it," Tyrone said.

Barry gritted his teeth. Carmine meant to get rid of him and Marcelo, and that made it his battle. Carmine had better pray he never found him alone in a dark alley or anywhere outside the restaurant. He'd pound that ugly mug with his fists like a pile driver. Yep, he'd do it every day of the week and thrice on Sunday.

"Who's got dibs on the new girl, Emily?" Tyrone asked.

"He does." Barry pointed to Marcelo. "I feel it in my bones."

"Last time you felt something in those bones, I lost a couple of hundred." Tyrone sulked and took a drink from a sweaty plastic tumbler.

"Don't play the stupid horses then," Barry said.

"Anybody who's not picking up," Tyrone said, "get the hell out of my kitchen."

Barry followed Marcelo into the dining room. Emily stood across the room talking to Monica, both with their backs against the emergency exit. He told Marcelo he wasn't interested in Emily, and that he could go out with her if he wanted. Emily was fresh and sweet and like a ripe mango at the top of the tree—out of his reach.

"You sure it's OK?" Marcelo asked, but then he shook his head. "She's not my type."

He knew he could count on his buddy not to scoop her up.

"Barry," Connie said. "You mixed up the two ladies' meals on thirty-two. You switched the broiled snapper with the grouper. When they realized it, they were halfway through."

"Why's everybody breathing down my back?" He shook his finger at her. "Worry about seating people and keep your nose out of my tables."

She stepped back. "Get a grip. They switched plates halfway through and thought it was hilarious. Next time you answer me like that, I'm going to Carmine and Sergio."

Yep, they'd put her up to it. Otherwise, why would she have mentioned them?

The father and young daughter had made a couple of trips to the salad bar and were done. The guy waved for his check, and Barry trucked to the kitchen. On his return, he placed an apple pie *a la mode* in front of the girl. He'd give away the whole restaurant if he could.

"Dessert's on the house tonight," he said.

"Thank you, mister," she said, wide eyed.

Children shouldn't have to suffer for their parents' failures.

Connie brought a family of four to his booth. Great! Connie wasn't going to punish him with deuces. The customers were on their way home from the beach, in shorts and T-shirts and with a red glow on their skin. All except for the mother had Dumbo ears, ready to fly off across the room at the slightest wind the next time someone opened the front door.

"Cokes all around," the dad said.

They weren't Floridians, or they'd be drinking iced tea. He went to the service bar.

"Carmine knows I'm married, and he still hits on me." Sherry poured the Cokes. "He's such a sleaze. If my old man knew, they'd find Carmine floating in Tampa Bay."

"He's a chump, but that's what we have to put up with. Don't sweat it."

"Not me, I'm getting my Florida cosmetologist license when I get my out-of-state transcripts. No more late nights. I'd rather be home with my son and old man."

"Dyn-o-mite," Barry said. "That'd be a bona fide reason to celebrate."

He delivered the sodas, and they ordered supper, including two king crab claws appetizers. He turned in the starter order to the salad ladies as Tyrone jabbered with mushroom-head Curtis. Roger waited for his turn behind the old guy.

"It really gets cold in Toronto." Curtis lowered his meals on the tray. "You ever been in below-zero weather?"

"Why would I do that," Tyrone said, turning steaks on the grill, "when I can live in Florida?"

"How are the foxes in Canada?" Roger asked. "I hear they're shaggable."

"Why you asking me?" Curtis said. "I was married with a newborn at the time."

"Then she woke up and left both of you for another guy." Barry looked away.

Curtis slapped the counter and faced him. "Stop dipping in my Kool-Aid, twerp." He shouldered the tray and stormed out of the kitchen and into the service hallway.

"You best cool it, tough guy." Tyrone shook his head and went back to his meat.

Tyrone was right on. Why did he get so irritated with Curtis? Was the hippie a snitch, or was it his imagination? He'd better worry about doing his job.

Barry returned to his station to see his latest party, two middle-aged couples. The ladies wore dark evening dresses and the guys wore suits, ready for a concert or a special occasion. He heard water running, just like the night before when he went to bed, but he hadn't left any faucet on then. No one else in the dining room seemed to hear anything unusual. He had to settle down. That party could be a decent tip for him. After he took the cocktail and appetizer order—Manhattans up all around and two escargots in mushroom caps—he looked up and saw Emily and Marcelo on the opposite side of the room. She laid her hand on his chest, and they laughed and smiled at each other, as if they were making some freaking Colgate toothpaste commercial.

So she wasn't his type, huh? He was dumb as a box of rocks to fall for that one.

At the station next to his, he noticed a family of four with two young boys.

"Is your food OK, dear?" the mother asked one kid while cutting meat for the other.

Barry couldn't forgive his older brother for joining the Marines years earlier and never keeping in touch. He smirked. The family in front reminded him of the Cleavers from the *Leave it to Beaver*

TV show. The mother fussed over her sons as if they were girls, as Beaver and Wally's mom did. "Wear your sweater, Beaver. It's chilly outside, dear," she'd say to him. Yep, that would surely guarantee raising a couple of sissies. Man, his parents weren't like that, and they raised no pansies. Most nights his mother passed out before chow, too drunk to cook or care how his meal was. And his father wasn't like that henpecked stuffed shirt sitting at the table neither, even if he wasn't around at suppertime or at any other time. Being on his own taught Barry to be strong and on his toes for whatever trouble came his way, and he was grateful for that—because trouble always came his way.

VIII

Marcelo

When Marcelo got to the Bull Pen, Barry was waiting for him at the bar. He sat on a stool reading the label of a beer bottle. The air smelled of fresh popcorn. On the TV sitting high in a corner, colorful mechanical beasts roared around an oval asphalt track in a stock car race. A dozen people milled among the tables and bar, sipping bottles of their favorite beer or taking a shot of liquor and a chaser. Marcelo took a stool and expelled a sigh of relief. His legs had traveled miles and his arms had lifted tons of drink and grub on a busy night. After a couple of beers, he'd go home to get up early.

"This is my 38th beer from the list." Barry tapped the Saint Pauli Girl bottle.

"We're going fishing tomorrow, so don't make it a late night."

"Nice of you to let me know I had plans tomorrow." Barry took a swig.

"You'll live," Marcelo said. "Smitty, a bottle of Bud. Thanks."

The barrel-chested barkeep wore an apron and was placing beer cans in the cooler. He brought the beer and pushed a bowl of popcorn in front of them.

"When I drink all hundred and fifty beers on this list, my name will go on the wall forever," Barry said and tapped the paper list under a thick, transparent finish on the bar.

The Bull Pen Bar claimed to have the biggest selection of bottled beer, lagers, and ales on Florida's west coast, 150 to be exact. And Barry had told him more times than he cared to remember about the high honor bestowed on the first person to drink one of each of the brews listed: to have his name engraved on the Hall of Fame plaque hanging high on the brick wall behind the bar.

"Yeah, forever means until they sell the place again," Marcelo said.

"Nothing wrong with having goals in life, is there?" Barry laughed.

The Bull Pen was a regular place, nothing fancy. But why did they call it that? There was no mechanical bull there, not even long-horns hanging high behind the bar. And it was all wood: wooden walls, wooden floors, wooden bar, wooden stools, wooden tables, and wooden chairs. It was a bonfire waiting for a match. Actually, they should've called it the Lumber Yard. Because when it rained, Smitty sprinkled sawdust on the floor. Then again, all wasn't wood, like the red brick wall behind the bar, the jukebox, the pool table, and the glass ashtrays everywhere.

"Sergio said Carlos starts as a waiter tomorrow," Marcelo said.

"Let's see if that really happens."

"You know," Marcelo said. "I don't see anyone at work having it in for us like you say."

"The signs are there, big as Billy, if you know where to look," Barry said. "Trust me."

On the tube, the newscaster announced the results of the Preakness Stakes. Affirmed had won the second leg of the Triple

Crown, beating Alydar for the second time. Up next was the Belmont Stakes, and Affirmed could become a Triple Crown winner the year after Seattle Slew.

"I'm grateful I didn't bet on Alydar," Barry said. "I didn't think Affirmed would beat my horse twice in a row. He's got to be from another planet."

"For not betting, you sure are following races pretty closely."

"It's a free country," Barry said. "I don't want to talk about this. Let's grab a table."

Barry pushed the empty bottle away from him, and Marcelo ordered a couple of beers. They took a table in the center of the room underneath a rotating ceiling fan.

"We can take the boat out tomorrow and go fishing," Marcelo said.

"I don't know about open water," Barry said. "Call me early, and I'll see."

"You love the open water as much as me."

"Probably nothing's biting anyway," Barry said.

"Grouper's biting, and grunt fish and Spanish mackerel. Isn't that more than nothing?"

It was a typical weeknight at the Bull Pen. At one end, a well-endowed girl in a halter top racked up balls behind the pool table. The light hanging over the green felt surface hid her face; only her shapely chest was visible. A rail-thin guy in denim shirt and jeans compared the weight of pool sticks at the wall rack, while the jukebox hungered for quarters.

The front door swung open, and the traffic noise rushed in with Angie and Emily, both balanced in black and white like keys on a piano. They placed their order with Smitty.

"I know you want Emily to go," Barry said. "Saw you two looking at each other starry-eyed at work."

"I swear. I don't know how you come up with half this stuff." Of course, he wouldn't mind getting to know her, but he didn't need to be so obvious. "Let's just make it the two of us."

Angie joined them, took a pack of Kools from her purse, and pulled one out. Barry gave her a flickering, blue-and-yellow flame and illuminated her face. The tip glowed when she took a drag, and then she exhaled to the side.

"I owe you a beer for helping out with that eight-top," Angie said to Barry. "But don't get any wishful ideas; been there, done that, and I ain't going back."

"Never heard you complain none before." Barry turned away. "Don't hang the meat in the window if it's not for sale."

Emily brought two bottles of beer, placed one in front of Angie, and then nudged the smoldering ashtray toward her. Marcelo noticed Emily's shapely breasts and torso that narrowed to a tight waist. Her eyes locked on his. Her lips were red and sweet like Plant City strawberries.

"What's the conversation about tonight?" Emily asked. "The student uprising in Teheran? Students there are demonstrating against the Shah's policies and authoritarian rule, and—"

"Why talk about that?" Angie wrinkled her nose. "That's got nothing to do with us."

Marcelo shrugged at Emily.

"Who's up for boating and fishing tomorrow?" Barry eyed Marcelo.

"I'll go if Barry's not going," Angie said.

"I'll stay behind if you promise you'll drown," Barry said.

"They're actually good friends." Marcelo nodded to Emily.

"Sure, I can feel the love." Emily rolled her eyes.

"Maybe not good friends, just friends," Marcelo said. "Maybe not even friends."

He was babbling, yet she seemed to find whatever he said amusing. He hadn't noticed her dimples before. And her skin was without imperfections.

Barry pushed off the table and stepped to the bar. It was his turn to buy. Smitty grabbed two golden bottles of beer and wiped each with his apron. Barry paid and carried them back.

"I'd like to go boating," Emily said. "Who's in?"

"I'm in." Barry gave Marcelo a terse glance.

"I guess I'm in, too." Angie puffed out a white smoke cloud. "But I won't drown."

It was settled. All four of them would go tomorrow—as friends. Marcelo found it difficult to tear his eyes from Emily's. But he had to be honest: the road on which they traveled forked for them in the immediate future.

"Weather's supposed to be nice tomorrow," he said.

The jukebox came alive with the Commodores' hit "Three Times a Lady" coming from its center speaker. On the pool table, balls cracked against one another and then thumped against the pockets. The beers had doused the tension in the air.

"I haven't fished much," Emily said. "Not in years."

"Nothing to it: bait, cast, and reel," Angie said between puffs. "Emily don't know about fishing, but she knows all about the mind. She's studying psych at State."

"I said I took a psychology class."

"Then I guess it's time for me to go home." Barry began to get up.

"You don't have to go," Angie said. "Everybody knows your mom's a psycho, and craziness runs in families."

"You know nothing about my mother!" Barry slammed the table.

Barry's mom had been hospitalized at the psychiatric center for a "nervous condition" a couple of times. After she was released from the center the second time, she refused to take medication and instead turned to alcohol. Once, a football had landed on Barry's front yard from kids playing in the street. His mom grabbed the ball and rushed inside. A minute later, she threw it out stabbed with a steak knife.

"His mother's known as the neighborhood crazy lady," Angie said.

Barry guzzled half his beer in one breath. "If anybody cares, I'll be at the bar."

As Barry climbed a stool, Marcelo said to Angie, "That wasn't necessary."

"It's called payback. He stood me up for the last time. This chick don't forgive or forget."

"Isn't this fun?" Emily rested her chin in her hand and her eyes on Marcelo's.

Smitty poured Barry a shot from a bottle of Jose Cuervo. Marcelo recognized the yellow label and gold liquor inside. Dozens of times he and Barry had had a couple of tequila shots at closing time—lemon, salt, and all. Barry gulped the drink down and pointed to the empty glass for another. Grimacing, he looked back at them. Marcelo went to him.

"She ticks you off, and you want to get drunk?" Marcelo asked.

"Close the shades on that and have a shot with me." Barry downed the second one.

Barry was wallowing like a boat in shallow water.

"None for me, I'm driving," Marcelo said.

"Who isn't?"

Barry signaled for another shot, and Smitty stopped washing beer glasses in the sink, dried his hands, and poured him another one. The girls got up from the table.

"You better get back to your girlfriend, Emily," Barry said.

"What's up with you?" Marcelo asked.

"I ain't going fishing if he is!" Angie yelled and went out the front door.

Barry stood up. "I was hoping to drown you! Yeah, I'll do it, too!"

"Hey, keep it together." Marcelo said. "You're freaking me out."

"That witch is the devil." Barry took the stool. "Have fun boating with your Emily."

Marcelo accepted the fact that he wanted to see Emily outside the Vineyard, but not like that.

"I'll take a rain check on the boating. See you." Emily followed Angie out.

Marcelo joined Barry for a shot of Cuervo and a beer from the list under the clear, thick finish on the bar. Fishing could wait. The Gulf of Mexico wasn't going anywhere.

"Last call for alcohol," Smitty said and turned off the window neon sign at 2:00 a.m.

IX

Emily

Emily brushed her wavy auburn hair in front of the trifold vanity mirror. If she saved fifty dollars a week for the next three months, she'd have ample spending money for her senior year at State. It was the last leg of her four-year plan, a well-charted journey culminating with a bachelor's degree in business administration. In contrast, it seemed that for most of the Vineyard crew, getting out of bed in the morning was a triumph of optimism.

"Your mother's on the phone, dear," Grandma said and stepped away.

"Hi, mom," Emily said and twirled the cord. "To what do I owe this pleasure?"

"I wanted to know how you are getting along with your grandma."

"I haven't brought up the subject, if that's what you mean," Emily said. "I've been busy with work, and we haven't spent any time together."

"Isn't spending time with her the reason you're up there?"

"I thought the reason was to persuade her to move into a retirement home." The telephone got heavy. "Mom, I have to go to the drugstore. Later."

She hung up. Nothing needed to be said or done that day.

"Honey, I've made you a cup of tea; come," Grandma said from the doorway.

Grandma didn't ask whether she wanted tea or whether she was hungry, she just served her. When Emily first arrived, she found the manner patronizing. After all, she was a grown woman and not a child. But it was her way of being. To Grandma, Emily would always be a grand*child*. She sure could go for a cup of tea.

"I'm going to Eckerd Drugs before going out tonight," Emily said. "Need anything?"

"No, but I hoped we'd watch *The Love Boat* tonight."

The show starred Gavin MacLeod as the ship's busybody captain who encouraged his passengers to discover romance while traveling from port to port aboard the *Pacific Princess*. He should've lost his job for meddling in people's lives. That wouldn't fly in the corporate world.

"I'm sorry, but I've made plans. We'll watch *The Love Boat* next week."

In the kitchen they took seats at the breakfast nook, a booth with a white Formica table and padded benches upholstered with red vinyl. A window overlooked the greenery of the yard and the concrete tile patio. Underneath the shade of the mango tree, a swing chair swayed lazily. On the table, a china teacup and saucer sat on each side. Next to them was a shoebox full of black-and-white photos. As Grandma poured hot tea into each cup, steam rose from the brew.

"Remember this picture?" Grandma pushed the photograph across to her.

Emily was seven years old, on a step stool, sharing the chopping block with her grandma, chopping away with a butter knife. She remembered making believe she was a famous French chef—hat, moustache, and all. Back then, she imagined all chefs looked like Chef Boyardee.

"I remember. Where do you suppose I got my culinary skills?" She sipped her tea.

Grandma's eyes shone with vitality as always—eyes that had seen much of what Emily had yet to see. Her hair was now gray and her skin wrinkled and loose, but her eyes still sparkled.

"What about *this* picture?" Grandma handed it to her.

Emily was nine. She turned the bingo basket at the First Baptist Church, where her grandma volunteered to help run bingo night for the senior members of the congregation. That was before Grandma became a senior bingo-playing member of the congregation herself.

"I haven't seen these in a century." She touched Grandma's hand.

"A century? Don't make me older than I already am." Grandma combed her hair back with her hand and stuck her chin in the air.

Emily spread a handful of photos on the table. Her parents looked so youthful then. There was her brother at his eighth birthday party, and Grandpa at the Million Dollar Pier in front of the Mediterranean-style building. "I forgot about the old pier." A photo at Webb's City showed Emily at the trained animal acts, pointing to a chicken walking the tight rope. "Why aren't these in an album?" Emily looked up from the photos.

"I've been meaning to, but when I put them away, I forget."

"Leave them out so we don't forget." She stacked the photos in the box.

They sipped the tea with honey and talked about her job and Grandma's volunteer work at All Children's Hospital, where she read fairy tales to sick and dying children.

"A teacher never retires," Grandma said as they finished the tea.

"Let's sit for a while." Emily refilled grandma's cup and hers.

"I could get used to this." Grandma clasped her hands. "It's nice to have company for a change."

Grandma had been alone since Grandpa died from a stroke the summer before.

"Next time I'm off we'll go out, but today I'll make lunch," Emily said. "I don't want my expert culinary skills to go to waste." She opened the refrigerator and looked in.

"I'm glad you're here," Grandma said.

After loading her arms with tomatoes, onions, green peppers, and mushrooms, she placed them on the chopping block against the wall. She returned to the refrigerator and brought out a package of beef cubes, and got metal skewers and kitchen knives from the silverware drawer.

"Come," she said with a grin. "I'm not going to cut all these on my own."

Grandma joined her at the chopping block. She was the shorter of the two—unlike the photograph in the shoebox—with wrinkled hands aged with spots. They peeled and sliced the onions vertically in quarters and then horizontally into eighths, working in unison. They continued with the tomato, green pepper, and mushrooms, and then skewered the kebobs, which Emily placed on a plate and wrapped in cellophane before placing it in the refrigerator.

"I'm going to the drugstore," she said. "We'll eat when I get back."

"I'll get the grill ready." Grandma washed the knives.

The steamy weather met Emily when she stepped out to the screened porch. A red VW Beetle pulled up in the driveway, and Angie got out. Emily had told her where she lived. Angie wore round sunglasses and an oversized orange Buccaneers football jersey. Her cheeks were flushed red.

"Let's go see *Grease*," Angie said. "I think it's playing at Pinellas Park Mall."

"It's a plan. I like John Travolta, but I don't know if the movie is playing yet."

"Then let's hit the Cheyenne Social Club," Angie said. "It's the happening place. There's a lot of cute guys in cowboy hats there, stone foxes for sure. You've been there?"

"No, but I wanted an early night."

"Not with me, sweetie. I'll call you later. I'll give Monica a ring, too. She's off tonight."

"Oh, OK." Monica didn't like guys, but that was cool with her.

Angie got back in her bug and stuck her head out the driver's window as she backed up. The smoke from the cigarette in her mouth made her squint.

"You come with me, and I'll make sure you get lucky tonight," Angie said and drove off.

It had been awhile, and getting lucky wasn't such a bad idea—but not like that.

At the drugstore Emily compared stationery and settled on a letter pad and envelope set with a gold-and-black monarch butterfly design. Not that she had much to write to her friends about. Next to the cashier, she noticed a photo album she was sure Grandma would appreciate. When she got back, Grandma had readied the Hibachi grill with a charcoal briquette pyramid.

"I got industrious and made a salad, too." Grandma swayed in the swing chair beneath the green and red leaves of the mango tree.

Emily squirted lighter fluid on the charcoal, threw a match on it, and stepped back in time to avoid the orange-and-blue flame that roared to life with gusto and settled down as fast. In minutes, the briquettes glowed red. She waited a few more minutes before the kebobs went on the grill. The charcoal sizzled from dripping beef and tomato juices. Burned charcoal scent permeated the air.

"Summer's coming," Grandma said.

"And I hope the rain comes with it." Emily flipped the kebobs over.

"It has to rain when it gets that hot. Otherwise houses would catch on fire."

A six-foot wooden fence enclosed the back yard, with peach hyacinths and rosebushes caressing against it. Thick St. Augustine grass bordered the concrete tile patio.

Emily squinted in direct sunlight. "How do you cook out when it gets real hot?"

"I do it in the shade." Grandma giggled.

When she finished, she had one kebob medium rare for herself and one medium for her grandma. The charcoal, white in appearance, still burned hot. Inside, Grandma brought out the salad from the refrigerator, and they took seats next to tall glasses of iced tea.

"Where are you going tonight?" Grandma cut into her meat.

"A movie, maybe dancing. Wait right here." Emily left the room.

On her return, she carried the bulky paper bag. It crinkled as it changed hands. Grandma's eyes brightened when she saw the contents.

"Why did you spend your money?" She looked up with bright pleasure and squeezed her hand. "Thank you, dear. Now I'll have something to do while you're out."

After dinner Emily looked in her closet. What to wear? Shorts and blouse would do for a movie, but what about the Cheyenne Social Club? She turned and noticed a picture frame on her nightstand. It had the photo she had seen earlier, the one with her on the footstool, chopping vegetables alongside her grandma. The telephone rang.

"I got it!" Emily reached across the bed and answered the phone.

"You ready? We'll be by in twenty minutes," Angie said. "We're in luck. *Grease* is not out yet, but it's Ladies' Night at the Cheyenne: two-for-one drinks all night, and how I love it all night. Let's skip the movie."

That didn't sound like luck to her, and she didn't intend to spend another night at a bar. There was a question she wanted to ask, and she didn't care if it sparked a fire.

"Why were you cruel to Barry the other night?"

"He's an ass, and he got what he had coming to him. He picked the wrong wildcat to tangle with."

Emily sighed and glanced up to see the picture frame on the nightstand. "Sorry, but I'm staying home with Grandma tonight."

"Why for, she sick? Even so, that don't mean you can't go out."

She didn't try to explain because Angie wouldn't understand.

"You don't know what you're missing," Angie said as she hung up.

In the living room, Grandma read the *Evening Independent* in her nightgown.

"Want to split half a bottle of Chablis?" Emily asked.

"Hmmm…I have nowhere to go in the morning." She snickered, covering her mouth. "But aren't you going out?" A hopeful expression sprouted on her face.

"I'd rather help you put those photos in the album."

Emily slipped into a nightgown and slippers. She grabbed the chilled bottle of Chablis from the refrigerator and poured two wine glasses before returning to the living room. They spent the rest of the evening putting old memories into the new album and watching *The Love Boat* cast off for adventure.

X

Marcelo

"**I**'m not going," Marcelo told Barry when he clocked out. Emily was among those waiting at the Bull Pen, and Monica and Curtis were headed there. Marcelo was ready for a fresh new routine to replace the tired old one at the end of the work day. Each night out melted into another, and all brought the slow promise of frustrated ambitions.

"OK, but I'm going when I'm done," Barry said. "Catch you on the flipside."

"You think you should go? Why don't you go home and get some rest instead?"

"What are you, a doctor?" Barry asked. "You should join us and relax yourself."

Marcelo didn't want to do anything lamebrain like asking Emily out. That wouldn't go over well with Barry. But then, Barry *did* say he could have her if—change the subject. In a booth, Carlos was in a napkin-folding race with Roger.

"Your bro brought in the mother lode." Roger took a breather. "He made more than me."

"Don't get used to the easy money," Marcelo said.

"Oh, I'm used to it already." Carlos stopped folding. "You going home?"

"I don't know, but I won't be late."

"I'm going home, I'm beat," Carlos said. "I'm not used to having to remember so many things at once."

There wasn't much to do on a weeknight in the Sunshine City. A drive across Tampa Bay might unwind him a bit. With the top down on the Mustang, he pulled out of the lot into traffic.

A JC billboard on 34th Street recruited students around the clock. Emily was a senior at State. What was that like? It was three years of coursework, all that studying and all those nights staying in. In comparison, he had completed one year at JC in that time, all because Barry, a frosted mug of beer, and a beautiful, new waitress always waited at the Bull Pen.

Marcelo took I-275 North and headed to Tampa. A green-and-gold billboard announced Rodney Marsh and the Tampa Bay Rowdies, Tampa's North American Soccer League franchise. "The Rowdies are a Kick in The Grass," the sign read. Professional soccer had found a permanent home in Tampa.

He crossed Howard Frankland Bridge and made out the Tampa skyline ahead: two skyscrapers sparkled against the blue night sky. The choppy waters reflected slivers of moonlight. Dishing out for the AC compressor had killed him. He'd have to bust his hump another month to catch up to where he'd been two weeks before. Then another unfortunate event would happen, and he'd be set back weeks again. The game never changed. It was the first of June, and he hoped the universe had more to offer him. The month of May hadn't been generous.

He turned on the radio. The main news topic that week was President Carter's upcoming trip to Panama. It was the president's first visit after signing the Panama Canal Treaty, promising to give control of the canal to the Panamanians by the year 2000.

He changed radio stations. Bob Seger's song "Still the Same" roared from the speakers.

Marcelo took the Kennedy Boulevard exit and headed toward downtown Tampa. The traffic light at the Ashley Avenue intersection turned red, and he stopped. It had been several—WHISH!

A white station wagon flew past him on the left, ran the red light and—CRASH—plowed into the rear panel of a black-and-gold sports car crossing the intersection. The Firebird went into a tailspin while the guilty driver sped away. It spun and skated and crashed head-on against a concrete light pole, which toppled over it. Marcelo turned off the radio and pulled to the side of the road, where other drivers joined him. They watched while flames burst underneath the hood of the car. There was an unconscious woman in the driver's seat: her forehead lay on the steering wheel, setting off the car horn. Liquid dripped underneath the car engine.

"Call the fire department," a round-faced guy behind him called out to the gas station attendant who came out to watch. The attendant gave him a thumbs-up and rushed back inside. Other cars stopped and crowded the intersection.

"I hope they get here soon, poor dear," said a lady with a poodle on a leash.

Yellow flames burst under the car engine.

"Mother of God!" A truck driver took off his baseball cap and ran his hand over his head.

Marcelo couldn't hear fire engine sirens or see flashing lights in the distance. The unconscious woman inside the Firebird didn't have much time. She lay on the horn, blaring into the night, crying for help. Then he noticed gasoline dripping under the trunk. Live electrical wires from the toppled pole danced behind the car. Still, he heard no fire sirens, and it was a quiet night. He took off running toward the flaming car and the woman trapped inside.

"Hold your horses!" yelled the truck driver. "The fire department's coming. You're gonna get yourself killed!"

When he reached the car and the unconscious driver, the volume of the commotion turned off and time slowed down. All he could hear was his breathing. All he could feel was the heat from the flames under the car. The driver's door was jammed, but the window was open. The downed light pole blocked the passenger door. He shook her, but she didn't respond. The heat, smoke, and fumes made him woozy and wobbly in the knees. The fire under the car spread with the leaking gasoline. The tank was about to explode. He reached inside and rolled down the window as far as he could. The chest-crushing heat wrapped around him, and he feared his slacks would catch fire. He was fading and unsteady, groggy from the heat and lack of oxygen. He grabbed her underneath the shoulders and dragged her out the window.

His hearing and real time came back as he carried her from the burning car. As the fire roared and exploded behind him, the pressure pushed him forward. Finally, he could hear faint sirens growing louder as he ran. A flash of light blinded him. A second later he realized a woman had taken his picture as the car exploded. People gasped, their faces illuminated by the explosion. When he reached the grass, he dropped to his knees and laid her down. He fell forward and rolled on his back. Two paramedics rushed to them.

"We'll take it from here." They tended to the lady beside him.

People encircled and looked down on him, asking if he was OK. All his attention was on the black sky and the moon and stars hidden behind a barrier of clouds. He remembered his last fishing trip to Key West. He and Barry had stopped the car in the middle of Alligator Alley at midnight to stare at the sky. The two-lane country road had no lights and only one flashing traffic light in its ninety-mile length from Naples to Fort Lauderdale. There was no moon that night, but it was bright when they stepped out of the car. The Milky Way above them was amazing: a thick band, a bright cluster of stars splitting the night sky in two. He'd never seen a billion stars before. Never seen the Milky Way.

Warm drops fell on his face. The rain brought him back to the present, to the people looking down on him and whispering about him. He was at peace. A sense of satisfaction circulated through his veins. A lightning bolt ripped the sky, and he found himself in the middle of a torrential downpour.

XI

Barry

Barry drove to the Bull Pen with buckets of water pouring from the heavens. Where did all that rain come from? Man, just because Marcelo wanted to be a goody-two shoes and go home after work didn't mean he had to. He was wound tighter than a rattrap and was ready to snap. Who wouldn't be? He'd been under watch all night again—Connie and Carmine, who else? They'd made him jumpy as a freaking toad. After a night like that, he'd earned the right to relax.

He pulled into a parking spot in front of the Bull Pen. Rainwater streamed down the face of the building like tears. Flashing neon lights on the windows called him. He dashed inside.

At a table in front of the bar, fuddy-duddy Curtis and the girls played cards around a pitcher of brew. Ha! The love of his life Angie was there too. If she gave him any flak, he'd make tracks for home and call it a night.

"It looks like rain." Barry took a barstool.

"No shit, Sherlock," Smitty said.

Smitty opened a gallon jar of pickled pigs' feet and sank his teeth on a pink foot. Barry could hear cries of pain, but that couldn't be: the pig was dead. He'd heard his mom say how she ignored some things she heard or saw because they weren't real, and he gave his back to Smitty.

"Come join us," Curtis called out to him and shuffled the deck of cards.

Barry shifted his view when Emily and Monica looked his way. From the jukebox, a country song told the story of a pathetic, sad guy getting to Phoenix. After he got a chilled mug, he joined them and poured himself a beer with an inch of head. Perfecto!

Roger rushed in from outside and shook the water off his crew cut, as if he had any hair to begin with. A guy and girl locked in an embrace and kissing followed him in. Both looked as if they'd fallen in love with the refrigerator besides themselves. He could park a Pinto and a Vega in their shadows.

"I got a couple of job applications at Tampa Airport." Angie eyed her cards. "One was for Pan Am and the other for Eastern Airlines."

"You can't go wrong with those two companies," Emily said.

"That be far out," Curtis said, "when you get hired as a stewardess."

"If you want to wait on people," Monica said, "you might as well do it in style."

A dude with pencil arms broke open a pool game. Balls cracked and scattered all over the table. Two or three thumped into pockets. The guy walked around the table looking for his best shot. In front of Barry, Curtis dealt cards to everyone, and he pushed his cards back.

"Anyone want to play pool?" Roger asked.

"We're playing blackjack," Monica said. "Why? I don't know." She eyed her cards. "Oh, I went to get stamps today, and guess what? First-class stamps are now fifteen cents."

"So it went up two cents," Roger said. "I have books of stamps at my place if you want to crash at my shag shack."

"I told everyone," Monica said. "I'm not dating until I finish school. I can't take the relationship BS and the stress of college and work at the same time."

"I thought you weren't into guys," Emily said.

"No, silly," Monica said. "Who told you that?"

"Nobody." Emily giggled. "I'm just playing with you."

"No card playing allowed!" Smitty shouted from behind the bar. They folded their cards.

"I guess we'll settle for stimulating conversation," Roger said on his way to the bar.

"The Buccaneers are going to surprise the football world this season." Curtis collected the cards everyone had shoved toward him. "The defense is solid, and this rookie quarterback Williams is going to make a world of difference." Curtis acted as if he could tell the future.

"Roger, Curtis is talking to you," Barry said over his shoulder.

Roger brought back a glass of white wine.

The Tampa Bay Bucs had finished their second season last December with a 2-12 record. That was only because they won their last two games, their only wins in two seasons. The "Orange Crush" defense was young and showed promise, but Coach John McKay was under fire for the team's poor offensive showing.

"We'll win a handful of games this year." Curtis poured himself the rest of the brew.

"Tell me when that happens," Roger said.

Barry didn't want to talk football with know-it-all Curtis. That hippie load-out believed he was a walking encyclopedia of sports. If he ever had to depend on Curtis for conversation, it'd be time to say good-bye to the cruel world and jump off the Skyway Bridge.

"Whoever didn't pitch in for the last pitcher buys next." Emily nudged Barry.

Was she using Marcelo to get close to him? What a fool to imagine that! He grabbed the glass pitcher and went to the bar. The gulps of beer had relieved his tension. In a corner high behind the bar, the tube showed the news in silence. On the screen, a dark-haired guy carried a lady from a burning car. Barry rubbed his eyes. Could it be?

"That's Marcelo!" he yelled. "Turn it up."

Smitty got up on the step stool and gave the picture sound. When the others got to the bar and saw what the fuss was all about, their traps fell to the floor. Emily's eyes grew wide, and she put both hands over her mouth. You'd think they'd seen a polar bear in the Everglades.

"Who is the Fearless Hero of Saint Petersburg?" the TV guy asked. "About an hour ago at the scene of a traffic accident at the Ashley and Kennedy Boulevard intersection in Tampa, Marcelo Robles risked his life to pull an unconscious mother of three from a burning car, just in time, before the gas tank exploded and engulfed the car in flames. Motorists who'd stopped at the scene were trying to figure out what to do when Mister Robles rushed and pulled the helpless woman to safety."

"Look what he's gone and done," Barry said. "Made himself a hero."

His eyes and ears weren't lying. Marcelo had shot himself through everybody's television and into their living rooms like a superhero. He could be his partner, and they could fight crime and corruption together. They were a team.

"Just imagine, if he'd been here, he wouldn't have been there," Emily said.

"Why don't you talk normal?" Angie rolled her eyes.

"No arguing now, girls," Roger said. "We'll settle it later with a wet T-shirt contest."

"There's a garden hose out back." Old fogy Curtis laughed.

"Put a lid on it and listen," Barry told them, and they shut up tighter than an oyster.

"An amateur photographer at the scene dropped off these Polaroid pictures at the studio," the TV guy continued. "The Tampa Police Department confirmed the accident and provided us with the identity of the fearless hero. We attempted to contact him earlier but haven't been successful. We'll have more information as the story develops. Meanwhile, the grateful woman rescued is in stable condition at Tampa Bay General Hospital. We cannot release her name until next of kin is notified. In other news, torrential rains hit the bay area, ending the drought. More when we come back." A cigarette commercial about a cattle drive came on.

"Can you believe that?" Monica said.

"That's super," Emily said. "Barry, what's his phone number, I'll call him."

Why did she have a happy, stupid look on her face?

Barry got back and took a seat, blown away by what he'd seen and heard. Man, he'd never known anyone who'd been on TV before. Even less someone they called a hero. The news had him psyched; excitement flowed through his veins. Why was he being such a jerk to Marcelo? They were brothers, soldiers in a war without mercy. At the pay phone, he stuck a quarter in the slot. It rang three times before Marcelo picked up.

"Man, why didn't you tell me what you did?" Barry asked.

"What did I do?"

"Save that lady and become a superhero. It was on the TV. Everybody saw it."

"You've...you've got to be kidding me."

"You're the Fearless Hero of Saint Petersburg, my man, and they're looking for you."

Marcelo told him that at the scene, the paramedics treated the lady for smoke inhalation and gave her oxygen before strapping her to a stretcher and putting her in the ambulance. The paramedics offered to take him to the hospital for a checkup, but he told them he was fine. So they gave him oxygen and checked his heart rate and blood pressure while he gave his statement to Tampa Police. After that, he got back to town and grabbed a bite at Sambo's.

"I'm no hero."

"We know that, but they don't." Barry laughed. "Call the TV channel, hero boy."

"I'm not calling them...and I'm not answering my phone, either." He hung up.

"What a fool," Barry said. If it were him, he'd call in a New York minute. He'd be tickled pink to have fifteen minutes of fame; be a "one-hit wonder" and then fade into darkness. But he never got breaks like that. Man, he had to make his own luck. No guts, no glory. The Belmont Stakes was coming up, and he had June's rent to play with. No freaking way Affirmed could beat Alydar three times in row. That was humanly impossible! It was his sign, and he had to take it. The race was a gimme, and he had to place a bet.

And he was going to have his name engraved on the Hall of Fame plaque hanging high behind that bar. So he stepped up to the bar and ordered one he'd never tasted before, a Cristal beer from Peru. After that, he bought a pitcher of brew and a round of shots for the gang. It was time to celebrate. The outlook was bright, without the shadows of clouds or the threat of storm. He'd make a mint on that race, and they'd become famous restaurateurs: kings of the industry. He could hear the cash registers ringing in his ear. As he drove home, Mother Nature unleashed a fury of lightning bolts, ripping the belly of black rainclouds, drenching the streets and limiting his ability to see down the road.

XII

Marcelo

"Sergio wants to see you," Connie told Marcelo.

Could that have anything to do with a promotion? It'd be great if he could catch a break, a springboard of hope for the future. He crossed his fingers, half nervous, half confident. Then he noticed Connie's swollen eye underneath a thick coat of makeup. He lifted her chin and moved her hair out of the way. "What happened?"

"It's nothing," she said. "I opened a kitchen cabinet and hit my face."

"I'm here." Curtis put on his tie. "Sorry, Connie, my ex was late picking up my kid…What happened to your face?"

"Enough already," Connie said. "Get ready to open, and Sergio is in the office, Marcelo."

Marcelo walked with Curtis through the service area.

"Is her boyfriend hitting her again?" Curtis asked. "She deserves better than that. The moron doesn't know what he's got."

"Everybody deserves better," Marcelo said. "But she keeps taking it."

It was a helpless, sad feeling, but there was nothing anyone could do to help someone who didn't want to be helped. She'd left him before, only to go back when he cried like a disgraced televangelist and promised never to do it again. Marcelo went into the office, and Sergio looked up from the paperwork on his desk.

"You're some kind of superhero." Sergio had yellow, pink, and blue invoices next to the adding machine on the desk. "What did the TV people have to say?"

It figured. "I never called them." He shrugged.

"You can't go saving lives and not expect to cause a stir."

"Never intended to do any of that."

People were making a bigger deal out of this accident than it was, a minor incident soon to be forgotten. He sighed, excused himself, and plodded through the kitchen and the linen-covered tables of the dining room to the lobby. Carlos met him there.

"Everybody's saying you're a hero," Carlos said. "What happened?"

"Don't believe everything you hear."

The telephone rang at the cashier's desk. Jackie answered it.

"It's for you." She handed Marcelo the phone.

The call left him stunned, like floating fish after an underwater explosion. Channel 9 News wanted to interview him at the restaurant at 5:00 p.m., for the six o'clock news broadcast. The reporter wouldn't say who'd told them where to find him other than to say it was a private citizen who'd called. His workplace was no longer a secret hideaway—he'd been unmasked.

"I'll have to ask my boss."

He returned to the office to speak with Sergio and filled him in.

"Is it OK if they interview me here?" Marcelo asked.

"Does a gator crap in the swamp?" Sergio asked. "Of course, it's more than OK."

With Sergio's unfortunate blessing, he accepted the interview. At least the publicity would help stuff the register and their pockets with cash for days to come.

Minutes later, Sergio called an impromptu meeting and gathered the crew in the dining room. The place came to a standstill: only the ice machine and air-conditioning made their presence known. The crew detonated when they heard the news, electrified with excitement.

"Geez, a real live celebrity." Curtis shook his head in disbelief.

Emily snuggled up to Marcelo. "Want to save me from my dull existence?" She held his chin and looked into his eyes—his heart dropped like a blacksmith's anvil.

"Thanks for the publicity. I'm proud of you." Sergio went to the office to get ready for the cameras. "Imagine, a hero working at my restaurant."

"Good going, bro." Barry put an arm around him. "Get ready to make the big bucks."

Marcelo waited upfront to meet the reporter. The television crew would arrive any minute. Across the dining room, Sergio supervised the salad ladies cleaning the fingerprints off the sneeze guard. Everything had to be perfect that night.

A lady in a housedress and sandals strolled in the front door puffing on a cigarette. He recognized her. It was Barry's mom. She neared Marcelo at the podium.

"Is Barry here?" she asked.

"How are you, Mrs.—"

"Is he here?" She stepped to the dining room entrance and scanned the room.

Jackie called Barry on the intercom, and he strolled up front beaming. His sunny disposition crashed when he saw the reason for the call.

"What are you doing here?" His head bowed.

"This is no social visit." She took a drag. "You got money?"

"No, I haven't started working yet."

"They're cutting the phone off tomorrow if it don't get paid."

Barry kept quiet with his eyes on the tile floor. She told him how part-time work doing laundry at $2.65 an hour didn't stretch far enough. She burned her fingers and dropped the butt on the floor, stepped on it and ground it out. Barry picked it up and put it in his pocket.

"I don't have any cash to spare," he said. "I have my own bills to pay."

"What you good for? Nothing, that's what." She headed for the door.

"Then why did you come here?"

She turned. "I hoped that maybe once you'd be good for something."

Barry grinned, stuffed his hands in his pockets, and went to his station. Marcelo started after him just as the television crew arrived.

Five in the afternoon was an ideal time for the interview. The Vineyard had just opened for dinner, and there wasn't much business to interfere with the TV crew. The cameraman set up in the dining room in front of the salad ladies, who giggled as they finished putting the fresh vegetable and fruit decorations on the salad bar. A few feet away, Sergio wore his blue pin-striped suit and fidgeted with his tie's Windsor knot. Marcelo had gone home to get dressed. He wore a blue blazer and a red-and-blue striped tie.

The television reporter brushed her hair and put on fresh red lipstick. Marcelo took a deep breath, but there didn't seem to be enough oxygen. She stood in front of the camera with Sergio and Marcelo out of the lens's sight. The cameraman counted down from three.

"Tonight we're at the Vineyard Restaurant in Central Plaza in Saint Petersburg. We're here to meet Marcelo Robles, known to most as the Fearless Hero of Saint Petersburg. According to TPD, Marcelo risked his life last night to save a helpless and unconscious mother of three from a burning car as others watched, frozen with fear." She turned to Marcelo, with Sergio at his side.

"First of all," she said, "thanks to Sergio Falcone for allowing us to meet Marcelo in his place of business, the Vineyard Restaurant. What's it like having a hero on your staff?" She put the microphone in front of Sergio.

"I'm proud to have him here." He looked into the camera. "He's a real respectable guy, works very hard, and goes out of his way to help others."

"Well, he's demonstrated that," she said. "Now, Marcelo—"

"One more thing." Sergio stuck his head in front of the camera. "Say you saw us on TV, and we'll give you a free appetizer with dinner for two. You'll see we have the best food and the best service in town. I guarantee it."

"That's an offer you can't refuse." She moved the mike to Marcelo. "Please tell us about yourself—who is Marcelo, and what makes him tick?"

He paused. "I'm a regular guy, not a hero, that's for sure." He looked into the black lens of the camera. "I've worked here as a waiter for over twelve months."

The bright lamps and the eyes glued on his every word made him warm under the collar.

"There's no better waiter than him." Sergio added. "And he's worked in the kitchen and the lounge, and he's going to open his own place one day."

"Open a restaurant? When will that come about?" she asked.

"It'll be a while. My partner and I are saving for it, but it's not easy."

Sergio stuck his face up to the mike. "He's a college student too."

Sergio's interruptions took Marcelo off the hot seat, and he didn't mind at all.

"Tell us. What college do you attend?"

"Well…I guess…I mean I go to JC. But right now I'm not going to school. It's expensive, and I can't do that and save for the business at the same time."

"That's fabulous," she said to the camera. "There you are, ladies and gentlemen. Our hero, Marcelo, is a courageous citizen, hardworking employee, and dedicated college student."

The lights went off and the temperature dropped, saving him from breaking into a sweat. While the crew packed their equipment, Marcelo answered questions for a *St. Petersburg Times* reporter and had his picture taken. Answering the second set of questions was a welcome breeze, without the light and the camera on him or the microphone in his face. The article was to run in the newspaper the next day. That he didn't expect.

"You were intense." Emily squeezed his hand. She offered a grin that knocked on his heart for admission. Barry watched at a distance but looked away when Marcelo's eyes met his. It wouldn't be right to fall for her.

"When you shake hands with the devil," Barry said later, "hell's the only place to go."

What was *that* all about?

After the six o'clock news showed the clip on Marcelo, the Vineyard telephone rang and rang, wearing out Jackie's ear. People asked to make reservations with Marcelo that night, but Jackie told the callers they never took reservations at the Vineyard. Plenty of time and energy went into keeping the place firing on all eight cylinders, and Sergio had decided a while back that they didn't need to spend further effort by taking them.

"You've got every single girl in Saint Pete waiting at the bar for one of your tables," Connie told Marcelo later that night.

Droves of curious customers came to dine and meet the Fearless Hero. Connie had to turn people away at ten o'clock when the overworked and spent kitchen closed. As Barry had said they would, they made big bucks that night.

Marcelo went home pleasantly surprised. His existence had been injected with a dose of satisfaction. Most of all, he was overjoyed to put this episode behind him.

XIII

Emily

"**E**verything is fine here, Mom." Emily blew the hair off her forehead.

Her mother's call had ended a welcome dry spell of non-communication. The ring of the telephone had turned her blue skies to the color of dirty dishwater.

"I asked your grandma when she was moving to Broward, and she said that was settled last year. Why haven't you talked to her about that?"

She objected to her mother's patronizing reprimand, not concerned with the whining in her own voice.

"I'd like to get to know her before I try to change her life."

"What have you been doing all this time then?"

Mother was challenging her, but Emily wasn't going to lace up the gloves. She had to tread carefully. With her mother, she had a razor-thin line between annoyed and incensed.

"We're doing this to be together again," Mother said, "like a family."

"Save it for Grandma, Mom, but I don't believe she'd buy that either. I've got to roll."

Sadly, there would be plenty of time and opportunity to resume their scrimmages in the future. It was sad, but her mother found comfort in the steady routine of conflict. Happily, Emily had a preferred alternative to their quarrels: Marcelo was living a cornucopia of amazing dreams, and she'd rather enjoy them with him.

Emily kissed Grandma on the forehead, rushed out the door, and drove to Marcelo's place. At a stop sign, she placed a dab of Estée Lauder White Linen behind each ear. If that didn't get him, nothing would. After the heroic rescue two weeks ago, Marcelo had laid low, waiting for the "hoopla," as he called it, to die down. The evening of the TV interview, she'd offered to buy him dinner and made it clear she wouldn't accept no for an answer. Could it be the night she cracked that hard exterior of his and got to his heart? Her eyes widened in anticipation.

Marcelo put the top down on the Mustang, and they drove to the beach. It was a modern-day carriage fit for a prince and princess. Minutes later, they parked alongside the Cyclone Restaurant under the fading light of day.

"Do you smell a distinct fragrance in the air?" she asked at dinner.

There was a pause that seemed to expand slowly, like the universe.

"Yeah, it smells like fresh fish," he said. "They make delicious burgers here, too." Marcelo seized his World Famous Grouper Sandwich two-handed and sank his teeth into it.

It amazed Emily that one of Marcelo's favorite places, the Cyclone, was practically a beach shack on Pass-A-Grille Beach, a peninsula at the end of St. Pete Beach. The small kitchen and bar offered a modest menu of fresh grouper, homemade conch bisque, and clam chowder. The rustic motif included a bar and a dining area. They took a table by the window. Across the road, emerald-green waves from the gulf ebbed and flowed onto the sand and caressed the sun-bleached shore. Pelicans glided across the horizon in their predator roles, searching the waters for their nourishment before turning in.

"How's Carlos doing?" she asked.

"I only see him at work it seems, but he's fine. We watched the French Open finals the other day. Borg beat Villas in three sets."

"Borg is intense. He might be the best to ever play the game." She appreciated the roar and the smell of the sea. "This is a beautiful location."

It hadn't been difficult for her to discover where to invite Marcelo. All she had to do was ask people who'd known him longer than she. Barry didn't offer much assistance, being vague and evasive. "He likes a hundred places; it's tough to think of one," he'd said, tight-lipped as a clam plucked from the sand of receding waves. Noticing Barry's non-cooperation, Angie was more that eager to help.

On the beach, half a dozen bathers lingered under a sun that eased into the gulf. She was pleased he'd accepted her invitation, happy to be alone with him. She blushed at the images that rolled across the screen of her mind: scenes of the two of them behind closed doors. A gentle breeze stroked her face and brought her back to earth.

"Nice article in the *Times*," she said. "How are you handling your newfound fame?"

His eyes darted off everywhere except at her, the source of the conversation.

"It's nice to be appreciated, but I don't know about fame, newfound or otherwise."

"You deserve all the praise you get." She shifted in her seat.

He amazed her with stellar new developments. The universe continued to shower him with gifts of cosmic proportions. WFTU Radio had invited him to be a guest on *Good Morning Tampa Bay*, the highest-rated morning rush-hour show in the bay area. It didn't end there. Channel 4 wanted to know if he would appear on *Faces of Tampa Bay*. The talk show recognized citizens who'd gone above and beyond the call of duty to serve the bay area.

"Don't think twice," she said. "Call them."

The manager, whose belly wore a strained belt for a smile, recognized Marcelo and picked up their tab after he autographed it for him. A teen girl in glasses eating with another, tables away, pointed at him and then to the newspaper in her hand.

"It's a privilege to be seen with the Fearless Hero of Saint Pete." Emily clasped his hand.

"I'm no hero. Actually, it was kind of dumb risking my neck for someone I'd never met."

"That makes it more remarkable. Would you risk death to save me?" She batted her eyes.

"I...I couldn't handle any more publicity." He took another bite.

Was he brushing her off, or did she have to hit him over the head for him to get a clue?

"At least it's a change from the routine, isn't it?" she sighed.

"You're not lying about that."

They strolled on the beach after sunset. The loose sand that filtered through her toes still retained the warmth of the sun. Moonlight rippled on the choppy waters and sparkled like a million diamonds under the night sky. A flock of seagulls gawked at a distance, preparing for the night. She held onto his arm as the wind whispered in her ear. He led her to the packed, wet sand. Waves crashed on the shore and white foam rushed to her feet.

"Isn't the full moon beautiful?" She rested her head against his shoulder.

"No more than any other night."

Not the most romantic guy in all of creation, but one full of passion, she was sure.

A cruise ship navigated on the horizon against a deep blue sky. She'd love to take a starry-eyed ocean cruise with him. She imagined a tsunami rushing onto the beach at that moment and then receding and carrying them to a waiting ship. A few feet away, a white-haired woman in a dark one-piece bathing suit slept on a blanket. Oh, no! Grandma had wanted to watch TV with her for days. Grandma hadn't said anything, which made her feel worse.

"I'm kind of nervous about more publicity." He brought her back to the sand.

"You've handled one interview, you can handle another."

"When will it end?"

"Never. You're a celebrity now, you need a manager." She laughed.

He was a rough sculpture in need of her finishing touches. He could be her David, and she his Michelangelo.

"Please, I'm no celebrity," he said. "But thanks for being a friend."

Just a friend? Oh, well. She knew he didn't have time for public speaking classes or a Dale Carnegie course before his next engagement. So as a *friend*, she could help him prepare. Her attempt to scale the wall built around him seemed in vain.

"We should get back," he said, and they turned around.

They had walked about a mile, but she could still make out the wooden "Cyclone" sign because of the floodlight shining on it. The fresh, clean gulf air revived her as they made tracks on the sand. Shortly, they neared his car underneath a flickering street-light. Across the road, the Sand Dollar Motel blinked "Vacancy" in red neon letters. How naïve to assume anything would've happened between them. They weren't even emotionally compatible, which was a basic requirement. At the car, he spun her around, held her against his body, and kissed her.

"What?" Her words muffled in the kiss.

"I'm sorry," he said. "I misunderstood…"

"You didn't." She kissed him back and lost herself in his passion under the streetlight, against the car, across the road from the motel. They expelled a collective sigh of relief.

"I don't want to pretend anymore," he said.

She glanced into his dark eyes. "Why would you have to pretend?"

"It's nothing," he said. "I've liked you since we met."

She kissed him again. Passion was vital to the soul as blood was to the body. Without passion, romance couldn't bloom and, certainly, couldn't explode.

"Come on." He locked the car door.

She held his arm as they crossed the road.

XIV

Barry

Barry couldn't believe it. It'd never happened before, and it'd probably never happen again. Not that it was anything of biblical proportions, like walking on water or parting the sea, but it ranked right up there: there had never been back-to-back Triple Crown winners until Affirmed beat Alydar at the Belmont Stakes. Who would've thought Affirmed could beat Alydar three times in a row? That was why he'd bet June's rent—and lost. Man, he was as penniless as the day he came into the world buck naked. If he didn't pay rent in the next week, he'd be living in his clunker of a ride. Then that phone call came.

Jackie had called everybody and their brother to come in an hour early for a meeting. Barry had no clue what could be so freaking important. Leave it to Sergio and Carmine to mess with his head at the worst of times. He torched up a tightly rolled joint of Acapulco gold to chase the nervousness away. Each day brought the familiar uneasy feeling of what the future held.

There wasn't time to iron his white shirt or wait for those black pants on the clothesline to dry. He slipped into the wrinkled shirt from the clothesline and fished out black slacks from the laundry basket. They didn't smell half bad. He had to hurry. Most of the time his life went at a donkey's pace; other times at that of an Oldsmar Racetrack thoroughbred. He filled his lungs to capacity with a monster drag and blew out like Puff the Magic Dragon.

He rushed out the door and jumped into his Catalina. "Crap!" The vinyl seats scorched his thighs. The lazy air conditioner had retired before he'd bought the car, and he'd had no time to air it out that day. He rolled down the window. Smoke snaked up from the doobie on his lips and stung his bloodshot eyes. The Pontiac cranked up and rattled down the dirt road before he floored it. His muffler dragged on the ground as he bounced and fishtailed onto Park Boulevard. Down the road, he flicked the burning roach out the window.

Hell, it wasn't the first time everyone had been called in for an emergency meeting. Whose head was going to roll this time? It'd better not be his. But he hadn't gotten any new call parties in a while; no one had written a letter to Sergio bragging about his excellent service; and he was no superhero. Actually, he'd been messing up lately. Did one of his parties walk out without paying, and Carmine and Connie were out to eighty-six him? That had to be the reason. The fear growing inside him was as real as the air moving in and out of his lungs. He could see terror in the air he exhaled. If he got canned, there would be blood, and he meant buckets.

Last time they'd called an emergency meeting was when beaucoup unpaid dinner checks turned up missing. They didn't actually turn up missing because if they'd turned up, they wouldn't be missing. They just didn't turn up. Sure, all restaurants had their share of walkouts: sons of bitches who drank and ate and then snuck out without paying. Mostly it happened on weekends, when waiters and waitresses didn't have time to bring the checks to Jackie. Or when waves of customers crowded the register and Jackie was too busy to see the termites sneak out. Not only did more checks than normal go missing then, but 100 percent belonged to two waiters, two gnarly dudes from California. They pocketed the money. That was what they did, though they never admitted to anything. Carmine had already given them the boot, and they were history by the time the meeting got going that day. Sergio didn't want to press charges because he didn't want to waste time with the police report and court and all, and he told all waiters and waitresses to watch out for walkouts. But Carmine put everyone on probation for six months, saying he'd fire anyone with checks missing during that period, no questions asked. The next morning, Sergio called off the probation that retarded Carmine had put everyone on. Barry was lucky—the very next day a couple of losers he'd waited on snuck out.

He pulled into the Vineyard parking lot to see the whole back of the lot full of employee cars. Man, Marcelo's car was already there. Was Marcelo involved in what was going down in any way? The engine backfired when he shut it off, shouting for a tune-up or another type of mechanical attention. Just die already. That car was going to be the death of him.

In the dining room, waiters and waitresses sat and waited for the crapola to hit the fan. He took a seat behind Carlos and Harry, but they didn't know what was going on either. A few feet away, Roger massaged his string-bean mustache as if he had something to worry about. The dude had nothing to fret about because the horny cheese eater was always kissing Carmine's and Sergio's butts.

Roger's head was on fire! Barry jumped up, "Hey!" He pointed but no one made a fuss. Everybody looked at Barry kind of weird. If Roger's head were on fire, he wouldn't be sitting there like nothing was happening. His eyes were lying to him! The fire went out, and he sat down and cracked his knuckles.

"What the hell are you lacing my dope with?" he asked Harry.

"Nothing, man. It's all orgasmic, like God made it." Harry scratched his scraggly face. "Like I was saying, if anybody needs to fry, it's that crazy nut, just like I'm going to torch up this number burning a hole in my pocket after the meeting."

What? "Who needs to fry?" Barry asked.

"He's talking about the Son of Sam killer in New York City," Carlos said. "He just got twenty-five to life for killing six people. But he's not going to roast because they don't have the death penalty up there."

"They don't got that?" Harry asked. "Isn't that unconstitutional?"

"Where's your brother?" Barry asked Carlos.

"He's around somewhere."

Barry swallowed hard and took deep breaths. A few struggled to act calm, but others seemed as if they didn't care. Curtis rubbed his bony thighs, worrying how he could he take care of his motherless child if he got canned. Tyrone bit his nails and had a blank stare. He had nothing to be concerned about unless he fell off the wagon and started bending the elbow again. Besides, he was the kitchen manager. Angie played it cool talking to Monica, probably about some unfortunate soul she dragged home from the bar. Man, it was getting warm and stuffy.

What? Marcelo came into the dining room with Sergio and Carmine, and he was all dressed up. He wore a coat and a tie and looked like a mannequin from Ermatinger's Men's Wear. Sergio held up his hands, and everyone clammed up real quick.

"We have good news for you today," Sergio said.

Everyone let out a giant sigh of relief. Barry's heart rate came down, and he could breathe again. Carmine had the hugest smirk Barry had ever seen on that loser.

"Tell us already!" Roger yelled across the room, and everyone agreed.

"I'll tell you," Sergio said. "Today, Carmine and I promoted Marcelo to assistant manager." The room swelled into a wave of claps and cheers. "He's worked hard, and if anybody deserves it, it's him. He begins his new job tomorrow."

That, he couldn't believe. Marcelo should've been promoted ages ago. The only reason Carmine had agreed to it was probably because it was good for business: Marcelo was the town hero. But there was always profit behind any business move. His buddy deserved it. They had to go out that night, get super wasted, and celebrate good times.

"Congratulations!" Sergio gave Marcelo a bear hug in front of the whole crew.

Everybody clapped. Roger got up and shook Marcelo's hand with gusto.

"We're not done yet," Sergio said. Emily waited behind Roger for her crack at Marcelo, but all had to sit down. "Marcelo has something to say."

"Tonight after the dining room closes, we're having a wine-tasting party to celebrate my promotion. We can also learn to describe each of our wines in one sentence. That way we can sell more wine and increase our sales and tips. And..."

Barry needed the cash badly. Marcelo choked up. Suck it up, man!

"I want to thank Sergio and Carmine for the opportunity. I'll do the best job I can."

They all got up, clapped like maniacs, and surrounded him like a movie star or something. Emily got to Marcelo, and Barry kicked back and took it all in while the rest made a fuss over his friend. Why did Barry let Emily, who didn't even like him, get between him and his best friend? Maybe she wasn't that bad. He got so paranoid sometimes.

Barry recalled being Mr. Big Shot once. When they busted hump at the Fogcutter Restaurant, Barry took first prize in a wine-selling contest between all the waiters and waitresses. Marcelo got second place. He couldn't believe he'd beaten him, because Marcelo was so smooth he could talk a dog off a meat truck. The night he won, a bunch of waiters and waitresses went home to get decked out, the guys in bellbottoms and killer platform shoes. They met at the Gallery Lounge and took shots of tequila and boogied into the night.

"We're going to party tonight," Barry said to Carlos.

"And celebrate good times. We'll let Marcelo pick the place."

Barry's belly shook like a bowl of jelly when he laughed, seeing Roger across the crowded room, taking an order from a party of six—the Waltons. Roger had named them that because the menfolk wore overalls and the clan drove up in a beat-up pickup truck. And what a mess they always made around that table, dropping bread rolls, half-eaten baked potatoes, silverware, and all kinds of junk. Roger had a difficult time keeping up that fake clown smile of his. Barry could see his shoestring mustache tremble across the sea of parties. Nobody ever wanted to get stuck with them, especially on a busy night. It was a sure way to get in the weeds.

"Why do they have to ask for me?" Roger always wondered.

They ran his rear off because nothing was ever right. They sent food back to the kitchen because it was undercooked or overcooked or because it didn't taste right. And they always asked for prime rib bones to take home to their pack of dogs.

"They probably make soup for themselves with them," Roger had said to Tyrone one night as he stuffed the meaty bones into a doggy bag.

Worst of all, they always left him a horrible tip—10 percent. Papa Walton made out as if it were a humongous tip or something special. Each time, he'd pull Roger aside and stick the 10 percent in his pocket while making some nonsense talk that had nothing to do with anything. What did he think, that he was going to get mugged for that dough?

Roger passed by. "Don't say a thing."

"I won't." He followed him. "You helping Marcelo celebrate after the wine tasting?"

Roger faced him at the service bar. "There's nothing going on tonight other than that."

"I guess you aren't invited." He cracked up.

"Sit on it." Roger got lost in the traffic in the service area.

Barry went to the service bar and poured himself a Coke. Carmine was working the horseshoe bar. His undivided attention was locked on two chicks revealing plenty of cleavage. Barry took a sip. In front of him, Sherry broke up the ice in the bin with a scoop.

"Need anything?" she asked.

"No," he said. "What's the skinny with your cosmetology license?"

"Can you believe the school hasn't sent me the transcripts?" She threw the scoop in the ice bin. "If it wasn't out of state, I'd get them myself."

"That really blows." He walked away.

Barry noticed Marcelo at the bread drawer, feeling rolls and sticking them in a basket. The next day, his buddy would be Mr. Assistant Manager.

"Where we getting down tonight, big guy?" he asked. "What's the lowdown?"

"Don't know, but Emily says it's special." He shut the drawer and booked.

What the hell? Why was she making the decision where everybody was going to party that night? He didn't like the vibes he was getting. Every muscle in his body tightened. His breath got shallow and quick. His palms got clammy. Barry was going to find out.

"What's cooking tonight?" Barry asked Emily when she joined the pickup line.

"I'm doing something just for Marcelo."

"We're not all going out?" He slammed the covers on his meals. "You can't do that."

She gave him a stare and then called for her table. "We can all hang out any time....This is a special night."

What! Barry gritted his teeth, shouldered the tray, and made tracks. She must be fried if she thought she was stealing Marcelo away from his friends on an important night. Ha! Marcelo wouldn't put up with any of that.

Barry totaled a massive check for an eight-top and laid it on a tip tray. Waiting for payment, he checked on his other tables. One of his parties came back from the salad bar. The chicks, about his age, had plates piled high like colorful pyramids. They'd be busy for a while. Next to them, four loud guys chugged down a second round of beers before chow. He wasn't going to rush them because he knew they'd take good care of him if he let them be. He never raced against time anyway because time always won. The check he'd just laid down had a Master Charge on top of it. He picked it up and headed upfront. The man and his old lady in his booth didn't look pleased. What were they still doing there? They'd already paid. His long whiskers and gray sweat suit reminded him of a manatee. Man, he'd forgotten his coffee.

Marcelo came up while Barry waited behind motormouth Angie at the cashier. She was slowing down Jackie. Shut up already! That place was going to be the end of him.

"I'm seeing Emily tonight," Marcelo told him. "We can go out another time."

Barry handed Jackie the check and card. "You couldn't tell her *no?*"

"It's complicated." Marcelo had a happy boy look on his face. "I'll fill you in later."

"That's pretty crappy, man." Barry got his card and receipt and took off.

"I'm sorry," he called out. "I've got a lot to tell you."

No, he couldn't trust Marcelo either. Even he had turned against him.

At his new table, Barry found three teenage chicks looking as if they'd bought out Mary Kay. They'd caked on that makeup to hide their pimples for one night. He took their order and brought their iced teas and bread while they were at the salad bar.

The people in his booth were still there. It was the manatee-looking guy, and he didn't look happy. Crap! He'd forgotten to bring his coffee again.

Barry filled half a thermos pitcher of coffee and grabbed a cup and saucer. It was clear as sparkling wine that Marcelo and Emily didn't want him in the picture. Why had Emily come to work at the Vineyard of all places? That wasn't a freaking coincidence, but a clear signal there was a plot in the making. He had a hyper sense of smell, and he smelled something cooking, almost ready.

XV

Marcelo

The wine-tasting party was a ton of laughs and cheers. Marcelo hoped to unify everyone at the Vineyard as a team, and just about everyone seemed to be on board. Barry was the odd man out: he left and didn't attend the party. Marcelo was learning not to expect much from his friend. Barry was the same guy who'd promised the moon and the stars for their business but instead delivered a black hole. Marcelo put his absence out of his mind. He had places to go and people to see.

"See you tomorrow—in my new life." Marcelo punched out. "Peace, man."

"Great wine-tasting party," Tyrone said. "Thanks for inviting the kitchen."

"You're the most important department in a restaurant."

"I know that's the wine talking." Tyrone laughed as Curtis entered the room.

"Marcelo," Curtis said. "What can I say? You've motivated me. I'm signing up for that real estate class I've had in mind. My son's growing up, and I don't want to wait on tables much longer." Curtis punched out.

"Anything I can help you with let me know."

He looked around the deserted and spotless kitchen. The next time he clocked in, he'd be part of the management team. He was ready for whatever route or detour his career took. On the way out, he heard footsteps running behind him. Carmine caught up with him at the back door out of breath.

"You've got to stop smoking those cancer sticks," Marcelo said.

"Mind your own potatoes." Carmine panted. "This came for you today."

There were five letters addressed to him. Who'd be writing him at the restaurant? The envelopes were different colors, two of them with perfume dabbed on them. In his car, he opened them. "This is too much."

He held money orders, checks, and cash totaling $275—the down payment on his new lease on life. The notes congratulated him for his heroism. They were gifts to help with his business or education. He couldn't keep the cash, could he? The public generosity was much more than he'd ever expected. Every molecule in his body vibrated with optimism.

Before getting to Emily's house for a late dinner, he picked up a bouquet of red roses.

"These are for you." He handed them to her at the door.

"Tonight's your night, not mine." She looked at them and beamed. "They're beautiful." The warmth in her eyes and the heated passion in her kiss told him he'd done right.

"Maybe later I can come over and spend the night," she whispered. "But I have to warn you. It's not ethical to have sex with your subordinates."

"I'm no Carmine," he said. "And *you* seduced *me*, remember?"

"You're no Carmine, that's for sure. And it's not sexual harass-ment." She opened a button on his shirt. "That's because you can't harass the willing."

"Either way," he lifted her chin, "I'm willing to face the consequences."

"Oh, boy…" She sighed. "I want you to meet Grandma." She led him by the hand into the living room. "Grandma, this is Marcelo."

Grandma sat on the couch in a robe and leafed through a *Life* magazine. She took her reading glasses off, and they said hello. The TV announced the miniseries *Dallas* at low volume. The five-episode primetime soap opera had intrigued the nation with the Ewings—a wealthy Texas family in the oil and cattle-ranching business—and their exploits, especially from that conniving older brother JR, whom everybody loved to hate. Marcelo didn't know why JR always wore a white Stetson hat when it should've been black.

"First time I've met a real live hero," Grandma said.

"I'm no hero, but thanks anyway." He settled into an armchair.

The only other time he'd been treated as a hero or anything close was when he wrestled in high school. He could still hear the cheering students in the gym stands as he and Barry turned opponents into pretzels on the mat. The adrenaline rushed through his veins and his breathing deepened, remembering. He returned to the present and his magical tour of cash and prizes.

"Nice of you to stay in for a change," Grandma said toward the kitchen where Emily had disappeared. "She came to spend the summer with me, but I hardly see her."

He didn't know what to say. "I like *Dallas*."

From the kitchen, he heard the faint hum of a blender. Grandma pushed herself off the couch and got to her feet. Emily came into the dining room with a bowl of pasta.

"I've already eaten, and it's late," the grandmother said. "I'll let you enjoy each other's company. Good night, dear." She vanished into the darkness of the hallway.

Emily set the table and asked him to join her. He'd worked the dinner shift for years, and late dinners had become a ritual. On the menu was spaghetti with pesto sauce. She poured two glasses of chilled sauterne wine. More wine? Why not?

"This is for the great person you are. I had to drive to Tampa to buy fresh basil."

"How did you know I liked this?"

"I heard you and Barry talking about it."

He frowned. "That's how you knew where to get basil."

He recalled Barry's visit to Haslam's Book Store to find a cookbook with the pesto sauce recipe in it and how he'd offered to make it for him—he was the same guy who hadn't stuck around for the wine-tasting party. When he glanced at her, Barry's research trip to the bookstore vanished from his mind. "This is tasty. What did you put in it?" He wanted a million insignificant words to fill the space between them.

"Cloves of garlic, pine nuts, salt and pepper, olive oil, grated Parmesan cheese, and fresh basil leaves. That's about it."

"Thanks for going to all that trouble."

"That's the kind of girl I am, always thinking of others."

After dinner they moved to the sofa, and she poured two more glasses of wine. On top of the TV, a younger grandma in a black dress and pearls watched them from a gold-plated picture frame. Back then, humanity had not yet been introduced to Kodachrome.

"I called back Channel 4. They want to interview me on *Faces of Tampa Bay*."

"That's wonderful." She swung her hands around him and kissed him.

He could fall for her like a penny to the bottom of a wishing well—and glisten in the sunlight. Perhaps he already had.

"What's the program about?" she asked.

Every week, *Faces of Tampa Bay* had a segment titled "Tampa Bay Resident of the Week." It celebrated people who'd performed altruistic acts for the community. Usually they were people dedicated to community causes or the charitable people who supported them. He'd performed a selfless act for another human being, they told him, when he risked his life to save another. It would be a fifteen-minute interview airing across the bay area for all to see.

"Sublime, but what are you going to wear?"

He jerked his head back. "I'm not getting dressed yet."

"Don't worry." She snuggled up to him. "I'll help with your new persona."

There was nothing wrong with his image. All the recent interest in him had made him pay attention to how he acted when meeting people, being polite and well mannered. That came naturally because of his upbringing, but he wasn't in the market for another image.

"I don't want to change," Marcelo said. "I like myself."

"Your life's changed. You've got to change with it."

He wasn't the type of person whom circumstances would easily change. There was a guy from the neighborhood who got an inheritance. He bought a Cadillac, expensive Italian suits, and jewelry, and he smoked awful-smelling cigars.

"He bragged at bars and restaurants around town, telling everyone that he was in the oil business," Marcelo told her. "He'd invested in a vacant gas station: one advertised in the newspaper looking for a partner to reopen."

As it turned out, two con artists swindled him and fled the state. The sucker sold his car and expensive clothes at twenty-five cents on the dollar, and when the cash ran out, he went back to live in his parents' garage, where he often went to bed with a growling stomach.

"You're too smart for that. You're a celebrity now, a shining star. You're going to meet different people and make new friends, and I'll be your manager." She laughed.

"I'm happy I met you," he said. "But I like my friends, and this is getting out of hand. Why change for people who'll forget me in a couple of weeks?"

"Just leave it up to me. I'll call the TV station and ask about the interview, and then we can have a practice session to get you ready so you can relax during the real deal. You don't want to fumble the interview in front of the whole bay area, do you?"

"That'd be no fun." The suggestion made lots of sense.

"And I'll be there in the audience, for moral support."

The next morning he would take his suit to the cleaners and get a haircut. Then he'd tell Barry and Carlos about *Faces of Tampa Bay*. But he'd hold off telling Barry about the money he'd gotten for their business—until all the cash that was to come in came in.

Later on, she accompanied him home, where they made passionate love and celebrated being alive. He fell asleep with her in his arms, dumbfounded by his good fortune and ready to continue to dream. He woke up with her in his life. He felt secure, like a vault with the combination locked inside.

XVI

Emily

Quarter-sized raindrops scurried across Emily's windshield as she drove to work. The rubber wipers squeaked and thumped across the glass. The blades showed their wear, streaks arched a path on the surface. Each swing was timely, clearing her view as she began to lose sight of the road. Torrents of rain swept cars into Central Plaza parking lots, where they idled with lights on and waited for the downpour to pass.

The Vineyard lot rescued her from the dangers of the road as "How Deep is Your Love" by the Bee Gees came on the radio. She sighed and smiled at the romantic she was and turned off the car. The wrapped gift with the red bow would remain in the backseat, to be presented to Marcelo at the end of his shift. Shielding herself with a brown paper bag, she ran in the back door.

The lunch crew had finished its shift. Angie and Monica added their tips at the service table next to silverware trays. Green bills and silver coins cluttered the countertop in front of Monica. Her golden hair was down over her shoulders.

"Working a double?" Emily asked.

"Yeah." Monica gestured to the other waitresses. "I don't have munchkins or a hubby waiting at home like these gals." She chuckled. "Maybe after I finish school, but not right now."

"Believe me, it's not all that's cracked up to be," a stout waitress said and strapped a purse over her shoulder.

"You don't have to tell me that." Angie stopped counting the coins on her hand tray. "Don't need to live it to know it."

"It doesn't sound like a bad setup," Emily said, "having a caring family waiting at home."

"Ha!" Angie said. "Wait until you get a slob that drinks beer, watches football, and farts up the room. Tell me how sweet *that* is."

"Damn, Angie. Why so cynical?" Monica wrinkled her forehead. "Good grief. You'd make a nun swear."

"Just 'cause you're gonna become an RN don't mean it can't happen to you." Angie poured the change into her pocket. "I've got to scarf down some dinner before going back on the floor."

"By the time I become a nurse," Monica said to Angie, "you'll be Flying the Friendly Skies as a stewardess, serving travelers thirty thousand feet above sea level. I'm sure of that."

Angie nodded. "I sure hope so. Thanks for helping me fill out the job application. Catch you on the rebound."

Monica turned to Emily. "You'll probably be glad to leave this place. But you'll miss us. At least I'd like to think you would."

"I'm not leaving yet," Emily said. "Don't push me out the door already."

It was inevitable and as certain as the next tick of the universal clock. Come the end of August, she would leave the Vineyard and everyone behind, including Marcelo. It was a thought she didn't want to entertain.

"I've got to do sidework." Emily turned to the sheet on the wall. "Let's see, for station ten, sidework is…bread baskets and bread. I guess there's a first time for everything."

Barry was rinsing coffee pots in the sink next to the massive stainless steel coffeemaker at the end of the hallway. She noticed that tables and shelves were also stainless steel in that place. Barry had once said that if he could help in any way, all she had to do was ask.

"Did you know Carmine and Sergio before starting work here?" Barry asked her.

"What? How would I know them?"

"By not answering my question, you answered my question."

"Whatever that means," she said. "Anyway, what's this bread sidework all about?"

"Can I work for you tomorrow?" Barry asked. "I need to save for the business."

"I need to save for college."

He kept his eye on task. Steam from the hot water rose around them. "Take the paper napkins out of the baskets, tap them over the trash can to get the crumbs out, then line them with cloth napkins and stack one on top of the other. Do about forty. That's all we'll need tonight." He coughed. "How did your private celebration go the other night? You know, with Marcelo. The one nobody was invited to." He shut off the water and lined up the coffee pots on the table.

"We had dinner at my house, and it was the ultimate. I made spaghetti with pesto sauce."

He gave her a double look and then dried the counter off with vigor.

She lowered her voice. "I have a present for him, and I can't wait to give it to him."

He finished drying the counter. "Why'd you do that for? I mean supper…and a gift?"

Hadn't Marcelo told him they were dating? At the other end of the hallway, Carlos looked out to the dining room and then around the service area. He went into the kitchen and stepped right out into the hallway. He looked both ways.

"Anybody seen Roger?" Carlos asked. "My guy forgot to sign his Bank Americard slip. He added the tip and totaled it but didn't sign it."

"Just sign it yourself," Barry said, "and don't be such a pansy."

"I'm not that corrupt yet," Carlos said. "There he is. Roger, do me a solid."

"What's he going to do?" Emily asked.

"I'm going to put my John Hancock on it," Roger said. "Should I sign it with a lightning bolt or a pig's tail?" He signed it at the speed of light.

Carlos examined it and shook his head. "It's a lightning rod."

"Now I'll know what to do when that happens to me," Emily said.

"I scribble crooked lines all the time," Barry said. "If nobody can read it, it's OK."

Harry brought out a rack of clean water glasses and stacked them on the service table. Damp hair fell over his eyes, which were as red as Mother's Day roses. He stared at them with a foolish grin, wagged his tongue, and went back to the kitchen.

"I got a beautiful silk tie for his suit," she said.

"Why, he getting married or something?"

"It's for his TV interview."

"What TV interview?" He had a question mark on his face, but then it evaporated. "Oh, I know all about that already. That's yesterday's news."

She breathed a sigh of relief.

"About the sidework," Barry said. "Grab eight bags of dinner rolls from the storage room and put them by the bread warmer. Turn one drawer on to medium and put two bags in and cover them with a moist towel. Don't worry about keeping it full. Anybody can put in another bag when it runs low. I got to get to the floor." He turned to her. "I'm on to everything."

Well, then why didn't he fill her in about it?

On the floor, Emily caught a glimpse of Marcelo in the foyer. The hairs on her arms stood on end recalling their night of bliss. His eyes caught hers. Even at a distance, she could see that he felt for her what she felt for him. She turned around so he wouldn't see her blush.

Connie was doing a swell job of assigning tables. It was a weeknight, and the dining room and her section were half occupied. That meant every department in the house moved at a slower pace, like cars through a school zone. It gave her the opportunity to pay more attention to her customers, thus increasing her tips. Emily had a question for Connie.

"I broke up with him," Connie said. "And you know what's funny? After going together for two years, I don't even miss him. It's nice not to be waiting for the other sandal to drop."

"You sound happier," Emily said. "Stay that way."

"Hey, Emily." Jackie scowled from behind the register. "Marcelo's girlfriends better stop calling and leaving messages for him. I'm not his freaking secretary."

"It's you and me," Roger told Emily. "As long as we're working next to each other, get ready for a dose of humility." He pulled out a blue disposable lighter, lit it, and placed it back in his pocket like a gunslinger from the Old West. "Prepare to lose." He reached over and gave one of her unsuspecting customers a flickering flame while the guy searched for a light with a cigarette dangling from his lips. The sudden light in front of his cancer stick startled him, but he took it as it were oxygen. She waved Roger off and went to place an order. He trailed her into the kitchen.

"I'm winning one to zero, nada, goose egg, nothing," he said. "You got a lighter?"

"I don't smoke."

"Now you got one." He gave her a blue one. "If I beat you to it and light one of your customers' cigarettes, it's one point for me. Then if you light one of mine, it's one for you. At the end of the night, whoever's ahead wins. I'm an accounting major, so don't try to cheat."

"I don't care who wins. But if you want to give my people a light, go ahead."

"You're a boatload of fun." Roger turned away and flicked the yellow light on and off.

Marcelo headed toward her. He looked handsome with his spiffy haircut and the new gray suit she helped pick out. The teal paisley tie, waiting in the car, would go much nicer with that gray suit than the hideous red-and-blue striped clip-on he always wore. She bit her lip; she couldn't wait to tear at his flesh.

"Jackie told me about the telephone calls you're getting," she said. "What gives?"

"I don't give them any thought. But let me tell you about the lighter game."

"That's the least of my concerns," she said. "I'm above juvenile games."

"Oh, OK then…"

That night, she was horrified to learn that Marcelo had started the cigarette lighting challenge, as he called it. Why had she called it a juvenile game? Still, it was a childish game devoid of her participation. Moments later, she met up with Roger and Barry in the kitchen.

"OK, OK," Roger said to Barry. "You can work for me tomorrow, geez."

Roger turned his undivided attention to her and closed the distance between them.

"Rumor around here is that you and Marcelo are going around?" Roger raised his eyebrows. "And by going around, you know what I mean."

"Yes, we're seeing each other," she said, "if you need to know."

"I don't need to know." Roger leaned toward her. "But if you kiss and tell, I'm all ears."

"I'll leave you wondering," she said. Barry hid his crumpled face behind Roger.

As the evening came to an end, she noticed Marcelo and Barry across the dining room. They exchanged words but, apparently, no pleasantries. Marcelo huffed and snapped off his tie, but it was the end of his shift. He came her way. The gleam in his eyes was gone.

"I told Barry about the TV interview, but he said he'd already heard it from you."

She stepped back. "I'm sorry. He said he knew."

"He didn't, and I wanted to surprise him." Marcelo dropped his shoulders. "I hope this isn't a window into what you meant by 'managing' my life?"

She knew it was a rhetorical question. Her eagerness to help him had become an accomplice in her sabotage.

He rubbed his neck. "Do me a favor. Let me tell others what's going on with me, OK?"

She lowered her eyes. "You're absolutely right. Sorry."

"I'm meeting Barry at the pier tonight. I have to find out what's going on with him. Catch you later." He squeezed her hand. "I can't be mad at you, not for long."

She had to clarify the parameters separating his and her life. And it wasn't as if she didn't have plenty on her agenda with her mother and Grandma. Sunday, she'd plan a day with Grandma and bring up the subject, just to get her mother off her back.

Monica strolled up twirling a strand of hair. "Want to go to the beach with us Sunday?"

"Sounds like a plan," Emily said.

XVII

Barry

In the Catalina, Barry crawled down Second Avenue North toward the pier to meet up with Marcelo. The moon and stars hid from him behind barriers of black clouds. Raindrops tapped on the windows asking to come in. Humidity fogged up his windshield. Along the sidewalk, lampposts looked like sparklers through the damp wet glass. With his sleeve, he wiped the damp windshield as his tires swished on the wet asphalt. It'd been a major downpour, with thunder, lightning, and all. The rain had rinsed off the streets and sidewalks but didn't cleanse the ugly feelings that stuck to him like ticks to a dog. It was too freaking late to celebrate Marcelo's promotion, and he knew it. Besides, he couldn't afford more than a couple of beers. *Why don't you just make a U-turn and go home?* He didn't listen to himself and kept on. He was going to meet a stranger, someone he didn't know anymore. The red alternator light on the dash lit up.

What now? It went out, to his relief.

There was not one soul fishing on the pier. He always told tourists this was the only concrete, mile-long fishing pier on the whole rotten planet. Actually, it looked more like a stretch of bridge with sidewalks than a fishing pier. It was eleven o'clock according to his watch. The inverted triangle-shaped building rose up at the end of the pier, against a night sky black as ink and broken up by distant lightning. A dim light on the top floor, the fifth level, illuminated the lounge where Marcelo waited. The rest of the building looked dark and eerie. He wasn't in a festive mood, but where Marcelo waited, he wouldn't be bothered by festivities.

The Catalina inched up past the bait shack and parked next to Marcelo's Mustang. Both cars faced choppy waters that beat themselves senseless against the pilings beneath his feet. The salty sea breeze strained to revive his mood, but he refused. A handful of cars overlooked the bay, leaving plenty of parking spaces for others that wouldn't come. On the ground floor of the building, abandoned retail spaces stood with For Rent signs taped on glass storefronts.

A shadowy lounge met him when he stepped off the elevator. A three-piece band played, and a chick sang "Blue Bayou" to a dozen customers on barstools and at tables. The singer sounded like a Memorex tape recording of Linda Ronstadt. The empty parquet floor waited for dancers in front of the stage. Marcelo sat at the bar in bellbottoms and a revolting disco shirt.

"Hey," Marcelo said.

"Hey back." He took a stool, ordered a beer.

"Let me buy you that drink." Marcelo reached in his back pocket.

"I can pay for mine." June's rent was three weeks late, and the landlord wanted him out.

Barry's black-and-white uniform announced to the world he was a member of the servant class. Marcelo had changed in front of his eyes: he'd gotten rid of the old clothes like a snakeskin and had traded them for a better look. Still, Marcelo was only weeks away from servitude. Their relationship had run its course, the divorce long overdue.

"Why the long face?" Marcelo asked.

"I don't see one." He took a swig. "You didn't tell me you were shagging Emily."

"I was going to," Marcelo nodded, "but I didn't have the chance."

"I know. You're too busy for your friends. Just change the subject."

"You're having a cow because of Emily? You said I could go out with her, remember?"

"I said change the subject!"

The bartender and the guy he was talking to glimpsed their way. What did they want?

"What's come over you?" Marcelo asked, but Barry didn't respond. "OK, I'll change the subject. How much do you think they want for the restaurant space on the fourth floor?"

"What, in *this* building? You don't have that kind of coin."

"I'm just making conversation," Marcelo said. "What's the deal with you?"

"Don't worry about it." Barry took a swig. "That place has opened and closed more than any other in town. That's where dreams come to die. Talk about something else."

"Well, Argentina beat Holland 3-1 in the World Cup finals in Buenos Aires." Marcelo cleared his throat. "I want you at the TV station Wednesday at ten a.m."

"I'm busy that morning."

The singer ended the song, and a few claps followed. Barry left the bar and went out to the terrace. He leaned on the railing where Marcelo joined him. Puddles of rainwater dotted the ground like spots on a gigantic Dalmatian. The wind wouldn't leave him alone:

it messed with his hair and made his eyes water. Below, the mile-long pier stretched away toward the St. Pete skyline. Two people were getting ready to fish, one on each side of the road. Two cars crawled along in different directions.

"I haven't swum there in ages." Barry meant Spa Beach to their right: a strip of shore about one hundred yards wide that lured bathers and then stung them with jellyfish.

"That was the last weekend of summer vacation before we started high school."

Just as they'd done since the end of fifth grade, that summer they rode their bikes to the beach almost daily. But in high school, it wasn't cool to be seen at Spa Beach—Pass-A-Grille and Clearwater Beach were the places to be. Distant crashing waves begged for his return.

"Did you ever imagine when we were ten that we'd be here, doing what we're doing?" Marcelo asked.

"I'm not doing what you're doing."

Moments passed.

"Too bad it's not that safe to fish here at night anymore," Marcelo said.

Sometimes change was for the worse. Spa Beach wasn't safe anymore, and people didn't go there after the sun went down like before. One couldn't go there at night anymore without fear of being mugged.

"Don't go in the bathroom at the corner at night or you'll get rolled," Barry said. He could sense them casing the place, hiding behind bushes.

"We can open that restaurant soon," Marcelo said. "Everything's looking up."

"Not for me." Barry frowned. "I don't want to talk about that, either."

"Suit yourself."

People only got one chance in life, if they got that. And when that happened, one had to make the best of it, because another chance might never come. Barry's had probably come and gone, and he had missed it because he never saw it.

"They're thinking about tearing the Vincent down." Marcelo pointed to the Mediterranean architecture building behind Spa Beach. It was encircled by a chain link fence and overgrown with palmetto trees and shrubs.

In the 1920s and 1930s, the Vincent Hotel was the pride of St. Pete. Royalty, politicians, and the wealthy from every corner of the planet vacationed there. Barry had seen pictures of the hotel in those days, with its driveway lined with luxury cars of the time.

"At least it got its chance to shine. Everything goes down the toilet in this town."

"I don't like how you're talking," Marcelo said. "You've got to get real."

Barry looked at the apartment buildings across the way, with lights glowing dimly in the distance. Were the people living there happy or faking it? Relief washed over him as he knew he wasn't alone after all. They went back inside and had a couple more beers, and then they rode the elevator down to their cars.

"I left my keys on the bar," Marcelo said. "I'm going back up. See you."

Barry put the key in the ignition and the motor turned, but it didn't fire up. He tried it again for five seconds and nothing, and then again for ten seconds and nada. The car refused to crank up. He banged the dash and then tried the key again and the motor turned, and turned, and turned, each time slower and slower until the battery ran down. Marcelo always carried jumper cables in his trunk.

The bay waters below splashed against the pier and invited him for a swim. He felt the pier tremble. It was fragile, with weak pilings, ready to collapse. He was resting on the hood of his car when Marcelo came down.

"You're still here," Marcelo said.

"I want to sit awhile before going home." *You don't need his help.*

Barry waited until the red of Marcelo's taillights disappeared down the mile-long pier. Then he went in his trunk, opened the fishing tackle box, took out his survival knife, and set off on his hike. It was a long journey home, and he would have to thumb part of the way. He picked up his pace and stayed on the left side of the pier to avoid the restroom at the corner. He could still sense them lurking around. Halfway up the pier, he got the urge to pee. He felt the sharp blade of the knife in his pocket, crossed the street, and headed into the restroom.

XVIII

Marcelo

The *Faces of Tampa Bay* audience clapped and cheered when Marcelo entered the brightly lit Channel 4 studio stage. The ovation swelled like a roaring river as he greeted the host and took a seat. The area beyond the stage was black as a moonless night, and he couldn't make out any faces. He knew Emily and Carlos were sitting among the shadows. They'd come with him that morning, but what about Barry?

His and the host's chairs angled toward each other in front of blue curtains. A philodendron overflowed its planter on the end table between them. Green leafy vines reached halfway to the hardwood stage.

"Welcome to our program," the hostess said, "where we recognize bay area citizens who have gone beyond the call of duty to serve our communities."

A brief introduction was followed with a description of Marcelo's response to the accident—actions people called heroic—and then the interview took a personal tone. Marcelo voiced to bay area residents what kept him going: his job at the Vineyard and his plans to go into business.

"I'm sure I'll get there," he said. "I can see my partner and me cutting the ribbon and christening our place." The picture, once vivid in his mind, was fading like footprints in the sand.

"Would you like to tell us about your partner? Who is he?"

"Barry's more than my partner." He felt his throat constrict. "He's my best friend and is like a brother. We grew up together."

"He must be a standup guy and a real winner for you to consider him."

"Yeah," Marcelo said. "He is."

The interview, though short, seemed endless to Marcelo. But in time, it ended.

"Marcelo, I hope all your dreams come true. You deserve it. Thank you for coming."

The program ended, and the audience applauded. The lights came on and brought the audience and its chatter to life. Emily was where she said she'd be, in the front row with Carlos. But as people rose from their seats and exited the studio, Barry was nowhere in sight.

"I can always count on you." Marcelo wrapped his arms around her.

Carlos looked about the studio. "This is unreal."

"You're right," Marcelo said. "It's not reality."

If he was a hero, why did he feel empty like a book without print?

"I'm going to Barry's," Marcelo said.

"He's different," Carlos said. "I think the cheddar slid off his cracker."

A wooden sign nailed to a pine tree announced the entrance to the Orange Blossom Mobile Home Park. Marcelo pulled onto the dirt road, drove to Barry's single-wide trailer, and parked in front. The

Catalina rested in the driveway between his and another home. It was an aircraft carrier floating on a sea of sand. Through the screen door, he noticed Barry on the couch, drinking a can of Bud, listening to Bad Company on the stereo.

"Enter at your own risk." Barry beat him to the greeting.

He took the invitation, stood inside the doorway. "You got home OK the other night?"

"I didn't get mugged, if that's what you mean."

Barry wore a BVD tank top and cutoff jeans. His hair was unruly as a haystack. A two-day beard growth darkened his face. His stare was that of a man in a deep, dark place. A packed metal pipe lay next to a baggie of weed on the coffee table. Sections of the *Times* were sprawled on the floor. A pile of laundry crowded a corner. The place stank like a barrack of soldiers.

"Fire up that bowl." Barry pointed to the pipe. "But don't Bogart it."

"You go ahead." Marcelo leaned back on the wall. "I have to work in a few minutes."

"Are you Mister Straight now? When did a job keep us from getting stoned before? And how many times did we wake up hung over like sheets on a clothesline? That's right, you don't do that either now."

He still remembered. It hadn't been that long ago. Countless times they'd huddled around and lit two or three bowls before heading to the job. Barry had always been more than generous with his cash, especially when it came to the smoke and brew he indulged in regularly.

"One time you surprised me with a Turbo Bong you'd bought at the Wooden Nickel, remember?" Marcelo said. "It was the latest technology in drug paraphernalia."

"We smoked three bowls of Colombian gold that time and got blitzed." Barry held his stomach when he laughed.

That day they'd sought a different kind of freedom and stepped into another dimension: one where fantasy and reality merged into one.

"You didn't know if you should go or stop at a red light," Barry said.

At that intersection Marcelo had inched forward and stopped every three feet. Cars blew horns and went around him, showering him with choice curse words. Somehow they made it back to Barry's place and called work to say they wouldn't be in—Marcelo's car had blown a fan belt and had overheated.

"We scarfed down a baker's dozen of glazed donuts that night." Barry squinted his eyes as he laughed. "We never did figure out who had the thirteenth one. Did we?"

"Well, that was then," Marcelo said. "This is now."

"You figured that out by yourself? You must be a detective."

A pile of dirty pots and pans rose from the sink, and overflow marked the stove. They cried out for hot water and a scouring pad. Two rancid garbage bags waited for a trip outside.

"What's going on with you, Barry?" Marcelo took a seat. "You can tell me."

Barry kicked the coffee table. "Nothing is going on; I'm fine. Change the subject."

"Don't you think you should see a doctor?"

"I said change the subject."

"OK. When you're up to it, we can talk about our place. About the money—"

"I don't have any, OK?" Barry glared. "Find another partner. Everybody thinks you're better off without me. They think you've hitched your wagon to a dog."

"What? Who's *everybody?*"

"Emily and everybody at the Vineyard, that's who. I hear things."

"Man, you've really lost it," Marcelo said. "If so, are you going to prove them right?"

"The manager at the Lobster Trap was right. I'll never amount to anything."

They were working as busboys then. Barry was accused of stealing tips after busing a table and got fired, but he'd never taken any. Earlier, the girl had told the guy he was leaving too big a tip, so he took a couple bucks off the table as they left. When the waitress got back, she didn't see the amount she'd seen before and accused Barry of stealing.

"I walked out with you then," Marcelo said. "That wasn't right."

It was the first time one had walked out with the other in support.

"Anyway," Barry said. "You should get going."

Barry lit the pipe, took a huge drag, and held it. A red flush colored his face.

"What are you going to do? Sit around and get high for the rest of your life?"

He exhaled a white puff of smoke. "It's a hobby of mine, like cooking."

"You make no sense." The sweet scent of marijuana reached him. "I've got to roll."

"Adios, amigo…Peace, man."

Marcelo started his car, pulled into traffic, and drove away under threatening skies. Barry was tripping, and the man needed to snap out of it, quick. He'd stuck his head up his butt and blamed Marcelo for the darkness. Go figure that one out. Marcello pulled into the Vineyard parking lot, grabbed his starched shirt from a hanger in the back of the car, and went inside.

"Would you drop two pieces of chicken for me, mixed?" Marcelo asked Tyrone.

Tyrone eased a breaded poultry breast and leg into the deep fryer to avoid the splatter.

"You know," Tyrone said. "With you becoming a hero and all, I don't know how my novel will end now."

"Now you know how I feel," Marcelo said. "Things are changing too fast, and not always in a good way. Sometimes I don't know which end is up."

"You have to take the good with the bad," Tyrone said. "Life's about change. Unless you change, you get stuck."

"I guess you're right. I'll be back in fifteen."

Marcelo put on his crisp shirt in the office and then slipped on the paisley teal tie Emily had gotten him. Then, at the desk, he opened the day's mail. Most were business advertisements and equipment service offers, from dining room furniture to heating and refrigeration. He put the ads aside for Carmine and Sergio to review. The rest were bills, which he opened and placed in the IN basket for the brothers to see and file in accounts payable. Then, he grabbed his meal and went to the break room and joined Roger and Carlos.

"Sorry, but I have to leave you ladies." Roger put his coffee cup in the bus pan. "I've got to make *mucho dinero* because I'm taking Saturday off. I'm going to see another boss, Bruce Springsteen, at the Bayfront Center."

"I heard that concert was sold out," Carlos said.

"That's for common folk like you two." Roger split.

"I saw Barry," Marcelo said. "I think he lost his marbles."

"You know," Carlos said, "your success has to be hard on him."

"I can't help that," he sighed. "I'm trying to do the best I can with what's been dealt to me. I never asked for it. What else can I do?"

"Not much any one of us can do at the moment," Carlos said.

Curtis popped his head in the room. "Marcelo, your back window isn't rolled up all the way. It's going to rain buckets."

Marcelo went out to the lot and rolled up his window. A breeze swept through the parking lot, picked up brown leaves, and swirled them in the air. A lightning bolt fractured the horizon in half where the earth met the sky, followed by a thunderous crack. Marcelo sought protection in the Vineyard from the storm about to develop.

XIX

Emily

"Don't forget my umbrella," Grandma said. "It might rain."

Emily pushed the curtains aside. The sky was a brilliant blue, and there was a slight breeze on the palm leaves across the street.

"It doesn't look like rain," she said. "But I'll get it."

She was rummaging through her dresser drawer when the telephone rang. It was Monica.

"I'm not going to the beach today," Emily said. "I'm going shopping with Grandma."

That afternoon, she and Grandma exchanged the ferocity of a subtropical sun for the air-conditioned coolness of Webb's City's main corridor. On the shelves, Florida souvenirs offered themselves at half price: foot-long rubber alligators, six-inch wood-carved pelicans on buoys, and magnetic starfish and sand dollars waited for refrigerators on which to cling.

"What's Marcelo doing today?" Grandma asked.

"He's shopping for clothes, but I don't trust his taste. He's not the most fashionable guy."

"Let him wear whatever he wants to wear."

Marcelo's wardrobe could have become a lightning rod for her unsolicited criticism, but she had refrained herself. She'd had to swallow her tongue to keep from uttering a word.

"Let's go to the tobacco shop," Grandma said. "Let's find those cigars your father likes."

"We'll have to mail them to him." She paused. "He's too busy in his new life."

"That happens in a new marriage. He'll come around." Grandma cleared her throat. "Look, everything's on sale. Webb's City is closing soon. I don't recognize this city anymore."

Known as The Store of Tomorrow Today, Webb's City had become The Store of Yesterday Today. It was fading into a memory, much like the flocks of snowbirds, northern winter tourists, that had sustained it throughout the seasons.

The lingering smell of tobaccos told her they were nearing that department. To her surprise, she could differentiate one blend from another: some sweet, some fruity, and some just plain nasty. How could chomping on a wet cigar be pleasurable?

"How are these?" Grandma held up a cigar box with pasted-on gold insignias.

"Hav-A-Tampa is what Dad likes." Emily placed the box back on the shelf.

"I don't see them. Let's ask a salesman." Grandma touched her arm. "Isn't this a wonderful way to spend the day?"

"It sure is."

Emily imagined herself oiled up with Coppertone as Sunset Beach, getting a pink glow on her body under a constant shower of sunrays. The evening would have ended with dinner at the Oyster Bar, with the feel of sand under her clothes and in her sandals. She sighed.

"There's the salesman," Grandma said.

A diminutive gent with a king-sized smile helped them with their purchase.

"Grandpa and I used to bring you here and make it a day," Grandma said.

Memories flickered in and out of existence like fireflies. Her grandpa had told her how Doc Webb began with a small discount pharmacy during the Great Depression. As businesses around him closed, he bought them out and expanded his store and merchandise. Eventually, his empire grew to several blocks west of downtown. He sold just about everything, from clothing to furniture to car tires. There was a supermarket, a barbershop, a plant nursery, a gas station, etc.

"People don't want to come to the center of town anymore," Grandma said. "They would rather go to out to the malls in the suburbs."

"Dad will love these." Emily patted the brown paper bag.

"Let's go see the animal acts," Grandma said. "We always loved them."

She remembered the trained animals on the fourth floor next to the toy department. As a child, she couldn't get enough of them. There was a bunny that would kiss the wooden figure of a female bunny standing at a picket fence and a chicken that walked the tight rope, each for a nickel. The elevator reached the fourth floor.

"Oh, my," Grandma said.

The trained animal act was gone. The area was now being used for storage of disassembled shelves that would no longer hold merchandise at that location, waiting for their next assignment patiently and silently, one stacked against the other on the wall.

"I'm hungry," Emily said to distract her.

They ate lunch at the luncheonette counter: turkey sandwiches and iced teas. After refueling themselves, they cooled off with a visit to the ice cream stand.

"This hits the spot," Emily said.

They shared a bench next to the stand, each with one scoop of chocolate ice cream in a cone. The barbershop across from them had mostly empty chairs.

"I remember Dad would get a haircut and a free ice cream cone, all for sixty-nine cents," Emily said. "He would let me have his ticket, and I would claim his cone. I always would ask him when he was going for his next cut."

"So many wonderful memories," Grandma said. "Let's head back home."

An afternoon storm had moved into the area. Flashes of light dimly glowed behind bulging clouds pouring their bellies below. Sheets of raindrops bombarded every inch of the lot, striking defenseless shoppers seeking shelter in their cars as steam rose from the blacktop.

"Let me have my umbrella," Grandma said, and Emily looked in her bag.

"I'm sorry. I forgot it when the phone rang. Wait here, I'll bring the car around."

She dashed across the lot, moving through the smell of wet asphalt and the dull roar of rain. When she pulled up to the entrance, Grandma climbed in, shivering like a soaked puppy. Emily covered her with a beach towel from the back seat. The showers passed quickly, a brief downpour on an otherwise sunny day.

"I almost forgot. Your mom called and wanted you to call her."

It had been a pleasant day.

When she got home, Emily called Marcelo. It was midafternoon, and he was probably in the office planning the specials with Sergio or ordering something. Jackie handled her call with the courtesy of a prison guard and abruptly transferred her. The phone rang once.

"Oh, hi," he said.

"What an exciting greeting," she said. "Everything copacetic?"

"Everything's fine." He paused. "It's work, nothing else."

"How did it go at the mall?"

"Terrible. I couldn't find anything I liked. You were sorely missed."

"I'll have to make my presence felt later, then," she said. "What are you doing?"

Mondays and Tuesdays were the slowest nights of the week, and he was working on plans for specials to bring in more business. To his surprise, Carmine liked his idea and gave him the go-ahead to explore the cost and profit margins. He was ready to turn in his report. There were two specials, one for each night, and for only five dollars: a prime rib and a live Maine lobster special.

"We put that on the marquee outside and we'll snag them in," he said. "We'll do tons of business without much sweat."

"Sounds promising," Emily said. "Are we doing anything tomorrow? You're off, right?"

"I'm working during the day," he said. "But I'm off at night."

"You know what they say: all work and no play makes Jack a dull boy."

"Jack's no dull boy." He laughed. "Not anymore."

Neither was she.

XX

Barry

"How can you forget your vest?" Sergio asked Barry. "Next time I'll send you home for the night. Turn this one in when you're done."

"How can I avoid doing something that I forget?" He put on the vest.

Barry left the office and headed up front to sign in. *They're lucky you dragged yourself in at all.* He'd found the motivation to clean up and show up with organic inspiration.

"What, I've got seven again?" Barry scratched his head.

What was going on? Station seven was next to the service area, closer to the kitchen and service bar than all others. He wouldn't have to hoof it all over creation to get rolls or coffee. And he could turn in his drink orders to Sherry and then wait on his people while keeping an eye on the bar for them. Man, he could make beaucoup bucks—just what he needed. Finally, he could pay June's rent four weeks late and get his TV back: the one he'd given his landlord when he showed up with cops to evict him. He shouldn't knock his good luck. Maybe the gods were finally smiling on him.

Marcelo wasn't working that night and that was fine with him.

Barry poured water into racks of glasses filled with ice cubes. Then he filled plastic pitchers with water and dried his hands. Down the hall, that horndog Roger stalked Monica the way a Florida panther stalked deer. Man, the guy was living in the sixties: he'd gotten another weekly crew cut.

"Forget it. I'm not going to your crib," she told Roger and shook her head.

Her head said no, but that smile said yes.

"Barry, what's the story?" Monica asked. "Where's everyone going tonight?"

"How would I know?" He puckered his brow. "Nobody tells me anything anymore."

"There you go," Roger said to Monica. "That bottle of Blue Nun is waiting in my fridge, waiting for us to pop the cork, waiting to see what develops."

"Yeah, up your nose with a rubber hose." Monica rolled her eyes. "I'd go anywhere but to a guy's pad. The playground is closed to men until I finish school. You all know that."

Carlos came out from the kitchen shouldering a tray. "I'm still a man-child. Is the playground open for me?"

"You're too young, maybe in a couple of years." Monica giggled. "Your brother better not hear me say that."

"I'm eighteen," Carlos said, "old enough to drink, old enough to ravage your body."

"Oh, brother, you're worse than Roger," Monica said.

"You're late in the chase, Carlos," Roger said. "Get in the back of the line."

Monica slapped Roger on the arm. "You don't have your filthy paws on me yet."

"You mean I've got a chance?" Carlos said, and Monica threw up her arms.

A smile broke on Barry's face recalling happier times. But he, Marcelo, and the gang were light years away from then—and heading in opposite directions in the universe.

"Two people who worked here won a singing contest at the Brown Derby last year," Barry said. "Remember, Roger?"

"I wasn't working here last year, my friend."

"Marcelo told me about it," Carlos said. "I was too young to go then, but I'm mature and legal now." He elbowed Monica, and she pushed him away.

On that Saturday night a year ago, they heard about a singing contest at the Brown Derby at midnight. And because the two had run their mouths about their singing talents, they decided to go try their luck. One was a blimp of a waitress, and the other was a prep cook, long and thin as a Cuban cigar. She belted out a disco tune, and he a twangy country one.

"I went that night." Curtis joined them. "The guy got first place and the girl second."

"They must've had talent to win." Monica slapped Roger's hand away.

"Actually, they sucked," Carlos said. "That's what I was told."

That happy night a summer ago, about twenty waiters, waitresses, and cooks took off to the Derby after work. Because the crowd's clapping decided the winners, and because the Vineyard crew clapped like a bunch of seals, they won. An excellent time was had by all.

"What were their names?" Carlos asked.

No one remembered their names, but the faces of the nameless memories were tattooed on Barry's mind. They were two of dozens of lives that had come and gone like passing ghosts. Reality erased his happy memories like chalk on a blackboard, and he came back to the present.

"There's Emily. I'll ask her where she wants to go." Monica caught up with her at the entrance to the kitchen.

Yeah, go ask Ms. Congeniality.

"Come on." Roger followed Monica like a horny senior on prom night. "The bottle of Blue Nun has your name on it."

They'd had a real fun time at the Derby that night. One of a thousand cool pictures stored in the photo album in his mind. All taken before Marcelo became a hero boy and Emily steamrolled into their lives and crashed their party uninvited. Since then, no more worthy memories had been added to his collection. He'd become yesterday's newspaper.

His first party of the night was a couple of lovebirds who couldn't take their glassy eyes off each other. It made him want to barf. He didn't have the intestinal fortitude for it that night.

"Bring us a dozen raw oysters to start." Their hands were clasped across the table.

"Let me recommend a bottle of Pouilly Fuisse with your appetizer," Barry said, but they weren't listening. "It's a rich, dry wine with an aroma of grilled almonds and—"

"OK, just bring it." The twerp waved him off.

He sat the sweaty wine bucket by the table, popped the cork, and poured for his taste.

Connie gave him a three-top—a middle-aged shrimp of a guy and his mummified parents. To them, he sold snails but no wine. He turned in the raw oyster order to the salad department. The ladies were peeling shrimp and shucking oysters.

"Two escargots," Barry called off to Tyrone as Harry brought a stack of clean plates.

"Like I was saying," Harry dropped off the dishes for Tyrone, "me and my brother Jim painted one house a day for a month straight last spring." He pushed his limp hair away from his eyes. "We made a thousand bucks a week each."

Tyrone pulled his eyes from the grill. "They must've been Barbie doll houses you girls painted to finish one a day."

Tyrone felt the temperature of the steaks by pressing the meat with his finger: the softer the meat, the rarer it was. Angie carried a large tray and meal covers into the area.

"Man, I was born with a paint brush in my hand," Harry said. "Nobody here has made a tenth of the bills I made painting. What do you make, two hundred a week?" he asked Tyrone.

"Nobody makes the money you make," Angie said. "That's why you're mopping floors and cleaning toilets."

Harry stuck his middle finger in the air and went back to his dirty floors and toilets buzzing with flies.

"You know," Curtis said, "the New York Yankees beat Detroit, and Ron Guidry improved to a perfect thirteen and zero. It's a new Yankee record."

"We don't talk baseball around here." Tyrone pointed the tongs at him. "This is football country. You dig?"

"I copy that," Curtis said. "It's sad that there's no professional baseball in Florida."

Tyrone looked at Barry. "What are you so quiet about?"

"I've got nothing to say." *You've got to watch Tyrone. You've got to watch everyone.*

He had a secret to guard like a national treasure because there was no one he could trust anymore. That morning he'd been offered a bartender job at the Starfish Restaurant. Actually, he went there to apply for a waiter job advertised in *The Times* Help Wanted ads. But when he got there, the freaking job was filled.

"We've got a bartender opening if you want," a big-haired waitress had told him when he was about to leave. "You can mix drinks, can you?"

"Do mushrooms grow on cow manure?" he'd told her.

Damn right he could mix drinks; every decent waiter knew how. What a lamebrain question that was. So he'd filled out the application and interviewed for the surprise job. He'd put on a super cool exterior, which didn't melt before the interview was up. They wouldn't say it, but he knew they'd wanted him for the bartender job all along. They'd placed the ad just for him.

"We'd like to have someone of your caliber join our team," the bar manager had told him. "Let me know in a couple of days if you want the job."

Had the Starfish heard he was an exceptional mixologist and wanted to take him away from the Vineyard to help them drive their competition into the ground? He thought so. The clues were there, big as Billy. Man, he would gladly do it.

"You OK?" Tyrone eyeballed him.

He came back to the world. "You got that escargot coming sometime tonight?"

"Keep your pantyhose on, youngblood," Tyrone said.

"Pickup twenty-nine!" Curtis called out.

"Pickup twenty-nine," Tyrone said to the other line cooks.

Tyrone slapped a New York strip on a plate, buried it with golden onion rings, and put it under the lamps. The strip sizzled on the metal liner, screaming to be devoured and be put out of its misery. The fry cook put up a fried seafood platter, and the broiler cook put up a broiled snapper. The fish shifted back and forth on its juices in the dish, trying to swim away. Curtis was garnishing his meat when Monica and Angie joined the line.

"Emily wants to go to the Quarterdeck Lounge," Monica said. "What about you, Barry?"

"Tell us where, Barry." Curtis covered his meals. "So we go someplace else."

Tyrone gave old Curtis the evil eye and put up the escargot in mushroom caps.

"It's hot," Tyrone said.

Maybe Tyrone isn't with them.

"The Bull Pen doesn't make the grade anymore?" Barry grabbed the appetizer.

They hadn't been there in days. Emily had barged into their lives, had cast a spell on Marcelo, and then had changed their world. And the witch wasn't even sorry about it!

"We're moving on up and leaving you behind." Angie faked another laugh.

"Emily and Marcelo wanted someplace different," Monica said. "Don't kill the messenger."

"Why do we listen to Marcelo?" Barry asked. "He might be assistant manager and a hero, but he's not the king of the world."

"Like that Meat Loaf song, 'Two out of three ain't bad.'" Monica giggled.

"When you're the hero and manager," Angie said, "then we'll give a hoot where you want to go. I just want to go where the good-looking men are."

Yeah, Angie tore into guys at the liquor lounge like a rat tore into a cheese factory.

Barry looked around and didn't see any friends, no support. One morning he'd woken up and found himself alone in the world. But he had himself and the talents he'd been blessed with.

"I have a primo new job," Barry blurted out. "It's a bartender job at the Starfish."

Tyrone looked up. "That place down the street is a money-maker—tropical garden restaurant, revolving bar, live music, dancing."

"That's Beaucoup Bucks City, no lie," Monica said, but Angie kept her loud trap shut.

Barry huffed, grabbed his snails and oysters, and took off to the dining room. The job at the Starfish was all that plus a bucket of fried chicken. It was a gold mine to be exploited, and he was the overburdened mule saddled with the tools to do it. He delivered the appetizers.

He gave a party of two their check, and they got up to leave. He was a giraffe of a man, bending at the waist to hide his height. She was dumpy with arms and legs plump like knockwursts on a grill. Jim came over with a loaded bus pan and rested it on his thigh.

"I hear everybody's going to the Quarterdeck." Jim's skinny arms trembled from the weight. "I need a ride home." He got closer. "I got a pound of killer weed."

"Why not go to the Bull Pen? Everybody agreed to the Quarterdeck?"

Jim shifted the bus pan to the other thigh. "Nobody could agree on nothing, so Emily decided. I know it's out of your way, but can you give me a ride home?"

"Sure." He didn't mind being out a bit if he could help somebody.

His number lit up on the dining room board, and he headed to pick up. Not only was he not going to the Quarterdeck, but he was calling the Starfish the next morning and taking the job. They wanted him and had put an ad just to get him to take the bait. *How did they know I'd had it here?* At the Starfish he'd make a fortune and open a place of his own without a partner. He wasn't Marcelo's flunky anymore. Their relationship had crashed, and it had left no survivors.

"How did you do on station seven?" Connie asked at the end of the night.

"I did all right." Barry counted a hefty wad of bills. "Thanks for giving me that station."

"Don't thank me. Marcelo asked me to give you that one."

I don't need his handouts. Come next morning, he'd call the Starfish and take that bartender job for sure. How was he going to sleep tonight, waiting to make that call in the morning? He could see himself fuming—with his stomach churning—pacing the floor all night.

XXI

Marcelo

Marcelo and Carmine looked over the dry goods inventory in the storeroom. Carmine counted the canned goods while Marcelo wrote down the quantity and content size on a clipboard. Tomato sauce and tomato paste went faster than hot dogs at a picnic. There was much to learn. Vendors delivered dry goods on a credit basis, invoices to be paid at a later date, which resulted in a considerable accounts payable balance. He was getting acquainted with that, and how important it was to know what the expenses were at every step of the way. He was learning, clearing hurdles in his way. Luckily cash came in daily in a restaurant, as it would in his and Barry's on the first day.

"Heard you on the radio this morning," Carmine said. "You sounded good."

"Thanks," Marcelo said. "I'm glad that's over."

He'd survived his last interview. This time it was the rush-hour radio program *Good Morning Tampa Bay*. But those fifteen minutes on the air seemed like an hour. He'd assumed they'd rush by as quickly as the commuters going to work. Still, after two TV interviews in front of cameras, the radio one was a breeze. It was still hard for him to imagine that he was the center of attention and the toast of the town. Surprisingly, he was soaking it up like ink into paper.

Connie came in. "Marcelo, a lady in the dining room wants a word with you."

He shrugged and motioned to the shelves of inventory. "Couldn't you handle it?"

"She specifically asked for you."

"You best go." Carmine winked. "I'll be here when you get back."

"Who is she?" Marcelo followed her through the red tiles of the kitchen.

"How would I know?"

Roger was filling glasses of iced tea when they entered the service area.

"Looks like you're getting lucky, my friend," Roger said.

"Oh, I doubt that," Connie said.

"Where is she?" Marcelo scanned the dining room. Every fifth table was occupied.

"It's the single one in forty-seven, next to the booth." Connie returned to the front.

The elegant woman looked to be in her eighties and sipped red wine. She wore a beehive hairdo and sparkling pendulum earrings and was wrapped in a mink shawl as if it were cold as a Buffalo winter night. That's what Curtis would say. It was typical: older people often complained that the cool, crisp air conditioning made the room too cold.

"I should give this hero worship a chance." Roger stood beside him, iced tea for two on his tray. "Maybe I can find an old broad who hasn't had a young stud in decades and bring joy back into her life. Wouldn't you call *that* heroic? Hell, the pope might even canonize me for that." He twirled his mustache.

"Well, you're one young stud short." Marcelo studied the woman. "And I didn't ask for all this attention."

"Milk it all you can…and then some." Roger went to his party.

It was the start of the Early Bird Specials before the dinner rush. Each special was two dollars off. Other than the lady asking for him, a dozen parties of golden agers occupied the dining room. Usually, most of the Early Bird crowd was retired and on fixed incomes. "We lost our life savings during the Great Depression," he often heard from them, even though it had been forty years since that had ended. But the lady who was waiting for him didn't appear to be strapped for cash. When he stepped up to her, she lifted her stare. Her skin was smooth as polished porcelain.

"Good evening, Mrs.…?"

"Call me Sally."

"How was your dinner this evening, Sally?"

"Is that really what you want to know?" She rubbed the base of her wine glass. "The food was outstanding. The service left much to be desired."

The older woman was done eating and had pushed her plate to the side. The empty breadbasket and bread plate, both full of crumbs, sat next to the check on the tray. He hoped the burgundy blot of wine on the white tablecloth wasn't the server's doing. He cleared the table.

"That was a courageous act, saving that helpless woman's life."

That answered the mystery. All that called for was to spend a couple of minutes and answer any question she may have about the incident. Then he would excuse himself and return to the store room and the work that waited for him.

"I acted before I had time to think of the danger."

"Modesty is a virtue…"

She was probably a lonely widow with not much happening in her life. A couple minutes of his time wasn't too much to offer. Work could wait.

"You're very kind," he said. "Is there anything I can do for you?"

Carlos watched from the next table where he served cocktails.

"I'd like to offer you a scholarship to complete your college education," she said.

Did he hear her right? He saw Carlos's jaw drop and almost back into the wall as he stepped away from his table.

"My education…?" Marcelo asked.

When would his good fortune end? A college scholarship was not only more than he expected, it was more than he deserved.

"Thank you, but maybe it would be better spent going to someone else."

"I make offers to deserving students as I see fit. Why? Do you know anyone more deserving?" She waited for an answer, still as stone.

"Me going back to college…"

"You could attend State if you wanted."

He wanted that when he was younger, but now? He had to be dreaming. OK, it had been a nice ride: all the attention he'd gotten the last few weeks, the cash and prizes had been unreal, but he was ready to wake up.

"The scholarship pays for housing, tuition, and books, up to four years at any state institution. Thus, you're guaranteed a bachelor's degree."

He didn't want to leave his job, his business plan, or his brother behind. How funny. For years he had been stuck in a rut, waiting for his life to change, waiting for breaks to go his way. Instead of waiting, he should've done something about it. He stood speechless, like a singer who'd forgotten the words to a song.

"Well?" she asked.

"Don't know what to say…"

She grimaced. "If you need to ponder about it, do so and give me a call." She handed him a business card. "And please bring me a very dry martini straight up with a lemon twist."

At the service bar, Curtis loaded two grasshoppers on his tray. The creamy green drink occupied champagne glasses.

"I heard you started your real estate class," Marcelo said. "Far out."

"Yeah, it's a lot more work than I imagined." Curtis coughed. "Do you know if Connie is seeing anybody? I kind of want to ask her out, but I don't know."

"I don't believe she's seeing anyone. Ask her out. All she can say is no."

"That easy, huh?" Curtis grinned. "I'll sleep on it a bit."

Before going home, Marcelo grabbed a pad of paper and took notes. The next day, he would propose a two-hour, mandatory training session for all waiters and waitresses. After that, it would be held once a month for new employees. The meeting would present a brief description of every item on the menu, how to take an order and serve, how to clear a table, how to converse in a friendly but respectful manner, as well as knowing the house liquor and wine brands. The goal was for every customer to get the same quality service from anyone at the Vineyard.

That evening when Marcelo pulled up in his driveway, he saw two bicycles next to Carlos's Camaro. Inside, the living room reeked of marijuana. Jim, Harry, and Carlos were listening to "Money" from

Pink Floyd's *Dark Side of the Moon* album and passing a doobie around. They looked up with heavy eyelids and ridiculous grins.

"Don't Bogart that joint," Jim said to Harry, and he passed it.

"You're just in time," Carlos said.

"Time's up is more like it," Marcelo said. "It's time to go home, guys."

"I guess it's not OK for the help to get high with the boss." Jim let out a sharp laugh.

Marcelo led the twins to the front porch and waited until they got on their bikes. As they rode down the street, each attempted to push and kick the other off his bike. In the living room, Carlos had opened the windows to air the place out and cleared the coffee table.

"That was an out-of-sight Wimbledon Finals yesterday," Carlos said. "I knew Borg would beat Connors. But in three sets? We should go hit a few."

"We could." Marcelo looked through the mail on the mantel.

Carlos cleared his throat. "Whatever I bought, we smoked it tonight."

"I didn't say a word. Just don't waste your time partying like I did."

They talked about the scholarship offer he'd gotten and about the money that continued to trickle in. The cash was for his and Barry's restaurant. He wouldn't ask his friend for any capital because Barry wouldn't do that if he were in his place.

"Are you opening that restaurant or going to college now?" Carlos asked.

"You know the answer. Maybe a couple of years ago I would've gone to State, but school doesn't pay the bills for me now."

He went to bed amazed at his good fortune but unsure of the next step. But he wasn't in any hurry, and if he kept one foot in front of the other, the next move would reveal itself. In moments he faded into a land of foreseeable dreams where he hiked toward mountains shimmering in the distance.

XXII

Emily

The Cheyenne Social Club was overflowing with Western enthusiasts when Emily arrived. Cowboy hats, boots, and ruffled skirts thrived that evening. A heavy blanket of cigarette smoke filled the saloon. On the parquet dance floor four steps below, couples corralled in close quarters got down to the sound of Donna Summers's "Last Dance." The vocals and notes vibrated from speakers and synchronized the crowd. She stood aside to orient herself and look for Angie.

Angie talked about the place as something special, but she failed to see it. The jovial crowd reduced her vision to a couple of feet as she trudged through the human mass to the bar, where she noticed Angie. There, a guy in a rhinestone shirt leaned on the counter and talked to her. Angie laid her hand on his forearm, and both were engaged in heavy eye contact.

"There you are." Angie hugged her. "I didn't think you'd make it."

"I said I'd be here." Angie smelled of ninety proof.

"I'd better mosey on to my friends before they miss me," he said. "Don't forget to save me the last dance." He shot her with an imaginary pistol and then blew on the imaginary barrel.

Gag her with a spoon! The song ended.

Angie lit a cigarette and waved the smoke away from her face. "Shadow Dancing" by Andy Gibb vibrated throughout the place. The energetic crowd clapped and whooped in approval.

"I might just get us lucky tonight." Angie winked. "You know, even a lady has to loosen her corset from time to time." Angie sipped from a tall colorful drink. "It's a Planter's Punch," Angie said when she tracked Emily's gaze. "It's Planter's Rum and—"

"It's more than I want to know," Emily said. "Who's the guy?"

"You like him?" Angie's blouse hung with awkwardness from her bony shoulders.

"I'm only making conversation." Emily ordered a gin and tonic.

"Good. He's some college student here on vacation. Sleep with him and I'll never have to see him again."

"How romantic…"

"Those are his friends over there." She motioned to three urban cowboys in hats sitting at a booth against the wall. "You can have your pick, but lay off my man."

Not a chance. Marcelo filtered into her mind. He was loyal and honest, qualities that didn't exist in abundance in the male species. She cleared her mind and told herself to have fun.

"Do you miss your books, college girl?" Angie asked.

"You must be joking."

A kid no older than eighteen came up to her. "Would you like to dance?" He kept his gaze of self-doubt at his feet.

Angie shook her head and gave her a thumbs-down above his bowed head. Emily didn't want to dance but didn't want to say no. It had taken courage for him to ask.

"I'm sorry, but I just got here," she said. "Maybe later?"

"Sure, I'll be over there." He pointed to a table with two boys who seemed too young to shave. He stepped away a couple of inches taller and with an air of encouragement.

"Who are you, Mother Teresa?" Angie asked.

Angie could be as cold as Jell-O, afraid a warm feeling might melt her heart. She ground out her cigarette in the ashtray, and Emily could breathe a bit more.

"Watch and learn," Angie said.

Angie walked up to a guy in a white Stetson hat and plaid shirt who was leaning his back on the wall with one boot up against it. He tipped his hat, extended his arm for escort, and they took the steps to the dance floor. Looking back, Angie stuck out her tongue at her in jest.

Why had she agreed to meet her there?

"Hi, I'm Jimbo." The guy wore a peach leisure suit. "Can I buy you a drink?"

"No, thanks." She showed him her full glass.

"You're friends with Angie, right?" He slid into the stool next to her. "Angie's a pretty cool party animal. You party like her, too?"

"I'm not Angie." She smirked.

"Listen, I live down the road." He pressed into her. "Let's go party some, I got some blow. We can trade like with Angie."

Her face flushed warm. "I'm looking away, and when I turn around I want your sorry self out of my sight." She turned and heard his voice fading away, talking about a female dog.

What could she expect? Angie called it the best pick-up place in town, and she ought to know. On the dance floor Angie and her new interest danced to "Disco Inferno" by The Trammps. Emily scanned the lounge and noticed the kid she had promised a dance. He caught her eye and nodded, but she shook her head.

Angie walked up. "Let's go party with this guy. He's got snow. Forget this weed crap."

"I don't want to, and I don't think you should go either. I came to see you, remember?"

"He's got two roommates, plenty to go around. Live a little, will you?" Angie put bills down to cover her tab and grabbed her purse. "Ready?"

She stayed put. Angie took the guy's arm, and they cut through the haze and the cramped crowd to the front door and into the darkness of the night. A girl, practically a child, took the stool next to her, leaving no seats at the bar. The clock behind the bar announced 11:30 p.m. The night had not yet begun, yet it was over for her. Before she went home, she stopped at the young guy's table. "How about a dance?" she asked.

The guy's two friends looked at each other with eyes wide as saucers. She took his arm and descended into the crowded dance floor to the tune of "Dancing Queen" by Abba.

The next evening she bought aspirin for her grandma's summer cold, the sneezing and coughing kind, and hurried home. All evidence pointed to the rain they got leaving Webb's City the other afternoon as the culprit for her condition. Emily had forgotten Grandma's umbrella. But all she had to do was quarantine the host and extinguish the parasite. At home, she readied to meet Marcelo while Grandma read the newspaper.

"There was a huge march on Washington, DC," Grandma said. "Almost a hundred thousand demonstrated for the Equal Rights Amendment."

Emily buttoned the back of her blouse. "There are a lot of people against it, but it'll pass. It's inevitable, just give it time."

"You're going out again?" Grandma asked and turned the page. "Are you seeing Marcelo again? He must be quite a guy."

"He's easygoing and caring." She couldn't mention his unbridled passion.

"I bet I got this cold at the hospital." Grandma bundled up on the sofa.

She had volunteered at All Children's Hospital two days before, as she'd done on a weekly basis since she'd retired. Working as a schoolteacher, she'd learned that children were human incubators and transmitters of common illnesses. As a result, during her career, she'd been exposed to various ailments and had built a robust immune system.

"Get to sleep at a decent time." Emily kissed her. "I have to go."

The sun had spilled its yolk over the horizon when she arrived at the Redington Shore Pier. The temperature had dipped into the low eighties, and a soft breeze whispered about. "I'd love to," she'd told Marcelo when he asked her to join him fishing.

She had given him more space in the last few days to manage his own affairs. It was a bad habit of hers, trying to help without permission. She meant well, but at times was a bit selfish in her pursuits. Sadly, Marcelo had managed before she arrived and would after she left.

The wind brushed her hair behind her shoulders as she stepped on the wooden planks of the pier. The water, green and clear, revealed the rocky bottom feet below. Ten yards in, olive green waters obscured the rocks. She saw Marcelo leaning on the railing, holding a fishing pole. Another pole stood against the pier beside him. Both lines angled into the water. He caught her eye and placed his fishing pole aside.

"It's great to see you." He wrapped an arm around her and kissed her. "How did your night with Angie go?"

"It wasn't a memorable night. I was hoping it would soon become a repressed memory."

When she was close to him, all was in balance in her world.

"Any bites?" she asked.

"Just nibbles." He peeked at his watch. "High tide comes in forty-five minutes, and that might bring decent-size fish with it."

"I was here years ago." A golden glow spread across the horizon.

"You must be an expert angler then."

He picked up a pole and reeled in the slack on the line submerged in choppy waters.

"I've been known to snag schools of them," she said.

The totality of her fishing experience consisted of holding a pole after it'd been baited and cast into the water for her, and then handing it to her dad or brother when an unfortunate fish snagged her line and fought to get loose. A defenseless fish wiggling on a line made her squirm.

"Don't you get bored to death staring into the water in a zombie-like trance?" she asked.

"You get bored?" He handed her the second pole. "Reel it in and see if it needs bait."

She reeled in the line, and the hook was bare.

"Sometimes small fish take the bait without you noticing it," Marcelo said. "Their mouths are too tiny to swallow the whole shrimp and get hooked, so they nibble it off the hook, like this one." He dangled the empty hook. "Just bait it."

"Why don't you?" she said. "You're closer to the bait bucket."

The stingers on the head of the shrimp scared her. Her finger had been pierced as a child, and it still hurt. The trauma of over a decade ago was still fresh in her mind.

He pulled up the bucket from a rope tied to the pier and baited her hook with live shrimp.

"I want to see you cast," she said and grinned.

"We'll do it together."

He embraced her from behind, placed his hands over hers on the pole, and guided her body in the back-to-forward casting motion. She was safe and secure in his arms. The hook, line, and sinker sailed fifty feet in the air before plunging into the gulf, announcing its arrival to the marine life below. He held on to her.

"About me managing your life—"

"I forgot about that already," he said. "All's copasetic."

He kissed her cheek from behind.

"I could've cast that." She looked back at him.

"You'll get the chance."

The pole leaning against the railing jerked toward the water, and he pulled it back and reeled in the line at a steady pace. But his enthusiasm waned when the line lost the tension.

"It got away..."

She didn't want to get away that evening. Later, they'd go to his place and make love.

"I...I can't believe you're leaving at the end of August," he said.

She turned to him. "We've got plenty of time." For what, she didn't know.

"Put a finger on the line coming from your reel. So when you feel the slightest bite, you can pull back at one o'clock to hook it."

"I prefer to pull back at one-thirty." There, she'd made him chuckle.

She hadn't seen those dimples much in the last few days. Had Barry's bizarre behavior fizzled out his bubbly personality? She hoped brighter days lay ahead.

"What's going on with Barry?" she asked. "I haven't seen him after work lately."

Moments passed. "He'll come around."

Shifting waters seemed to sway her taut line left to right.

"I know one thing," he said. "I'm going back to school."

"What?" Were her ears functioning well? Why would he say that if he didn't mean it?

"I've been offered a four-year scholarship."

She heard about Sally's visit and about her generous offer. Just when vivid dreams of his restaurant had begun to infiltrate his nights again, it seemed life had thrown him another curve.

"Before now," he said, "the farthest idea from my mind was going back to college."

"A four-year scholarship?" she said. "Oh, you're going to love it at State."

"Whoa. Not so fast. I didn't say State."

She lowered her eyes to her line and the choppy waters. It wasn't her decision to make.

"I'm thinking about JC because of my job and all."

"Of course," she said. "That's practical."

"I wasn't thinking about school," he said. "But it makes sense going into business."

High tide arrived with a pale moon watching. By then, anglers of all ages had invaded the pier and staked their claims, equipped with fishing poles, tackle boxes, bait buckets, and Coleman lanterns. Baited lines sailed into the dark, splashed, and sank into the gulf. Gawking seagulls, the smell of the sea, and the breeze on her face—was she enjoying the serenity for which fishing was known?

"How's your grandmother?" He baited his hook.

"She's fine, probably watching TV tonight."

It was another week that she hadn't stayed in with her grandma. In her purse, she looked for a piece of gum to get rid of the sour taste in her mouth. Instead, she found the bottle of aspirin she'd bought for her grandmother's cold earlier. The one she'd forgotten to leave with her because she was too busy looking ahead to her date with Marcelo.

XXIII

Barry

In the employees' restroom, Barry pressed the front of his vest and pants with his trembling hands, hoping the warmth would iron them out some. *If only these hands could heal.* Man, his vest looked like crumpled paper in front of the mirror. He'd left his clothes in the laundry basket after coming home from the Laundromat and forgot to hang them up. Hell, they were clean, and he didn't smell like the Vineyard menu: he didn't smell like surf and turf. Wrinkles were the least of his problems. He didn't want to go out on the floor, and he didn't know why.

He scooped up two glasses of ice water and peered into the dining room. Droopy eyelids and a headache bugged him for their medicine—a decent night's sleep. Man, he hadn't had a decent snore in days. The harder he tried to catch some shuteye, the more uptight he got. And when he finally dozed off, he dreamed his soul wandered over a landscape of bare rock and howling wind. He had to keep on keeping on. But he had something to be happy about: he'd rung the Starfish and taken that bartender job. He'd start in two weeks, and he could tell the Vineyard to shove it. First, he'd give them something to remember him by. *The way to keep from getting burned is to torch the place yourself.*

He took a giant deep breath and went to his first party of the evening.

"Good evening, ladies."

He wasn't telling them his name, and he couldn't care less if they just called him waiter. All he was to everybody and their uncle was a trained animal act, like the dolphins at the St. Pete Beach Aquatarium. *Relax, don't sweat it.*

"My glass has too much ice." She pushed it away without the courtesy of eyeball contact. "How's yours?" she asked her friend, who didn't utter a word.

"I'll bring you another. How about wine this evening?" He picked up the wine list from the table, but she snatched it away. *Don't let her get to you.* He remembered July's rent was two week's late, and he didn't have a five-spot to his name.

"Bring me another glass of water." She buried her face in the menu.

He scanned the room and spotted Carmine behind the register watching him. Did he put her up to this? *Don't let her get to you.* He ran into Carlos in the hallway.

"You look like hell," Carlos said. "Are you feeling OK?"

"Are you a psychologist now?" Barry asked. "Man, this witch is squeezing my lemons."

"You want me to take the party for you? I'm not that busy."

"I'll take care of her myself; don't you worry."

Connie looked in from the dining room. "Barry, you have a party of four."

Crap! "Take that one for me," he said to Carlos. "I can't deal with it right now."

The lady at his table didn't know who she was messing with. One time, he got a customer good. Yep, he could still hear those squeals. Why not give everyone at the Vineyard a performance to remember? It would be his final curtain call. He was ready to savor immortality.

Roger shouldered a loaded tray and trudged through the service area.

"You believe I tell a customer the fish of the day is sea bass." The hefty load strained his voice. "And he asks if it's a freshwater or saltwater fish? What a doofus."

"I believe anything." Barry looked around. "Watch what you say and do around here."

Jim lugged a crammed bus pan down the hallway to the dishwasher. He stopped and rested it on a thigh. "Your lady wants her glass of water now, but she didn't want me to bring it."

"Take the dishes to your brother and mind your own business."

Barry strolled into the kitchen. It smelled of dead flesh burning on the grill. If the two ladies were in no hurry to order, he was in no rush to take it. Monica and Curtis were yakking to Tyrone while Harry mopped the floor around them. It was a slow night, but the old guy Curtis had a nice-size party going. Nine covered meals waited on an oval tray ready to go. There was no freaking way the scrawny guy could carry that out.

"Tyrone's the best at pool," Curtis said to Monica. "He cleaned my clock and ran the table at Club 29 the other night." He shut his trap long enough to hoist up the tray. He strained but got it up. "Tell her. You were there, Barry." Curtis grunted and left.

"Don't drag me into this," Barry said.

"Tyrone ran the table because I wasn't there." Monica laughed and took a king crab claw appetizer from the refrigerator. "And it doesn't matter what Barry says."

"I said don't drag me into this."

"I don't play women, period." Tyrone hit the spatula on the counter. "You load-outs get the hell out of my kitchen if you're not picking up."

Barry got another glass of water with a couple of ice cubes and a basket of hot rolls for his ladies. When he got back to the floor, he stopped in his tracks. His customer was rotating her head around like Linda Blair in *The Exorcist* looking for him. *That's not real, my friend.* How was he going to make it through the night?

He put the glass and the rolls on the table.

"What took you so long?"

Not only was she squeezing his lemons, she was making lemonade!

"You act like you don't care about your job," she said. "Get us two gin and tonics, and don't forget the limes."

Who told her I don't care about this job? A snitch must have ratted him out after he spilled his guts about the Starfish job the other night. At the service bar, he placed his order.

"I swear," Sherry said. "Next time Carmine walks behind me for no reason and rubs against my behind, I'm going to slap him into the parking lot. Who does he think he is?"

"Maybe he thinks he owns the place or something."

"You OK?" She looked at him weird. "I should call his wife and tell her about his floozy at the register."

Carmine was discreet as a neon sign in his affairs, Marcelo had said. The sleaze had gotten Jackie in the sack with gifts and bonuses for keeping walkouts to a minimum. *That's why Carmine wants you gone.* With him out of the picture, there'd be one less witness to blab to his wife about his sex romps in the office while preparing the bank deposit for the next day.

"Is Sergio working tonight?" Barry asked

"No, just Marcelo and Carmine," she said.

The lounge had a decent late happy hour crowd. Working as a bartender at the Starfish, he'd take all the business away from the Vineyard lounge, and they'd have to board up the doors. He imagined the lounge empty, full of cobwebs, and Sherry at the unemployment line.

"Guess what?" She squeezed the limes in the gin and tonics. "My school transcripts came in, and I sent them to Tallahassee. When I get my cosmetologist license, I'm out of here."

"I'm glad you'll have something to fall back on."

"This is the reason I keep going—besides my old man, of course." Sherry showed him a picture of her son crawling on the bed. His fresh eyes were pools full of potential.

When he turned around with the drinks, he spotted Carmine and Marcelo down the service area. He could hear them buzzing like dragonflies. He kept his eyes low, on the plastic runners, and let them pass.

"That jerk's got to go," Carmine said.

"What?" Anger boiled in his veins. "What jerk has to go?"

His vision went to black-and-white and to slow motion. His heartbeat sped up. He could hear it. It was fight or flight, and he didn't know how to fly. The vein in his forehead thickened and throbbed. He was ready to stomp Carmine's head like an eggshell. *It's show time!*

"What the hell's wrong with you?" Carmine asked, retreating.

Marcelo stepped up. "What's the matter? What's the problem, Barry?"

Color and motion came back to normal. Barry came back to the world.

"I heard what he said about me." He pointed at Carmine.

"Nobody said anything about you," Marcelo said while Carmine hid behind him.

"OK." Barry nodded. *That's how they want to play it.* "We'll forget about this."

Marcelo looked puzzled as Barry turned and went on to deliver the gin and tonics. Connie had sat him a party of three, a grandma with two kids under ten. Man, he couldn't handle a doting grannie and devil children that night. He served the gin and tonics.

"This drink is nice and strong," she said. "And the rolls are soft and warm."

"I'm not just a pretty face," he said.

Monica was glad to take the three-top for him. The night hadn't picked up.

He couldn't handle much of anything on the floor anymore: busy nights ruffled his feathers. He'd learned to hate the nights when they were crowded as a chicken coop, and customers clucked for this and clucked for that! When that happened, he imagined going from table to table wringing their feathered necks.

Moments later, the woman who'd been squeezing his privates let out a bloodcurdling scream of anguish in the dining room. And Barry rolled up his sleeves, ready and eager for his showdown with Carmine, *mano a mano. Let it all hang out!*

"What happened out there?" Marcelo asked him in the office.

"Where the hell's Carmine?" Barry looked around.

"He went home early. I'm handling this."

He sighed. "I was watering my tables, tripped, and poured half a pitcher of iced water down her bare back. You know, by accident."

Marcelo nodded. "I know better, but we'll leave it as an accident. You're lucky Carmine's gone, or you'd be out the door this minute."

"Oh, I'm disappointed, too. Believe you me."

Marcelo sighed. "Do you want to work here anymore? You haven't done a good job lately. Why don't you take a few days off and decide what you want to do?"

Marcelo is just Carmine and Sergio's flunky. "I want to go home for the night."

When he left the Vineyard, it would be on his own terms. Then they wouldn't have him to kick around like a worn-out soccer ball anymore. Working at the Starfish lounge, he'd drive Sergio and Carmine into bankruptcy. There he'd find a new playground, new playmates, and a fresh new start. And no matter how much the Vineyard begged him to come back, he wouldn't. They would miss him—big time. Yep, soon he would come into money, and lots of it.

XXIV

Marcelo

Marcelo and Sergio met with John Copper and his agent in the empty lounge. A three-page contract fluttered on the table alongside four tall glasses of iced tea on coasters. The John Copper Band had been playing at the Vineyard for the last three months, and their contract was up. The document waited for signatures to legalize the renewal. Marcelo knew the lounge customers enjoyed the group and their music selection: top-forty songs and Elvis tunes. Renewing the band's contract wasn't in Marcelo's job description, but Sergio asked him to the meeting to learn the ropes. Marcelo learned daily.

"It's not about getting the best deal for you and screwing the other guy," Sergio had told him before the meeting, "but about coming to an agreement you both can live with."

They signed the contract and toasted with glasses held high. Sergio and Marcelo returned to the office. John Copper and the band had a reason to be relieved; they wouldn't have to break down and pack up their equipment for another three months.

"You're a natural for this business, like me," Sergio said.

"I don't know about that," Marcelo said. "There's a lot to learn."

"Let me ask you this," Sergio said. "What is the best marketing plan for a restaurant?"

"You can't beat location and word of mouth—satisfied customers, that is. Word of mouth will keep them coming. The advertisement will only bring them once if they're not happy."

"It works for us," Sergio said. "Be careful because once this business gets in your blood, it's impossible to find a cure. More than that, I believe in what I'm doing here. It's my reputation. My life."

Sergio cracked a window into his past. He was born and lived in Tampa's Latin Quarter, Ybor City. At thirteen, his first job was dishwasher. In time, he became a prep cook and then a cook. Sergio never took the next step in his career unless he was well planted on the one he was on. The owner, and chef, noticed Sergio's dedication and took a liking to him. He taught him all his culinary skills, and eventually he became general manager. When the opportunity presented itself, he took his life savings and leased the Vineyard. Carmine joined him after the place he managed was sold and he lost his job. But Marcelo had heard the rumor that Carmine had been given the boot for taking unauthorized loans from the business bank account.

"I want to pay back the favor," Sergio said, "and teach you what I know."

"You're doing it already. Thanks, I'll give you one hundred percent."

"One more thing," Sergio said. "Since I'm bringing you along, you report to me and not Carmine. I know my brother, and he's more of an operations manager, not a personnel manager."

Marcelo made his rounds: from the kitchen to the dining room to the lounge. He made sure every department was ready to spring into action when called on. Just as he'd made sure he was visible to his dining customers when he was a waiter, Marcelo made sure he was visible to the workers in his new role. In the lobby he helped Connie write up next week's work schedule. The mailman arrived, tipped his cap, and dropped off mail on Jackie's counter.

"Three more letters for you." Jackie sniffed the envelopes. "No perfume this time." She laughed. "Is that what I have to do for you to notice me, write you?"

"You're too much. Anyway, what would Carmine say?"

"Carmine and me are just friends." Jackie folded her arms.

Marcelo went to the employees' restroom to read the mail in private. When he opened the door, he was greeted by a sweet cloud of marijuana smoke.

"We're just about done, sorry." Roger took the roach from Curtis.

"Don't do that here again, guys," Marcelo said. "Can't you wait until you get off work?"

Roger let out a big puff. Curtis took the last drag and put it out with his shoe.

"Now, I have to air out before going back in," Marcelo said. "That was the last time, no joke."

He went out the back door, walked around the lot, and opened the first envelope. He halted when he realized what was inside. The check came with a typed note that read:

> Dear Marcelo,
>
> Sorry I didn't get this to you sooner, but I was waiting for my quarterly dividends. Please find enclosed a cashier's check for $300 to help you with your restaurant. Humanity is better off with people like you.
>
> God Bless

In total, he'd received over $3,600, more than enough to open the breakfast-and-lunch place he and Barry had talked about. The day before, he'd gone downtown to pay his car insurance and drove by the luncheonette they'd had in mind. A red-and-white For Rent sign hung on the front window. He had kept driving: he wanted to tell Barry before he spoke to anyone.

Marcelo tallied the employee time cards at the desk. Barry was working that night. He would talk to him about the cash he'd gotten and the place for rent before he went home. Curtis knocked on the open office door.

"I heard you and Connie have been seen around town together," Marcelo said.

"Don't believe everything you hear." Curtis laughed. "Connie's working lunch tomorrow, and I want to wax her car then. Could you make sure she keeps busy from noon to one so she won't go out to her car and ruin the surprise? She's been talking about detailing it."

"Why would you do that if you're not seeing each other?"

"Maybe because I'm a nice guy," Curtis said. "And maybe because we're dating."

"Good for you," Marcelo said. "It's torture to wax a car in the middle of summer."

"The heat I don't mind. And since I'm kind of strapped for cash because of my kid and all, at least I can save her the money for the car detail."

"I think I could keep her busy tomorrow," Marcelo said.

"Thanks," Curtis said. "I still can't believe she's going out with me."

Rod Stewart's "You're in My Heart" came on the radio as Marcelo went to the file cabinet to pull the most recent employment applications for the dining room. Back at the desk, he reviewed and numbered them from one to ten, based on the attractiveness of the candidate. He would know whom to call when the need arose. The others he tossed in the wastebasket.

"How's it going, cowboy?" Emily leaned against the doorframe.

"Not getting much done with the interruptions." He chuckled.

"Well, I'm here on business," she said. "And you know how I take care of business."

Emily's smile would leave an imprint on his mind long after she'd walked away. Man, she even made that ordinary uniform look extraordinary.

"Come in," he said.

She took a seat across the desk from him. "So this is where it all begins."

"You could say that." He gazed into the warmth of her eyes. "How's your grandma?"

"She has some sort of respiratory problem." She sighed. "But I would rather not talk about that. She'll be fine soon."

"Do you need time off?" Marcelo asked. "To take care of her, I mean."

"Everything's under control. What are you doing?"

"Going over employment applications to see who we call when a position opens. I was a Boy Scout, and as the Boy Scout motto says, be prepared."

She cleared her throat. "You seem to be really getting into this."

That was an understatement. He told her about the meeting with John Copper and Sergio to renew the band contract, and about how Sergio was going to teach him all he knew about the business, and about how he would make sure Sergio would never regret it. Marcelo's dreams were bright stars, and he was racing toward them.

"Learning this business was what I always wanted," Marcelo said.

"Wasn't what you always wanted to go to State?"

He turned off the radio and paced the room. He told her she was right, but that was when he was younger. He was twenty-one, too old for a sophomore. His job, his brother, and his life were in St. Pete, and that was where he belonged.

"What about us? I'm not part of your life?"

He took a seat and searched for the words to express what she meant to him.

"You're a big part of my life," he said. "If it hadn't been for you, I don't know how I would've handled all the attention. You make all the difference in my life."

"You do, too," she said. "Then you must know what day today is."

The question caught him off guard. There was nothing significant to the date. Was there?

"Today's the fifteenth of July," he said.

"Yes, our one-month anniversary. You remembered." She stared him in the eye. "Tell me you're going to JC."

Yes, he would take two classes that fall and use part of the scholarship. He would continue to take two classes a semester until he finished his associate degree. School and his job would keep him plenty busy. With business courses added, his business plans were rock solid.

"I'll sign up for accounting and management," he said.

"Radical." Emily came around the desk.

She kissed him on the lips, and he pressed back. She was supple and tender and made his breathing difficult. He had just caught his breath when Carlos entered the office, and not looking happy.

His brother's face was easier to read than the alphabet. Marcelo stood.

"Carmine fired Barry and told him to punch out." Carlos caught his breath. "Then the coward locked himself in the liquor room when Barry told him to step outside. Barry gave the check from a deuce to a four-top by mistake, and they paid it and left. Then he gave the big check to the deuce hoping they wouldn't notice, but they did."

Marcelo cringed.

Barry stormed into the office, his face red, his eyes glaring.

"It's time to leave this dump." Barry was hyperventilating. "We don't need this crap!"

"Maybe we can fix this," Marcelo said.

"Too late for that," Barry said. "I told Carmine he could take his job and shove it where the stars don't shine in front of everybody before I told him to step outside. Then he ran."

Marcelo held his forehead. "Why did you do that?"

"Screw him. Let's go." Barry took a step and waited. His chest rose and fell.

Carlos looked at Barry, then at Marcelo. Barry waited with anxious eyes.

"I...I can't go," Marcelo said. "I have a job to do."

Barry swallowed hard and retreated. On his way out, he punched the time clock. Splintered glass fell on the hallway tile.

XXV

Emily

Emily clenched the steering as she drove to work feeling responsible for Grandma's delicate condition. She put on sunglasses to combat the glare of the setting sun. Grandma's sneezes had escalated into severe chest and nasal congestions. What type of a granddaughter was she, to have forgotten Grandma's umbrella and then the aspirin? She wouldn't win any awards or medals for her dedication. No use fretting. Grandma would be better soon.

Emily joined others in the break room for a quick bite before her shift. The subdued conversation that late afternoon was about how the lovable Carmine had thrown out Barry like an old pair of shoes.

"When I graduate," Roger said, "everyone's invited to see me tell Carmine to kiss my beanbag."

"You can't blame Carmine totally," Curtis said. "Barry wasn't doing his job."

"Carmine isn't doing his, and he's still here," Carlos said. "Whose side are you on?"

"I'm not taking sides, just saying."

"Don't take this personally, Carlos," Roger said, "or it'll eat you up."

"It is personal. Marcelo and I should blow this place. Carmine isn't going anywhere, that low bottom-feeding letch."

Barry and Carmine had become detriments to the restaurant, more trouble than they were worth. But Carmine was still one of the owners, even if he was fair as loaded dice. On the other hand, she could see that Marcelo was becoming an important piece that kept the Vineyard running smoothly. That could be difficult for even Carmine to undermine.

"Maybe I should go to Ringling and Barnum and Bailey Clown College," Carlos said. "Venice is as close as I'll ever get to State. This place is a circus, complete with freak show and all."

"What would be your major?" Roger asked. "Circus clown? Rodeo clown? Party clown? I'd say circus clown. The highlight of your day would be making the fat lady sing in the middle of the night."

Carlos failed to find the humor.

"You know," Curtis said, "I'm planning on a new career. I've got to be honest. My acting career was over eons ago, but I wasn't ready to admit it."

"Barry told you when he met you that it was over," Carlos said.

"And you know what?" Curtis laughed. "That fool was right on."

Carlos put on his vest and picked up his plate. The rest of the guys followed him.

Emily cut into the medium-rare chop sirloin with her fork. It was red—she took a bite—and cold. For a few minutes she'd been distracted from Grandma's illness, and that hadn't been a bad thing: she hadn't felt guilty for her condition for that time. When she called her mother later, she would tell her she didn't want to be an accomplice in her twisted plan.

"Hey, girl," Monica came in. "What it is?"

"Barry got fired, and Grandma's all congested," Emily said.

"Barry's days were numbered in this place." Monica stirred her iced tea. "But be careful with your grandma at her age. Colds can have complications. How did she get sick?"

"She'll be fine," Emily said. "I'm taking care of her."

"Who's looking after her now?"

Emily lost her appetite. She wanted to see Marcelo when she was through with her shift. The moon was brighter, the colors deeper when she was with him. But she needed to care for Grandma, and clean up the mess she'd made.

Emily brushed her hair in front of the vanity mirror in her bedroom. She'd gone to Marcelo's for a few minutes the night before, concerned about how he'd been handling Barry's firing. He seemed to be taking it in stride. That was how he'd presented himself. Perhaps Marcelo would have a better chance without Barry: the heavy tail that kept his kite from soaring.

"Emily, come here!" Grandma's desperate plea came from the back of the house.

She rushed to the back door and gasped. Grandma lay on the concrete patio at the bottom of the steps holding her forehead. Emily stepped down to her side and sat her up.

"I don't know what happened." Grandma panted. "I…I feel cold."

"Come inside." Emily helped her up the stairs.

She lay Grandma in bed and brought her cold water to drink. Her breathing was shallow and quick. Though she complained of chills, her skin was warm and moist.

"Do you have a thermometer?" Emily asked.

"In the medicine cabinet over the sink."

Emily read the thermometer: one hundred and one degrees—a fever, as she suspected. Grandma held her chest, coughed, and found it difficult to breathe.

"I'm calling an ambulance." She dialed and made the call.

"What did you do that for, dear?" Grandma coughed. "I always get chills in the winter."

"I know, Grandma," Emily said. "Just rest and don't talk. It's making you cough."

She placed a wet washcloth on her forehead, paced the floor, and waited and waited. It was true; it was possible to slow down time if you concentrated on it hard enough. Mound Park Hospital was a few blocks away, only half a mile. Medical attention was minutes away.

Within ten minutes the paramedics arrived. One technician checked her grandmother's vital signs: pupils, pulse, respiration, and her temperature with the back of his hand. Then they strapped her into a stretcher and lifted her into the ambulance. Emily rode to the hospital holding Grandma's hand.

"Where are we going?" Grandma's voice was heavy with pain.

"We're going to see the doctor…and you'll be fine," she said, more for her own benefit.

In the emergency room, the intake nurse took her grandma's vital signs again and wrote down the symptoms: cough, shortness of breath, quickened pulse, chest pain, fever, and confusion. Grandma coughed greenish mucus. The nurse finished her assessment, and Grandma faded off.

"You brought her in just in time," she said.

"What's going on with her?"

"The doctor will give you the diagnosis."

The young emergency room physician shed light on the mystery. The diagnosis was bacterial pneumonia, and the treatment was daily antibiotics.

"Pneumonia often develops during or after an upper respiratory infection such as a cold," the doctor told her as Grandma slept soundly with the aid of an oxygen tank.

"She had a cold recently," Emily said. "I should've taken better care of her."

"No use in blaming yourself now," he said. "But she's going to need someone to care for her when she gets home. We'll keep her here for a couple of days until she's out of danger."

"Can I stay with her?"

"See the nurse's desk about that," he said. "But when she goes home, she's going to have to take her medicine, drink plenty of fluids, and get lots of rest. We have to be more careful because of her age. Resistance against disease is not what it used to be."

Emily went home after talking to one of the nurses. She could come back and be with Grandma. She brought a book to read while Grandma rested. She realized that love was a lemon, sometimes bitter and sometimes sweet. That night, Emily wrapped herself in a blanket next to Grandma and wept.

XXVI

Barry

Barry wrung his clammy hands and waited in his car before going into the Bull Pen. Man, he didn't want to go in that place and didn't know why. He'd been there a thousand freaking times before. He mustered the nerve, slammed the car door, and went in. A half dozen strangers were scattered about the bar and tables, sucking on their favorite poison. It wasn't his home anymore. The regulars changed with the seasons like leaves on a tree. He slid onto a barstool.

Behind the bar, Smitty balanced on a stepstool and reached to change the tube channel for a guy in a sleeveless shirt wearing a baseball cap four stools away.

"Give me a draught and a shot of bourbon," Barry said.

What are all these strange faces here to see? Smitty put up his brew and shot.

He downed the shot. It relaxed every muscle in his body and made his stomach glow. *Ahhh…* He took a gulp from the frosted mug and shifted his eyes about the place. Two middle-aged guys were pouring the last of a pitcher of beer at a table near the jukebox, but their attention wasn't on their brew. Instead, they eyed two young chicks playing pool unaware of their lustful eyes. They huddled their balding heads together like football players and whispered to each other with idiotic grins on their faces. So near, yet so far. Man, neither girl was much to brag about, one bony and the other one flat, but they were probably better than what the poor saps had at home: saggy old broads in curlers and slippers. A real pickle of a problem, but it wasn't his.

The Vineyard crew would be there soon, tripping and stepping over their thirsty tongues. It was Thursday, and that was when their weekend began. Yep, he knew the drill.

"Aren't you having a beer from the list?" Smitty wiped the bar.

Barry stared at him. *What had he done to those beers?*

Drinking the 150 brews on the list under the clear finish of the counter was a goal once. All because he wanted a thimble of recognition, a token to justify the air he breathed. But no new generations of regulars would see his name engraved on the plaque hanging on the brick wall behind the bar. Man, an uneasy feeling told him he wasn't coming back after that night. Then he remembered his business plan with Marcelo, cracked up, and choked on his beer.

"What a joke." He wiped his mouth with his sleeve.

A bunch of guys and chicks came in laughing and making noise. What the hell was so funny? Had they heard Flip Wilson or Carol Burnett? *Sit down and shut up already!* One of them had a goatee and a face only someone who'd given birth to it could love. The five other guys could pass for normal. They pushed three tables together and played musical chairs before parking their behinds. Goatee ordered two pitchers of brew at the bar and nodded at him.

"Do I know you?" Barry asked.

The guy carried the pitchers to the table and didn't utter a sound. Two guys came for the beer mugs. Someone grabbed Barry by the shoulders! *What the hell?* He spun around and jumped off the stool with clenched fists, his knee ready to connect and bring him down.

"What in creation brings you here?" Tyrone asked.

He dropped his fists and returned to his seat and drink. "Don't be sneaking up on somebody." He took a gulp of beer.

"Last time I checked you weren't somebody." Tyrone ordered a 7-Up. "You must be working at the Starfish, or you'd be kissing Carmine's pimply butt for your job back." He laughed.

He was in no mood for jokes.

"I miss your crazy self, though." They clinked glasses and took a swig.

The front door opened, and Barry winced to see Emily and Angie. The girls grabbed a table and waved them over to join them—or maybe waved Tyrone over to join them. Tyrone took the invitation and deserted him. *Crap!* Emily came to the bar.

"I'm sorry you were terminated," she said.

Only an imbecile would believe you were sorry. Barry turned away.

"Join us for a drink before you leave." She paid for her drinks and left.

What did she mean? He wasn't invited over until he was ready to leave? Oh, she wished he'd disappear to have Marcelo eating out of her hand like a mama's boy. Hell, he didn't care about anything anymore. One of the chicks from the group of twelve, wearing a cowboy hat, came over and ordered a glass of Chablis. *Hubba hubba.* Her eyes oozed curiosity and mischief.

He leaned toward her. "Hey, can I buy you a drink?"

"I wish, but my boyfriend wouldn't like that." She pointed him out.

It was the doofus who hadn't said anything to him earlier. The one who'd just walked away. Man, he should tell him his chick wanted to have a drink with him. His eyes followed her back to her table, and then he ordered another bourbon and beer.

Curtis, Roger, Carlos, and Marcelo walked in and joined the rest. He spun around and caught his reflection on the smoked mirror behind the bar. He was making like he was reading the labels on the bottles on the shelf when Marcelo came up to him.

"You haven't answered your phone," Marcelo said. "Sorry I couldn't leave with you the other night."

"You could've, but you didn't want to." He talked to him through the mirror. "You get a couple of lucky breaks and you forget about your friends."

Marcelo sighed. "It's not like that. Come join us when you're ready."

He noticed Monica arrive and join Emily, Angie, and the others. He'd expected to run into a couple of the guys, but why was everyone there? The girl in the cowboy hat was eyeing him again. Their eyes locked for seconds before hers darted away. He downed the shot and grabbed his mug. *It's time to join the party.*

"You guys hear about that test tube baby born in England?" Carlos asked. "It was five pounds, twelve ounces."

"Where you read that, the *Enquirer*?" Angie asked. "Now, how can you grow a five-pound baby in a test tube? That's impossible."

"I heard it from Walter Cronkite on *CBS Evening News*," Carlos said. "But you're right. Growing a five-pound baby in a test tube would be impossible."

"I'm playing pool," Monica told Tyrone. "Put your quarter up to play me next."

"You've got to win first." Tyrone said. "Anyway, I don't play girls."

Tyrone swallowed hard and shifted his eyes about the place.

"When Monica wins, you'll have to play her," Carlos said.

Tyrone crunched on ice from his 7-Up. "She might beat you, not me."

Around the table the talk was about the Vineyard and what had happened that evening. Barry listened, but it was nothing he hadn't heard before. When he looked her way, the girl in the cowboy hat winked, with her boyfriend beside her. The guy looked like a scruffy goat with that hair on his chin. He grabbed her chin and kissed her, and then he pulled up his jeans and went to the wall rack to pick a pool stick to play Monica. Thunder cracked above the Bull Pen.

"When did you start at the Starfish?" Emily asked him.

He wasn't there to talk to her.

"Lots of women go there for the live music and the revolving bar," Roger said. "My friend tended bar there, and he told me that married women in their late thirties and early forties went there looking for some strange, and he gave it to them. I'd have done the same thing, too."

"You'd mess with married women?" Curtis gave him a hard stare and then turned to Barry. "How do you like it there?"

"Don't want to talk about it."

He wasn't there to talk shop or to listen to others doing it. He had another interest.

"My turn," Curtis said after Monica beat the goat.

"She's lucky she beat that guy." Tyrone tapped the table with his fingers. "I don't play girls because beating them means nothing."

"But losing to one does." Curtis stroked the pool stick with hands covered in chalk.

"Come by the house tomorrow," Marcelo told Barry. "I have things to tell you."

What did he have up his sleeve? "I'm busy. I'll have to see."

"Get out!" Smitty shouted to a girl standing at the front door.

The chick was about fifteen, a juvenile with no business in a bar. Her red hair was matted down, her clothes wet. She turned to the downpour that had just started and then, with empty eyes, turned to the people inside.

"I told you to leave once already today." Smitty's arm pointed outside.

She turned and walked into heavy curtains of rain.

The goat was putting quarters in the jukebox, probably to play some redneck song. His cowgirl smiled at Barry. *She wants you.* Being a gentleman, he guzzled the rest of his beer and went to go make her acquaintance.

"I've been looking for a Stetson hat like that." Barry stood beside her.

"It was a birthday gift from my boyfriend."

"Yeah, the guy over there," an inbred butted in and pointed to the goat. "You better mosey on before he sees you."

"Who's talking to you?" Barry devoured the chick with his eyes.

He felt a tap on the shoulder. The boyfriend's ugly mug got in his face.

"You want to glue your eyes back in your skull?" he asked.

Barry held his nose. "You better try Scope. Listerine isn't doing it."

"You a funny mother, aren't you?" He slammed his pool stick on the floor. It rolled and came to rest at the foot of the pool table. "Maybe you'd like to step out the back door."

Barry was grabbed from behind and pulled away from trouble.

"Sorry, but we have to go." Carlos led him back to his seat.

The goat gave him the evil eye and then pulled up his pants and got back to the jukebox.

"That idiot would've gotten a knee to the nuts if he'd tried anything," Tyrone said.

"Why?" Curtis asked. "Barry was messing with her before knowing she wasn't alone."

"I knew she wasn't alone," Barry said.

"Then why did you do that?" Curtis looked as if he'd sucked a lemon. "People got to respect that. We're not *cavemen*."

The cowgirl blew him a kiss. Why listen to Marcelo or any of the Vineyard guys? He wasn't one of them anymore. If he had to strike out on his own, why not with her on his arm?

With her in his life, relationships wouldn't be mirrors that shattered with his presence. Was he being tested to see if he would rescue her? She could be his Adrienne, and he'd be her Rocky. Together, they'd triumph against all odds. If Marcelo could be a hero, he could too.

"She's mine now, goat breath," Barry said.

The guy pushed him and put up his fists.

"You're choosing the wrong square dance partner, hayseed," Barry said.

The goat pushed him again, and he tore into him like a tornado through a trailer park....

When the dance ended, Barry nursed his bruised knuckles and a bump on the back of the head. It was difficult to stretch his fingers, and some inbred had broken a pool stick across his skull. Overturned chairs, tables, and broken glasses and pitchers littered the floor. Having had more than they could handle, the goat and his herd had hightailed it out of the joint.

"You guys get out before I call the law." Smitty swept the broken glass.

He would've called them already if he were going to. Smitty didn't want the fuzz there, either. It wasn't the first time fists and bottles had flown at the Bull Pen, and it wouldn't be the last. The blowhard was worried he'd lose his license.

"I don't want *you* in here again." Smitty pointed his shaky finger at Barry.

"I'm done with all this." Marcelo's red and puffy face wasn't one of joy. "I don't want Carlos in any of this."

Carlos rubbed his swollen jaw. "I was just getting warmed up when they ran out."

"Are you happy?" Curtis had lost a front tooth. "All this crap for nothing!"

"She was blowing me kisses," Barry said. "She wanted me to rescue her."

"Are you *dumb* and *blind?*" Roger wiped his bloody nose. "She was looking at you with disgust."

"She didn't even want you looking at her," Carlos said.

"I never got in a bar fight when I drank." Tyrone's left eye was shut. "I had to quit drinking to do that. Man, I gave better than I got."

None of the Vineyard guys said another word, not even Marcelo. They stood mute, as if they'd bitten off their tongues in the dance. He got the message…he was no idiot.

"I've got to roll," said Barry. The room spun when he stood up. Marcelo grabbed his arm.

"Don't go yet." Marcelo held on. "They might be outside. We'll leave together."

He jerked his arm free and went for the exit. *You don't need him!*

"Wait," Tyrone said. "We're coming with you."

The rain had drenched the parking lot. The cars resting under the lights belonged to them. No one was hanging around the lot. Palm trees waved their leaves, warning of an oncoming storm— too late for that. Barry cranked up his Catalina, squealed tires out of the lot, and snaked onto the wet road. Lightning flashed and rumbled in the night sky. Another storm was approaching, one with menacing rumbling clouds and thunderbolts that could pierce the heart.

Down the street he turned on the radio. It was the traffic report. Man, he was wired with adrenaline, and he needed to mellow out real bad. He searched in the glove compartment for a doobie. There was no inside light, and it was impossible to see anything. THUMP! The front of the car rattled. *What the...?* He slammed on the brakes. Through the rearview mirror, he could see a lump on the road. It looked like a car tire in the dark, but then it moved. *It's somebody's poor dog!* There was nobody on the road at that time of night, and that meant there were no witnesses. He floored it and drove away with the hounds of hell gnawing at his bumper.

XXVII

Marcelo

The registration line at Pinellas JC went out the front entrance and wrapped itself around the administration building. The late July sun sparkled through clear skies. Marcelo and Carlos made it inside the building before dehydrating in the subtropical heat and joined different queues. Marcelo rubbed his cheek, still sore and lumpy from the brawl. Despite their aches and bruises they didn't forfeit their plans and enrolled for school. Mission accomplished, Marcelo drove to work.

"Get the hell out of my storeroom!" Marcelo heard when he walked in the back door.

Jim and Harry darted out of the room, and Tyrone followed them with a meat cleaver.

"I catch those two toking weed in my kitchen again," he said, shaking the cleaver at Marcelo, "I'll make a beeline for Carmine, and they'll be history. You know that guy loves to can people. He's got the compassion of a psychopath."

"You're a bigger man than that." Marcelo punched in for work. "I'll talk to them, now put away that weapon."

He wouldn't run into Barry at the restaurant that day. It was odd. But from time to time, it slipped his mind that he no longer worked there. The night before, for one second, he started off to find Barry to tell him a joke he found amusing. His only consolation was that he'd tried to reach Barry, to offer a helping hand, but he'd been met with a reinforced wall of resistance.

He went into the break room. There, he found Emily with Monica and Angie.

"I want to work as an emergency room nurse," Monica said. "That'd be exciting, going to work not knowing what the day will bring."

"That's freaking wacked," Angie said. "You'd get mangled, bloody bodies from car wrecks or from bar fights like the other night. No thank you, I'll keep waiting on tables."

"Are you OK?" Emily examined Marcelo's bruised face. "That Barry is a real zero."

"He's a loser with a capital L," Angie said. "A jive turkey."

"Don't talk about Barry," he said. "He might be messed up, but he's not a zero or a loser." He turned to Emily. "That's not what I wanted to talk about."

"Tell me. What's wrong?"

"Nothing's wrong." He exhaled. "I signed up for accounting and management classes."

"That's heavy." Emily beamed. "Two classes are plenty, especially with your job."

"Congrats," Monica said. "Maybe I'll see you on campus. I've got another two semesters before I finish school." She twirled her finger in the air. "Yippee ay yay."

Barry was gone, and it would be a while before he got used to that. Still, the other night at the Bull Pen would go a long way in helping him adjust to Barry's absence. But what would his days be like when Emily left? The end of one phase was the beginning of another.

"Why can't people be happy where they are in life?" Angie asked.

"Have you heard about your applications with the airlines?" Emily asked.

"No." Angie stood up. "I've got to hit the trail."

"I've gotta go, too." Monica put her dish in the bus pan. "When she gets home, make sure your grandma gets lots of rest and drinks plenty of juices. Soup is best for an upset stomach."

Marcelo and Emily were left to themselves. He brought her lips to his and kissed her. She was a bright spot on a dark day, and he had much for which to be grateful.

"I wanted to sign up for more classes," he said.

"You can't make up for lost time. Just make the best of the time you have," Emily said. "What will you do with the money you've gotten, if you're not going into business yet?"

"Keep it in the bank for now."

"You might want to consider investing in gold. An ounce is up to two hundred dollars."

He nodded. "What's happening with your grandma?"

"She's not well…"

Harry dragged a trash can by the door. "Tyrone wants you in the kitchen."

"Hold that thought," Marcelo told her. "Duty calls."

The last time Tyrone had called for him, the chicken delivery that had arrived two days earlier stank. It reeked of rot, though it had been transported in a refrigerated truck and in waxed cardboard boxes topped off with crushed ice. Marcelo had called the company to exchange the delivery, but it wouldn't arrive until the following day.

"Tyrone knows what to do," Carmine had told Marcelo when he asked him if he could send Harry to the market for fresh poultry that afternoon.

Marcelo relayed the message, and Tyrone soaked the rancid chicken in water with baking soda until the stench disappeared. That night, none of the employees had chicken for dinner. Carmine was always tripping. That wasn't cool.

"Check it out." Tyrone showed Marcelo a slab of prime rib and cut a piece. "It's cooked medium already."

Brown edges surrounded the rose middle of the cut.

"By the time I drop it in the au jus to heat it up and serve it, it'll be medium well." Tyrone dumped the slab in the steam table and slammed it shut. "We only got medium-well and well-done prime rib tonight." He wrote that on the board.

"Are all of them like that?" Marcelo inspected the other slabs.

"I bet they are. All four were cooked this morning by our buddy Carmine." He shook his head. "If Barney Fife was a cook, he'd be Carmine. And Useless would be his middle name."

"Nothing we can do about it now," Marcelo said.

"Can't you tell him to stay the hell out of my kitchen?"

"That's not my decision to make. Sorry."

Harry turned on the vacuum cleaner in the service area and ended their conversation.

There was no need to tell Sergio about the overcooked prime. It hadn't been done on purpose. It was an oversight on Carmine's part and probably wouldn't occur again anytime soon. Besides, he didn't want to step into a quagmire by angering Carmine: a man enamored with the idea of revenge.

"More mail for you, Mister Popularity." Jackie handed him two letters.

He opened them in the office in private. It was so wicked! He held two letters and checks totaling $325. One came from a guy who hadn't gone to college because he couldn't afford it, and later when he could afford it, he had a family to support. Even though he'd done well in a car-towing business, owning five trucks and contracting with major road assistance companies, he wished he'd gone to college. He encouraged Marcelo not to give up his dream. The other letter came from a wealthy woman who had plenty of children and grandchildren who would eventually inherit her wealth but didn't deserve it.

People had different reasons for helping him out. Part of him wished the checks would stop coming. On the other hand, if they continued, he'd have more than enough to strike out on his own if the need arose. Still, his good fortune rang hollow. Curtis popped his head in.

"Two cops up front want to talk to you," he said. "It's about Barry."

Marcelo landed back on solid ground. He had to keep it real.

XXVIII

Emily

Emily found Connie writing Tonight's Specials on the chalk-board in the foyer. A grapevine with green leaves and ripened concord grapes twisted itself around the borders of the board. A Moses-like figure with a silver beard was servicing the cash register next to Jackie. The machine's outer shell was off, revealing metal gears and mechanical levers.

Grandma had been released from the hospital that morning.

"I can't give you the time off." Connie kept writing. "Not even Marcelo can do that, not for an indefinite time."

Emily exhaled. "It's only for a few days, until my grandma gets better. It's not like I'm going on a Caribbean vacation."

"Carmine's in the office." Connie glanced at her. "Sergio won't be in until later."

"That's bogus," Emily said. "I'll wait, thank you very much."

From behind the counter, Jackie stared Emily down through her eyeglasses while the bearded guy inspected the workings inside the machine. What was up with that jelly-brain? She had no intention of asking Carmine for anything. Emily picked up her guest checks.

"You know something?" Jackie said. "The last waitress who got time off indefinitely didn't have a job when she wanted to come back."

Emily didn't acknowledged her comment with a reply, and found her section. It was next to Roger's. He leaned on a chair and wiped each shoe on the calf of the opposite leg, and then admired them. They were black and shiny like the boots of an army recruit.

"You and me close tonight," he said.

"Yeah, but I'm not playing the lighter game," she said. "I don't even want to close."

"I hear you, but it won't be so bad. We'll have the whole kitchen to ourselves."

Connie came to her station and told Emily that Sergio wasn't coming in. She'd have to ask Carmine for the time off. Connie wished her luck, as she hadn't worked there long.

"She's been here long enough if her grandma's sick," Roger said.

"Well, I hope you get it," Connie said. "You haven't had any time off since college. Not that this job is as hard."

"What you mean by that crack?" Angie wedged her wiry frame in the picture. "You saying this job takes no brains?"

"Nobody said that." Roger took off and looked back. "I've got to get rolling."

"You best run, freak," Angie said.

"Both of you make sure your sidework's done." Connie returned to the unfinished Tonight's Specials board.

Emily's sidework was condiments. In the service area, she uncapped ketchup, mustard, and steak sauce bottles and soaked the caps in a bowl of tepid water, rinsed them clean, and dried them. She wiped each bottle with a napkin soaked in soda water. Beside her, Angie scooped whipped butter from a plastic bucket into miniature paper cups. Yellow matter lubricated her arm to the elbow.

"You got to marry those ketchups." Angie pointed to two half-full bottles. "Like this." She wiped her shiny hand with a paper towel and inverted one bottle on the other, mouth to mouth. The contents poured from one to the other. "Never take a half-empty one to a table. If you do, shake the hell out of it before so it looks full."

Down the corridor, Carmine opened the bread warmer, felt the temperature inside, and then resumed his path toward them. He greeted the waitresses who passed his way. The guys cherished the lack of attention and their insignificant status on the Carmine totem pole.

"Hi, Emily," he said. "Everybody's treating you OK?"

"Just swell, thanks."

He reminded her that his door was always open, and then went into the kitchen.

"He's such a pig. Screw him." Angie launched a finger in his direction.

"I can still be polite. But you should apologize to pigs for that comment."

"This girl don't apologize to nobody." She pressed the lid back on the bucket of butter.

"There's no shame in apologizing if you're wrong."

"There you go. This chick's never wrong."

It was no use. Angie's mind had closed the window on introspection.

Angie carried the bucket back to the walk-in cooler in the back. Emily finished capping, wiping, and lining the bottles on the shelf. Angie returned to clean the counter.

"Has Marcelo heard from Barry?" Angie asked, wiping. "I don't care what he says, Barry's a bodacious loser."

"Nobody is totally bad," Emily said. "But it's like he's evaporated."

Could his firing and disappearance be attributed to a fortunate act of fate? Hurricane Barry had left sorrow and destruction in his path. They were living the calm after the storm.

Emily returned to the floor. In the foyer, Harry wrung a mop in a bucket and slapped it on the ceramic tile. It ate the dry floor as he swung it left to right. Curtis came her way with his hair puffed out like cotton candy. He played with his front tooth and winced.

"Got a temporary crown today," he said. "I think Barry's lost it, but you believe I feel for that fool? You'd imagine I'd be used to people coming and going all the time, but I'm not."

"There's a lot of turnover in this business, huh?"

"It's always like that," he said. "I could come back tomorrow, and you'd be gone."

"Well, I'm not going any place just yet," Emily said. "How's the real estate class going?"

"I'm keeping up with all the work, but I'm having second thoughts about having no salary and depending on sales commissions only."

"That can be trying."

Carmine brought a long-limbed lady and a small girl with a tight upper lip to her deuce. He pulled the chair out for the lady and placed the menu in front of them. He signaled to Emily that it was her party, as if she didn't already know.

"May the force be with you if you ask that letch for the time off," Curtis said over a shoulder and went into the service area.

Connie led a couple to Roger's section. She was a vocal woman of generous physical proportions. He was a minuscule, silent gent who walked in her shadow.

Emily went to her party.

"Hi," the lady said. "Bring me a vodka gimlet straight up and iced tea for my daughter."

At the service bar, Sherry stirred and poured the chilled drink: vodka and Rose's lime juice. Emily served them to her party as they read the menu. The young girl strained to be elegant and grown-up wearing her mother's pearls.

"We'll have two shrimp cocktails first," the girl said.

Tables away, Roger and Carlos snickered at something amusing transpiring between them. Sergio crossed the dining room. *What?* Emily rushed to him.

"Sure, no problem, as long as it's OK with Marcelo," Sergio said when she asked him for the time off.

Within the hour, the Vineyard hummed. Servers circulated throughout the corridors of the restaurant in a synchronized manner. They crossed station boundaries and helped each other in the spirit of cooperation. Fast-firing cigarette lighters jumped boundaries in friendly competition.

"I got the time off," Emily told Monica at the pickup line.

"Check it out," Monica said. "Life has sent you, Marcelo, and Barry in separate paths. Freaky-deaky, huh?"

She couldn't speak for Barry, but her and Marcelo's separation was temporary, only for a definite time, and only until Grandma got better. Then she'd return to the Vineyard, and they'd work and be together as before.

XXIX

Barry

"Oh, crap." Barry came to with a throat as dry as sandpaper and a headache beating like a bass drum. He struggled to suck air. With great effort, he dragged his bare feet through the living room carpet and kicked aluminum beer cans going to the refrigerator. Since the fight the other night, he'd been lying low, under the radar. He gulped down OJ from the carton and turned on the tube. The juice chilled his insides. They were showing her photo on the tube. It was…*That's the girl who got kicked out of the Bull Pen the night of the fight!* He turned up the volume and dropped into the recliner.

"The hit-and-run victim was a fifteen-year-old runaway girl from Atlanta, missing since last month. Her parents worried about her drug addiction and how that placed her life in danger. Saint Petersburg Police continues its investigation. If you have any information about the victim or the hit-and-run vehicle, please call SPPD."

Florida was always attracting runaways for some unknown reason. The dead girl on the tube looked like a chick who'd bused tables at the Vineyard while staying with her uncle. Later on, he'd found out she was a runaway and that the older guy she stayed with was no uncle. The chick had been drawn to Barry like a magnet to a refrigerator.

"I'm sick of the old guy," she'd told to him one afternoon. "But he won't let me leave. He's afraid I'll tell. Can I stay with you for a while?"

"Don't you think it'd be best if you went back home?" he'd asked. No jailbait for him.

The next evening the busgirl didn't make it to work. Connie had called her, and her uncle said she'd found another job. She never came in for her paycheck. When Barry went to drop off the check, the landlady told him they'd gone and left no forwarding address.

Barry switched channels and found another station reporting the hit-and-run.

"Poor chick." He went into the bathroom. "Some guy mowed her down and just left her there like a dead dog."

He splashed water on his face and dried off with a towel. In the mirror over the sink, he saw his reflection: one weathered by a short and troubled life. His eyes lost focus, and when it returned, his face had transformed. The girl from the news report was staring at him! "Why did you leave me to die?" she asked, and he ran out the room.

He didn't do it! It couldn't be! She'd been gone by the time he left the Bull Pen. And he drove straight home that night. He only stopped once, when he hit that…It wasn't a dog? *The TV station knows you're watching.* That was why they wouldn't let the story die— different from how he let her die on that deserted street. *How could you get so ugly in one lifetime?*

The cops will want to pin whatever happened to that chick from Indiana on him too.

"RINGGGG…"

He jumped up at the sound of the telephone. He reached for it but then retreated as if it were hot. After a couple more rings, he answered it.

"Hey, what's happening?" It was Marcelo.

"I'm on my way out."

"About the Bull Pen the other night—"

"I've got to split." He hung up.

The dead girl lying on the road crept back into his mind. He'd left her there like road kill, like a dead armadillo. In his short life, he'd seen good people turn bad and bad people turn worse. There was no escape. He was on a collision course with the electric chair. Old Sparky waited for him—

"RINGGGGGG…"

Heart attack! He let it ring until it died. When it rang again, he picked it up.

"Want some butt-kicking weed, man?" Jim cracked up. "Just got some Hawaiian herb, man. Believe that? Hawaiian."

"Where are you?" He looked over his shoulder.

"You buying weed or what, man? I smoked two bowls and—"

He hung up. On the tube screen, the dead girl's picture came back on searching for him.

"As we informed you, SPPD is looking for a late-sixties Pontiac Catalina or Bonneville in connection with the hit-and-run last week. A witness has come forward to report he observed a white male running to that car and driving away from the scene of the accident."

He hurried to the window and took a look outside—his car was there, under overcast skies. The old biddy across the way was watering her weeds with a garden hose, in a faded house dress and a head full of plastic pink curlers. The lazy hag sprayed the bald car tire and rusty gas can on the grass. When she turned around and pinned her eyes on him, he hid from view. The witch had eyes in the back of her head! She would turn him in if she knew anything, and the heat would come knocking in a heartbeat. He could feel their hot breath on the back of his neck.

The neighbor went inside her trailer, and he went outside to check out his car. A crumpled right fender and bumper gave the Catalina an unhappy look. How could he get that fixed not to attract attention? He was broke as always. At least the headlight wasn't broken.

"RINGGGGG…"

"Damn it!" He dashed back inside.

It rang and it rang until it died. He stared at the telephone and swallowed hard. What did the strangers at the Bull Pen and the chick provoking him into a fight have do with this hit-and-run or with anything? All he knew was that he wasn't safe, and he didn't know who to trust anymore. He looked out the window and scoped the landscape. The gray skies cleared and brightened his perception. The Pinellas County Sheriff posse would be after him soon with bloodhounds biting at his heels, ready to throw him in the cooler for the rest of his days. He could hear the dogs yelping and barking and coming after him.…

XXX

Marcelo

Marcelo pulled up in front of Barry's trailer but didn't see his Catalina. Still, he knocked on the door. Seconds later, he turned the knob and pushed the door open. Barry wouldn't leave his place unlocked: he kept his home more secure than the Federal Reserve. Inside, drawn window shades darkened the living room. A pressed wood entertainment set with saggy shelves stood empty against the wall. The worn leather couch and recliner were angled out of place. In the bedroom, the bare mattress and the empty hangers in the closet told him Barry had left. What then?

"He's been gone a couple, three days." A middle-aged woman stood in the living room in a faded sweat suit. "I stay across the way. I can't say I miss him, though."

When he neared her, she backed up. "You know where he went?" Marcelo asked.

"If I did, I'd have told the law that when they come looking for him." She alternated scratching her arms. "Days before he left, he was up all night with the TV until it gone off the air, then he'd turn on the radio."

"Do you have the landlord's number? He might know where he went."

"Have his number? He don't own my place." She headed for the door, but then turned. "You best be careful. He's got the devil in him. I ought to know."

Without another word or explanation, she stepped across the sandy lot and into her home.

"Crazy old hen." He took a seat on the couch and dropped his shoulders. Where else could he search? An empty Folgers can rested against the wall. Marcelo smiled.

A couple of summers ago, Barry had gotten in the habit of betting big and losing bigger at Derby Lanes Greyhound Track. One Sunday night, Marcelo drove him home after they'd guzzled several boilermakers and scarfed down smoked mullet at Peterson's Smoked Fish. Once home, Barry packed the bong with some primo Panama Red, and in minutes, both of them had reached the stratosphere without help from the Cape Kennedy launch pad.

"Hold on to my money." He'd handed Marcelo a wad of bills from the can that night. "Man, I don't want to blow it at the dogs when you leave."

Marcelo took the cash knowing Barry's pockets were sieves, unable to hold on to anything of value. The next morning Barry woke up and found the empty can.

"I blew all my cash last night," he'd told Marcelo at work that evening.

The story still made him laugh. He locked the door when he left.

Marcelo drove down Thirty-Fourth Street to the Starfish. He hadn't been to see Barry tending bar. Queen palms surrounded the building. The dining room was a garden with an abundance of subtropical plants. In the lounge, happy hour customers revolved like satellites to the round liquor cabinet at the center. Barry wasn't anywhere. Two older guys with red vests and black bow ties served the rotating clientele. One with curly hair and a mustache greeted him.

"A draught beer, please," Marcelo said.

The pilsner of beer he brought had a flat head.

"Would you like to run a tab?" the bartender asked.

"No thanks, I'll pay cash." A five-dollar bill went on the counter. "I came to see a friend of mine, Barry. Is he working today?"

"Barry?" He crossed his arms. "You mean as a bartender?"

"Yes, he started here a couple of weeks ago."

"Let me get the bar manager." He stepped over to the heavyset man with sideburns working with him. The hefty guy eyed Marcelo, then came his way.

"I remember him," the manager said. "I offered him the service bartender job in the dining room and asked him to call me, but he never did."

Marcelo's shoulders slumped.

The marquee at the Vineyard announced a five-dollar live Maine lobster special. Carmine and Sergio had accepted Marcelo's suggestion, and it had boosted business by 35 percent on Monday, the slowest day of the week. That night had become as profitable for the waiters and waitresses as a weekend night, making it easier for them to take a Friday or Saturday off when necessary.

He parked in back and headed inside. Jim and Harry dragged a hefty garbage can outside.

"No smoking weed behind the dumpster or anywhere on the property," Marcelo said.

Tyrone carried a tray of New York strips from the butcher's block.

"I just cut these, twelve ounces each," Tyrone said. "I'll give you a buck for each one that's off more than a quarter ounce, and you give me one for each that isn't."

"No thanks, I'd like to hold on to my cash. By any chance, have you heard from Barry?"

He gave a pitiful smile. "No, and I don't want to with the law after his butt."

Curtis was polishing a wine glass at the service bar. A bottle neck stuck out of an ice-filled wine bucket in a stand. Marcelo had introduced a wine-selling contest as another way to motivate the waiters and waitresses. It awarded a fifty-dollar prize to whoever sold the most bottles each month and thirty-five to the second-place finisher.

"I'm in first place," Curtis said. "I jumped to an early lead, and I'm racing to the finish line and the winner's circle for those fifty bills. But Roger is only one bottle behind."

Curtis showed him another wine glass. "What's with all the water spots?"

"We've been trying a different detergent."

"You mean a cheaper one. I know whose idea that was." He wiped the glass and placed it in the bucket to chill. "Don't mind me, just griping."

"It's cool. We won't be using that brand once we run out," Marcelo said. "I just found out Barry never took the job at the Starfish."

Curtis puckered his brow and picked up the wine bucket. "Does anything surprise you? Sorry, but if I see him I'm calling the cops, for his own good."

Curtis and Roger snarled at each other when they crossed paths at the entrance to the dining room.

"I just sold two more bottles of wine," Roger said loudly. "I'm in first place now."

Curtis looked back at Roger but kept walking with the wine bucket and ran into Angie. She shoved him back and out of her way.

"Just joking about the two bottles sold," Roger said to Marcelo and rang the bar bell. "One of my guys has been waiting for his date for over an hour. When they eat, he's going to wolf down his chow like a starving war camp prisoner." Roger cocked his head back. "You look like you're not getting any."

"I don't know what's going on with Barry. That's all."

Sherry poured Roger's two Cokes, and he put a maraschino cherry in each glass.

"Do yourself a favor and forget him," Roger said. "You got a first-rate deal going here, you're back in school, and you've got a nice piece of tail to boot."

"That's what everybody tells me, except for the tail part. That only comes from you. Anyway, nobody knows Barry as I know him. He's an OK guy."

"When you get a chance, check out the brick house at my booth, and tell me she's not stacked." He returned to the dining room.

"Barry was OK with me." Sherry broke the ice with a scoop. "If you see him, tell him I still haven't heard from Tallahassee about my transcripts. He'll know what I'm talking about."

Marcelo looked out to the dining room. A lady at one of Roger's tables took a flickering yellow light from Curtis, who showed a grin wide as a canoe. Two tables away, Roger's jaw tightened, and his face reddened as if he'd been slapped, insulted, or both. Next to Curtis, Monica's smile had fallen victim to the Waltons. She picked up rolls and utensils from the floor. Behind her, Angie was engaged in a heated discussion with a customer about a steak. He wanted to give her his plate, but she refused to take it, but then took it and stormed off with it to the kitchen. Later, he'd remind Angie the customer was always right. He went up front.

"Let me bring you up to date." Jackie pushed the glasses up the bridge of her nose. "Nobody cares if they ever see Barry again." She pulled an envelope from beside the register and handed it to him. "But he'll have to see you if he wants his paycheck."

Marcelo took the check and headed to inventory the liquor and wine. They had to place an order the next morning with the distribution company. On his way, he saw Carmine and Angie with the man who'd sent the steak back. The guy's body language told the story: he leaned away from Carmine. The cowering lady at his table played with the macaroni salad on her plate.

"Her filet mignon is cooked medium rare, just like she ordered it." Carmine took her salad plate without asking and put the steak in front of her.

"We told the waitress." The man looked irritated. "We want it cooked pink."

Angie stuck her wiry body between the two. "She ordered medium rare. Pink's medium."

"This is my restaurant," Carmine said. "You saying I don't know what's medium rare?"

"Of course not, all I'm saying is that it's undercooked." The helpless man looked up at Marcelo.

"I can take care of this, Carmine," Marcelo offered.

"I'm doing just fine, thank you." Carmine continued. "Medium rare has a cold, red center, just like what you ordered."

"Really," Marcelo said. "I want to take care of this."

Carmine glared at him. His nostrils flared. "Get away from here."

Marcelo wanted to drop him right there and then. No one would blame him for that.

"We're not getting anywhere," the lady said.

"No, we're not," Carmine said. "Let's forget this ever happened. You two leave and never come back to my place, and we'll call it even for the night." He stormed away.

"Smell you later," Angie mumbled and followed Carmine.

"I'm sorry for everything," Marcelo told the eyes fixed on him. "He's not well."

That was an understatement. And Angie's behavior was unacceptable, but what could one expect? She would never grace the society pages.

"I've never been embarrassed like this in my life." The guy led the shaken lady away.

An older gent at the next table cleared his throat and gave Marcelo a stern look. Marcelo glanced at the four ladies next to him.

"We're fine here," one of them said, and all broke eye contact.

"Again, I'm sorry," Marcelo said to those watching.

Could he complain to Sergio about Carmine, his brother?

Marcelo opened the door to the liquor room. Shelves of bottles lined three walls of the room. As it turned out, he'd need to order a case of scotch and two cases each of vodka and gin. He'd do the wine inventory later. First, he had to get Sherry's liquor. He read the list on the clipboard and took the bottles from the shelf and placed them on the cart, one by one. When he had all her booze, he locked the room and wheeled the cart to the lounge.

He found Sherry and Connie glued to the TV in the bar. Pioneer 11 transmitted images of Saturn and its rings from eight hundred million miles in outer space. No humans had ever seen such close images of the planet in the history of mankind. The scene made his worries insignificant, if only for a few moments.

He placed the bottles on the bar and helped Sherry store them in the cabinets above and below. Then he went to see Carmine in the office. He was behind the desk and on the phone.

"Don't ever talk to me that way again," Marcelo said.

Carmine ended the phone call and put his feet up on the desk.

"Don't you ever get in my business again," Carmine said. "I took care of the matter."

"You have no business being out on the floor."

"Watch it." Carmine leaned forward. "You mess with the bull, and you'll get the horns. You'll be history. You dig?"

"If that happens," Marcelo said, "I'll make it worth my while."

Carmine lost his smirk and backed down.

XXXI

Emily

Emily pulled dry sheets and towels from the hot dryer in the garage and folded them on top of the machines. The sheets crinkled with static electricity. The laundry basket, though topped high, wasn't heavy. It was full of fluff. She carried it inside to the linen closet and stacked the laundry on the shelves. In the living room, newspapers and magazines had been picked up, cushions and pillows were in place, tables were dusted and polished, and the carpeting was vacuumed. All seemed sanitized, sterilized, unlived.

Grandma slept in her room, and she didn't want to wake her. She'd been sleeping around the clock since she was released from the hospital two days earlier. Her fever had dropped, and when she had last touched her it remained low, her breathing, relaxed.

Emily drove to the A&P on Fourth Street. It was midafternoon, and the parking lot was practically empty. She pulled into a spot near the entrance and greeted the paper boy going in. She bought a few essentials: milk, OJ, eggs, sugar, corn flakes, and coffee. Leaving, she bought an *Evening Independent* for Grandma from the kid at the door.

At home, she put the groceries away, folded the paper bags, and made coffee. It had been an exhausting day, and she needed a pick-me-up. The shopping list on the table had every item checked off. The coffee percolated and filled the air with a robust aroma. The telephone rang.

"Hey, girl, how's your life of leisure going?" Monica chuckled.

"I'm preparing for my future domestic role. There's more involved than I realized in running a household."

She poured herself a cup of coffee and opened the carton of milk. It smelled sour. She checked. It was days before the expiration date. She'd have to take it back.

"Don't quit school and have six kids now," Monica said.

"No, but I might change my major to home economics." That wouldn't happen either. She'd make her contributions in the boardroom, not the kitchen or the bedroom. "What's new?"

"Just got home from class," Monica said. "Marcelo hadn't heard from Barry as of last night. I thought you might want to know."

"Thanks, I'll call him later on. Check you later."

She looked out the window. It had rained in the last couple of evenings. The lawn had experienced a growth spurt and sprouted halfway to her knees.

There was half a tank of gas in the lawnmower, enough to do the job. She pushed it to the patio and pulled the cord. It cranked up and purred on the first tug. The overgrown grass entangled the mower blades and bogged down the machine. She raised the front wheels off the ground and slowly lowered them on the dense grass to trim it gradually and keep the machine from bogging down. She mowed around the orange trees and along the rose bushes and shrubs, and then the machine stalled. She tried a couple of times, but it wouldn't crank up. It was odd. There was plenty of gas in the tank, but then she wasn't a mechanic. The bag on the mower had caught the clippings. She dumped the grass in the trash and returned the mower to the garage. The rest of the yard would have to wait for another time. Soaked in sweat, she took a shower.

She checked on Grandma. "You're up."

"I can only sleep so much." She yawned. "You find everything at the A&P?"

"Yes…but there was something else you wanted me to do."

"Oh, yes. Bills need to be paid." Grandma pointed to the dresser. "Top center drawer."

Emily followed her cue and looked inside. She found the light, telephone, and water bill.

"Please fill out the checks and I'll sign them," Grandma said.

Back at the breakfast nook, Emily wrote out the bills, addressed the envelopes, and licked and adhered the postage stamps to them. Then she put them in the mailbox and lifted the red flag.

It was late in the afternoon and a good time to call Marcelo. She'd love to see him later. They could visit and catch up on the latest, but Grandma needed her attention most.

Emily was about to pick up the telephone when it rang. It was her mother. She told her about Grandma's pneumonia and about her hospital stay, how her condition could turn from bad to worse without notice, how the illness had a life of its own, and how she felt responsible for her sickness. Mother's quiet was unsettling.

"No use taking responsibility when the damage is already done," Mother said. "Make sure you look after her this time." She paused. "Maybe I should come up…"

"She's much better now," Emily said. "No need to do that."

"I'll call you tomorrow," Mother said. "Can I talk to her?"

"Grandma, pick up the phone!" she called out. "It's Mother."

Grandma came into the living room after the brief conversation had ended.

"You shouldn't be out of bed," Emily said.

"I'm much better, dear," Grandma said. "I told her it wasn't anybody's fault."

Emily fixed Grandma's dinner: a grilled chicken breast with broccoli over pasta. It was Grandma's suggestion. She'd had plenty of soup and wanted food that would stick to her bones. They ate in her bedroom.

"The lawnmower gave out on me earlier."

"I'm surprised it still runs," Grandma said. "It's pretty old."

The telephone rang, and Emily answered it. "It's Marcelo."

"How's your grandma?" Marcelo asked.

"Much better, thanks. What's cooking?"

"I was thinking," he said. "Can I come over this evening?"

"I'd love to see you." She sighed. "But I have to take a rain check."

She wanted to unwind and relax. It had been a trying day, and Grandma was not quite back to herself, though her eyes were wide and fresh from restful sleep. She hung up.

"What's on TV tonight?" Emily asked. "Want some hot tea?"

"That'd be nice." Grandma opened the newspaper. "Let's see what's on tonight."

Emily put water on the stove and got a cup and a saucer from the cupboard.

"I've got a chill." Grandma wrapped herself in her robe.

Emily touched her forehead. Was her temperature warmer than earlier? She couldn't tell. But she didn't want to bring out the thermometer and make more of it than it was. The teakettle whistled.

XXXII

Barry

The bug-eyed desk clerk looked over the registration card Barry had filled at the Georgian Hotel. He'd pay for his stay with part of the $100 he'd gotten for his TV and stereo at the pawnshop. Man, if the clerk's face were a road, it'd be full of potholes. Barry turned around. Tattered armchairs and a faded rope throw rug hosted a couple of derelicts reading newspapers. One of them eyed him thoroughly. The duplicate driver's license his brother left behind when he abandoned him masked Barry's identity. Sunglasses hid his eyes and drew shades on the windows to his soul. He put his transistor radio on the desk and his duffel bag on the floor.

"What brings you to beautiful downtown Tampa, business or pleasure?" the clerk asked.

"Yeah, that's about it."

You can't trust anybody here. Barry had to be alert in that flophouse, like a wolf at full moon, or he'd end up at the Grey Bar Hotel. He could hide in Tampa. More happened there than in St. Pete: assaults, rapes, and murders. The Tampa fuzz had enough of their own crimes to solve to worry about him. He heard footsteps and turned, but there was nobody there.

"You got a four hundred engine in that Catalina?" The clerk jingled Barry's room keys. "My brother's got that in his Bonneville. You believe it gets him eleven miles per gallon? At seventy-five cents a gallon—"

Barry snatched the keys out of his hand and went to the elevator. Had the lamebrain caught the news about him, or did he just want to rip off his car? The guy could make a telephone call, and he'd be carless in the morning. But he had outsmarted them—the distributor cap was hidden in his duffel bag. He felt bug eyes watching his every move and burning holes in his back. The elevator took its time.

"I almost forgot," the clerk said. "We've got a cookout on Saturdays on the patio. We furnish the fire and iced tea, and you bring your meat and your potato salad."

"I'm a vegetarian." The elevator clanked open.

Barry got off at the fifteenth floor. The soiled carpet smelled mildewed. He found his room at the end of the hall. He looked both ways down the deserted hallway and opened the door. The hinges cried for oil. A double bed with a faded plaid bedspread took up the main room, along with a scratched dresser and a worn recliner. Two open windows allowed curtains to flap in the wind; they waved him over to take a closer look. He threw his duffel bag on the bed and went to them. Dusk had fallen, and night was squeezing the life out of day. Traffic lights stretched out along I-275 below. A yellow snake traveled toward him and a red one moved away.

From his bag, he took out a pint of vodka and a quart of orange juice. He didn't want to travel with weed on him. It was too freaking risky. Two paper cups stood upside down on the dresser, but there was no ice bucket in sight. It didn't matter. On the side of the bed, he mixed himself a screwdriver

and leaned back against the headboard. The chilled OJ and the warmth of the vodka bathed his throat. The King stared at him from a velvet painting across the room. Beneath it, fake red roses in a plastic vase decorated the dresser. For whatever it was worth, it was his sanctuary: it offered protection and peace of mind.

Watch your back in this place. Only bums and criminals stayed at that hotel, some of them probably on the run. To guys like that, a criminal history was a feather in their caps.

Two knocks on the door, and he shot up at the waist, spilling the drink on his stomach. He pulled out a baseball bat from his duffel bag and neared the door. Two more knocks followed, and he swung the door open.

"WHAT?" The bat rested on his shoulder.

A guy in a stained tank top and ragged shorts stepped back. "I'm from next door, didn't mean to bother you none." He wore a piano keyboard for a grin, with a few keys missing.

Barry stuck his head into the hallway and turned both ways—nobody there.

"The clerk downstairs said someone moved in, so I—"

"Are you the Welcome Wagon lady?" Barry gripped the bat handle with both hands.

"I'm not a lady. I just—"

"Don't knock on my door again." The idiot was about to buy a date with his fists. Across the hall, another loser looked on from his room. "Nobody knock on my door, and I won't knock on yours." Barry made sure Peeping Harry got the message and shut the door.

"What a horse's ass," Piano Man said from the hallway.

Barry locked the door, shoved the dresser against it, and shut the lights off. He was trapped, a prisoner in lockdown. Whispers slipped in from the hallway through the awning window over the door. Their tone warned him of unfriendly intentions. *Something's going down.* In the shadows, he gripped the bat with moist hands and hissed. He was a serpent ready to strike at the slightest provocation.

XXXIII

Marcelo

"Hey." Marcelo leaned on the doorway to his brother's bedroom.

Carlos emptied his closet: tennis shoes, roller skates, and a football crowded the wooden floor in front of the dresser. They'd enjoyed playing sports while growing up. It was the cheapest form of entertainment. Sports had taught them to play by the rules, win with grace, and lose with dignity. Carlos tossed a baseball glove on top of the sporting goods pile.

"Have you seen my tennis racket?" Carlos knelt at the closet.

"Use mine," Marcelo said.

"I've got yours. I need to find mine. I'm playing Jim later."

"Jim plays?"

"He says he does," Carlos said.

"Yeah, like a vampire takes to a sunny day at the park."

Carlos reached under the bed. "Found it." He tossed the sporting goods back into the closet. "You heard from Barry?"

Marcelo hadn't seen or spoken to Barry. Their daily conversations had been as dependable as summer afternoon rains. Even when the telephone company had disconnected Barry's phone for nonpayment, he'd always called. Once, Barry ran to the telephone booth around the corner from his trailer park so often, people driving by must've thought they were remaking Superman.

"The police came looking for Barry at work," Marcelo said.

Carlos took a seat. "Why? Is everything OK?"

The police had called Barry "a person of interest." The detective told him that Barry's car fit the description of the one that had struck and killed the teen girl a few blocks from the Bull Pen. They wanted to interview him and inspect his car. Marcelo had hoped that after Barry got the new job, he'd straighten out his life. Instead, it seemed that Barry had put out a fire and jumped into a volcano.

"You mean the girl who got kicked out of the bar the night of the fight?"

"That's her. They went to Barry's place, but he wasn't home." Marcelo rubbed the back of his head. "His neighbor told the cops where he worked."

"That's serious stuff. You think he did it?"

"The way he peeled out of the parking lot that night, he could've hit anything."

"Barry wouldn't run over somebody and drive away, would he?" Carlos asked. "What can we do?"

"Just wait. He'll turn up soon and clear up his name. You'll see."

That night, Marcelo dreamed about the time their Boy Scout troop had gone to a jamboree at Camp Soule in Tampa. There, Troop 207 completed every event they competed in, from making a fire to providing first aid. He and Barry led their troop against many others. Marcelo awoke and sat up. He had to find him. There was still much between them, even if it was an ocean....

"We have a four-top available and a deuce coming up," Connie told Marcelo.

People gathered around the podium. Every time a party was called, a pigtailed girl peeked over to read the name on the list. A guy whistled and jingled the change in his pocket, letting them know he was still waiting. Next to him, a shy boy hid behind a red bow tie between his Adam's apple and the rest of the world. The bar still buzzed with lounge lizards from happy hour. The prime rib special that evening was a success.

"These ladies have been waiting in the lounge," Connie gave Marcelo four menus. "They go to Monica." Each of the women had a drink in hand.

"You're Marcelo," one of them said. "Does the hero have a heroine waiting at home?"

Marcelo cracked up. "I don't know about any hero, but I have someone waiting."

"Well, what do you know?" she said. "He's got dimples and everything."

He led them to a table near the salad bar and pulled out the chair for her.

"Thank you, mister." She pressed something into his hand and closed it. "If I see you opening it before you get up there, I'll get mad, and you don't want to see me mad."

When he got back, Sergio was serving complimentary glasses of wine to those waiting.

"Got any more moneymaking ideas for specials?" Sergio asked. "This is going to break the sales record for the day. Where have you been all these years?"

His profitable ideas were mushrooming, expanding and multiplying.

"I've got a couple more I'm toying with." Marcelo opened the folded one-dollar bill placed in his hand. It had a red heart and a telephone number written across Washington's face. "Look what I got." He showed it to Sergio. "All I did was take her to the table."

"Get rid of it before you-know-who sees it," Sergio said.

"Jackie," Marcelo said. "Give me a pack of Juicy Fruit. I don't even chew gum."

Marcelo went to help Connie. The dinner rush still wasn't letting up. The list was long.

"Would you take these two people to Curtis?" Connie asked. "He has a deuce open."

"Welcome to the Vineyard," Marcelo grabbed the menus. "Please follow me."

At their table, Marcelo pulled out the chair for the lady and dusted it with the napkin that hung over his arm. They were only imaginary particles he was dusting. It was just a gesture that people liked because it made them feel special. Besides, it looked nifty.

"Would you be interested in a nice bottle of rosé wine this evening?" Marcelo said. "It'll go with whatever you have tonight, including our prime rib special."

"We're not drinkers," the lady said.

"I haven't had a drink in ten years. Two iced teas with lemon." The guy peeled the cellophane wrapper off a Hav-A-Tampa cigar, bit off the end, and stuffed it in his mouth.

"Coming right up," Marcelo said.

Marcelo returned with the ice teas to the couple, who were so far unattended. There were no glasses of water or a basket of rolls on the table.

"Is this your first time at the Vineyard?" Marcelo asked.

"Yes, we're from Tampa," she said. "I had to fight to get him out of the shop to take a drive to the beach. You have beautiful beaches on the gulf. All we have are bay beaches."

"We do have nice beaches," Marcelo said. "What do you do in the shop?"

"I'm a furniture maker by trade."

The cigar smelled strong. A girl from a nearby booth looked around to see where the scent that her wrinkled nose had detected was coming from.

"You must love what you do," Marcelo said.

"It's a craft, but my children are in college, and they didn't want to follow my footsteps." He cleared his throat. "What's on your mind, young man? You seemed troubled."

"All's well." Could the furniture maker read his face? Marcelo met Curtis on his way to the table.

"How's Florida's next real estate tycoon this evening?" Marcelo asked.

"I got to tell you I dropped the class. Working only on commission isn't for me."

"It's not for a lot of people," Marcelo said. "Got any other plans?"

"Maybe restaurant management," Curtis said. "That's what I know best."

Curtis introduced himself to the couple and began to take the order.

Marcelo opened a box of ketchups in the service area and lined them along the others on the shelf. They'd been running low. Carlos stuck his head in from the dining room.

"You just missed Barry," Carlos said. "He was up front talking to Jackie."

He stopped breaking the cardboard box down and hurried up front.

"He was just here," Jackie said. "I told him you had his check, and he left."

He darted out the front but didn't see Barry or the Catalina. Someone was walking down Thirty-Fourth Street, and Marcelo took a closer look. Tree branches blocked the streetlight above him, and whoever it was faded into darkness. Marcelo went around the lot but didn't see Barry's car.

"Carmine told me to call the police," Jackie told him inside.

SPPD interviewed Jackie, questioned Marcelo, and filed a report. They couldn't do much. No one other than Jackie had seen him, and no one knew where he'd gone. He was nothing more than a ghost of a man who'd disappeared into the night.

At night's end, Marcelo spotted Curtis handing the dinner check to the Tampa furniture maker. The guy put the cigar out in the ashtray, and the couple made their way to the lobby and exited the building. Jackie dimmed the lights of the vacant dining room and finished totaling the cash register sales. Then she turned off the lobby lights and dropped by the booth where Marcelo flipped through a catalogue. Carmine and Roger emerged from the service area.

"I'm taking off," Jackie said. "My ride's waiting out front. Carmine, the bank deposit for tomorrow is on the counter up front. Lock up after me." Jackie strapped her purse over a shoulder and disappeared into the black lobby. The front door creaked open and then shut.

"I got all my sidework done, boss," Roger told Marcelo.

Carmine jiggled his large key ring. "I'll be glad when the fuzz collars your buddy…And they will."

The front door creaked open, and all eyes turned in that direction.

"We're closed!" Carmine yelled.

Then the front door slammed shut, and car tires squealed away.

"The money!" Marcelo said.

He rushed to the cash register and palmed the counter in the darkness, but there was nothing there. He dashed out the front door, with Roger and Carmine close behind. A dark sedan with the lights off sped down Thirty-Fourth Street. Carmine screamed and stomped the concrete.

"Let's call the police," Marcelo said.

SPPD took their statements and dusted the counter for prints. "Do you suspect anyone?" the policeman asked. "Perhaps a disgruntled employee who was fired and holds a grudge?"

"Yes." Carmine stared at Marcelo. "I know exactly who that is."

A rusty tin roof topped the small wood-framed house with cracking paint. A dozen cats of every size and color lay around, sleeping on the porch, on the overgrown lawn, and underneath unkempt bushes. One kitten amused itself with a tall blade of grass, pawing at it while on its side. The wooden steps leading to the screened porch sagged under Marcelo's weight. He knocked on the screen door. On the living room couch, Barry's mom drank from a can of Schlitz and watched *The Gong Show* on TV—a talent show where talentless contestants got "gonged" before their minimum time was up if one of the panelists didn't like the act.

"Say something," she said but didn't get up. "Don't just stand there."

"Hello—"

"What you want?" She neared the door, took a swig.

"I need to get in touch with Barry. He might be in trouble."

She kept her eyes on the tube. "He don't live here. Who sent you here?"

He found out she had no idea how to get in touch with Barry. And she didn't know about the hit-and-run. Marcelo didn't tell her about the theft. It wasn't necessary.

"He don't use my address no more." She sipped from the can. "Besides, my phone's cut off 'cause I can't pay for it."

"If you hear from him, would you ask him to call me?"

She was consumed by the TV. A mature lady with a scratchy voice belted out a tune.

"I won't hear from him," she said.

When the singer got gonged, Barry's mom laughed a smoker's rough, congested laugh and returned to the sofa.

Marcelo had to do whatever he could to find him because Barry would do that for him. Above all, Barry had been a dependable and loyal friend when the need arose.

XXXIV

Emily

Emily shook the can of starch, sprayed, and ironed her white shirt for work. Heat radiated from the iron's path. Her black work pants and vests, pressed and hanging in her closet, anticipated their return to service. Her domestic role had been a temporary detour and not a destination. With Grandma much better, Emily looked forward to getting back to work.

With all her chores completed, she leafed through a *Life* magazine and smiled when Marcelo slipped into her mind. Love was a magic carpet ride that had transported her to undiscovered territory. The phone rang, and she leaped to answer it. It was him.

"I guess I'll have to take a rain check on the London Wax Museum," he said.

They'd made plans to visit the museum days before Grandma fell ill. It pleased her that he'd remembered even though they couldn't go. He'd been thinking about her, too.

"I haven't been there in years," Emily said.

"Well, it's still in Saint Pete Beach." He chuckled.

She had been to the museum with Grandpa ages ago, when she was barely old enough to remember and when her innocence made it difficult to differentiate between truth and fiction. She was awed by Batman and Robin, John Wayne, and Maxwell Smart, among others. She believed Grandpa when he shared a secret he'd held for eternity: the wax statues came alive when the museum closed, when the lights went out and the blanket of darkness fell. She was disillusioned when he shattered her fantasy world at the end of the day by telling her the truth.

"I want to see you tonight if I can," Marcelo said.

"Sure, if you don't mind coming over. And I wouldn't worry about catching pneumonia unless you have a weak or compromised immune system. That's according to the doctor."

He laughed. "That's one area of my life that's not compromised."

She hung up, opened her closet, and searched through her wardrobe, pushing aside hanger after hanger. As when shopping for something to wear, she didn't find anything. Nothing met with her approval. But it didn't matter what she wore as long as they spent time together.

"Grandma?" Emily stood at the foot of her bed. "Marcelo's coming over tonight."

Grandma nodded and strained to shift her weight. The newspaper lay beside her, where Emily had placed it hours before. That couldn't be good.

"I'm sore from lying down," she said.

"Why don't you lie down on your stomach now?"

Grandma needed to alternate positions. The doctor explained that the pressure of her weight could cut off blood circulation to those areas, and she could develop bedsores. The red blisters and shallow wounds developed easily but didn't leave without putting up a fight. Grandma rolled onto her stomach, and Emily covered her with a sheet.

The photo album Emily had given her weeks earlier lay on the night table. She picked it up and joined Grandma on the side of the bed. She opened the heavy album on her lap.

"Let's see what we have here."

A five-year-old Emily was center stage in the first photograph. She was feeding roasted peanuts to pigeons in front of the Williams Park bandstand. She could still hear the cracking and crunching of peanut shells in her fingers. Retirees occupied half-filled benches in anticipation of another performance. Oak trees offered shelter for squirrels that competed with dozens of pigeons for the peanuts. Blue-and-white city buses lined the perimeter of the park.

"I remember that day," Emily said.

The afternoon sun had begun to descend on Central Avenue in the next set of photos. Emily and Grandpa sat on one of St. Pete's green benches lining downtown streets. Behind them, the State Theatre featured *It's a Mad, Mad, Mad, Mad World.*

Grandma had dozed off when the doorbell rang. At the door, Marcelo held a paper bag.

"I picked up Chinese for us so you wouldn't have to cook," he said. "And chicken soup for your grandma."

She helped with the bags and kissed him, giving him a preview of coming attractions. She'd missed him more than she'd like to admit to herself. He accepted a Michelob beer, and they sat on the couch in the living room.

"What's new with you?" she asked.

"Let's see." He sighed. "Hired a couple of waitresses."

"I meant what's new with *you.*"

He seemed distant, and she hoped she wasn't the cause of his detachment.

He ran his fingers through his hair. "It's Barry. I don't know where to begin."

"Start at the beginning."

He told her Barry was missing, and about the police coming to the restaurant and about Barry's deserted place. She could see the anguish on his face and hear the frustration in his voice in trying to decipher what had become of his friend. She did the best she could—she listened.

"About me coming back to work…" Emily said.

"Could we not talk about work for now? I just want to enjoy your company."

"OK…sure."

After dinner they grabbed a couple more beers, took the couch, and turned on the TV. They'd missed *Charlie's Angels*. That was fine. The show hadn't been the same since Farah Fawcett left. Still, they welcomed the chance to tune out for a bit.

The next day, Grandma's temperature had risen. And she found it difficult to hold down solid food. Emily called the doctor: if her symptoms worsened, Grandma would have to go back to the hospital. She had to keep Grandma rested and well-nourished to keep up her strength and fight off the pneumonia. Emily made soup, beef with vegetables. It gave Grandma another choice besides the chicken soup Marcelo had brought. That, she hoped, would do the trick.

XXXV

Barry

"Three hundred bucks is my last offer," the guy in the mechanic's jumpsuit said as he looked under the hood of the Catalina 400 in the salvage yard.

Two Dobermans chained up in the rear of the lot sniffed the air, trying to catch a hint of Barry's scent. Man, those devil dogs made the hairs on the back of his neck stand up. *Don't look at them.* Three hundred bucks was a great offer. The tranny was about to blow: it screamed in agonizing pain when it shifted gears. Around them, car fenders, hoods, and trunk lids littered the lot. The junkyard dogs snarled at him, wanting to tear at his flesh when he looked their way.

"I'll take it." He had to get rid of the evidence, and the buyer wasn't asking questions.

In the office, worn tires lined walls to the ceiling. Two giant cardboard boxes held red and white tail light covers and electrical connections. A blood-red, half-eaten roast beef hoagie bled by the cash register. The guy chomped on the sandwich and opened the register with grimy fingers. Barry counted fifteen twenty-dollar bills, stuffed them in his pocket, and started for home.

"You need work?" the guy asked Barry as he reached the door.

He turned. "What you got in mind?"

"Tearing cars down," the cannibal said, red flesh stuck in his teeth. "You write down the parts you take off and tag them by model, make, and year, like you see here." He swung his arm around. "You can start with your car. I pay forty bucks cash at the end of the day."

"I can handle that." Barry sized him up and down. "But I got to get me something to eat." The juices in his stomach had turned on him and were devouring him inside out.

"There's a Burger King down there." He pointed and then took a bite of flesh.

Barry walked out of the yard and went the opposite way: he wasn't about to end up in a trap set by cannibals wanting to devour him—*Stop it! Why am I thinking that way?* Maybe it wasn't smart for him to hang around this place after dumping his car there, but he had a chance to break down the car into a thousand parts and scatter them all over the yard. It was a gift, like a repo man finding the car keys in the ignition. Golden Arches down the road called his name.

He burped and again tasted the burger and fries on his way back to the yard. The strawberry milk shake soothed his throat. *What?* He dropped the shake on the pavement when he saw a cop car pulling into the junkyard. He backed into the bushes. The pig and the cannibal were talking, and then the flesh-eater pointed to the Catalina. The cop walked around it and then knelt and looked at the damage on his fender. It was time to split, so he cut through the back streets of the rundown neighborhood and hopped on a bus. He would find a job on Kennedy.

A sign with shapely dancers hung above the Seven Oceans on Kennedy Boulevard. He'd been there in his other life, with Marcelo and other friends from high school. But Barry had to save his dough. He couldn't afford to go in even for an eyeful. Angie had wanted to go there once after he'd told her about it. *Imagine that.* Taking her there would've been like bringing fish and chips to a seafood festival. Man, but did she ever wail like a banshee in the sack.

"We need a cook," a teenaged, pimply kid in kitchen uniform told him through the screened back door. "You cooked before?" Pimples stepped out and lit a cig. He had the face of a cheese pizza. The joint sold birds by the bucket.

You can handle it. "I've cooked chicken before." Breading and frying, that's all it was.

The kid went to get the manager, and he waited outside. Cig butts littered the ground.

The manager's neck was saggy with chicken skin. "You ready to work?" he asked.

No, he wasn't, but he didn't want to look for a job, either. He'd stopped at every greasy spoon, burger joint, and choke 'n' puke on Kennedy in the last two hours. If he didn't find work quick, he'd end up wrestling gators for tourists at roadside attractions on US 27.

"I'm more than ready to work."

"Good, you can fry bird now." He let him inside. "We'll do the paperwork later."

"Right on!" the kid said.

Ten pressure cookers were lined up side by side on gas stoves like a production line.

Pimples got the chicken from an iced cardboard box, dipped the pieces in an egg-and-milk batter, and breaded them in a secret recipe he couldn't care less about, and then they were ready to fry. Barry stirred the pot for a minute until the pieces browned and then capped it, dropped the next batch, and stirred. By the time he'd capped the last pot, the first one had finished cooking. Then he'd repeat the whole thing again and again during the whole shift…nothing to it. He could do that job because it was repetitious, and there were no people coming at him from all sides.

Why were all kitchens always so hot? The heat was draining his bodily fluids.

"Hi, I'm Eve," a chick with deep, dark, inviting eyes said. "Who are you?"

She was a mango in September—ripe, juicy, and ready to eat. Eve took care of the front counter, waited on customers, and collected for the orders the manager would box up and pass to her through a window.

Keep your distance from everyone. "I'm…I'm Mike." That was his brother's name, the same one he had given to Chicken Neck and Pimples. But the cannibal had his real name from when he signed over the car title. That he couldn't avoid.

"You're a stone fox of a few words." She poked his belly and returned to the front.

"She's nice, huh?" The pimpled kid wiggled his tongue like a snake. "Forget her, dude." He opened a box of chicken on the floor. "Her boyfriend will kick your ass. He's an ox."

"Who's messing with her?" Barry stirred the pot and tried not to hear the cries of horror from the birds flapping in the boiling grease.

The manager stuck his head into the kitchen. "Yellow bird," he said.

"YB it is," the kid said.

Man, yellow bird meant the cooking time was cut from ten to six minutes. That happened when they got busy and golden-brown cooked chicken ran low. The barely cooked yellow bird went to take-out customers. *That was so sick!* At the end of the night, he couldn't avoid Eve at the time clock by the office. She punched out and raised her eyebrows at him.

"You work tomorrow, Mister Man of Few Words?" she asked. "Where do you stay?"

He had to remain unknown, but she kept asking question after question.

"You be here tomorrow." She blew him a kiss over her shoulder.

"Her boyfriend treats her bad," Pimples said. "He's got a first-degree cheating heart."

Eve wanted him, her Adam, and he wasn't afraid of her Paul Bunyan boyfriend. He'd chop him low and hard and watch him hit the ground like a redwood tree. Then he'd fan his feathers, scratch the ground with his toes, and strut in celebration. *I'll come to her rescue. I'll be her Underdog, and she'll be my Polly Purebred, just like Saturday cartoons.*

The news on the radio in the office interrupted his imagined heroism. Thousands of mourners were filing past Pope Paul VI in Vatican City in Italy, but he couldn't care less. The Catholic faith had abandoned him, and Satan had made eternal camp in his soul.

There was an update on the hit-and-run in St. Pete and that interested him, but there were no new developments to worry about. Still, he couldn't shake the guilt, even with a heart buried under a veil of lies and deceptions.

On the walk home, his heart raced every time a car drove by. Maybe there was more to his so-called accident. Maybe President Carter and the CIA wanted him for his special skills. The Cold War was messy, and the Soviet Union was a formidable foe. The accident was just a ploy to get him in the cooler and out of circulation, so he could go on his special mission. *What the hell am I thinking about?* The CIA didn't want him. The cops wanted him, to lock him up for eternity for running over that poor chick. No special mission waited for him, just the cooler: three hots and a cot at Raiford State Prison.

Headlights drove up behind him…and he dove into the bushes.

XXXVI

Marcelo

Marcelo drove to work in a rush at three in the afternoon. Why had Sergio called him in? He found Carmine and Sergio at a table in the back of the lounge. A handful of businessmen worked on their four-martini lunches with Sherry. She rolled her eyes at Marcelo as he took a seat. A suit looked over from a stool as if wondering what the secrecy was about.

"Carmine wants to ask you some questions about the robbery," Sergio said.

"Why?" Marcelo asked. "The police are investigating it."

"Tell me what you know about Barry taking that money." Carmine cocked his head.

"All I know is you didn't lock the door," Marcelo said. "What do *you* know?"

"You're thick as thieves, the both of you," Carmine said.

As the barrage heated up, Marcelo kept a cool demeanor. Carmine reminded them that Barry had paid them a visit that evening, and that his presence was more than a coincidence.

"What was your part in all of this?" Carmine asked.

"I've never been accused of taking my employers' money," Marcelo said. "You have."

Carmine kicked Marcelo's chair and shot up.

"Cut it out, the both of you," Sergio said. "This was a stupid idea. The insurance will cover the forty-six hundred dollars. Let the cops sort the rest out."

"Are we done here?" Marcelo asked.

"Not quite," Sergio said. "I want you guys to work together and—"

"I'm done here." Carmine left.

"Do both of us a solid," Sergio said, "and stay away from Barry."

"I haven't seen or heard from him since Carmine got rid of him."

"Tell me. Anything going on between you and Carmine I should know about?"

That was an understatement. He had a basketful of concerns, but it wasn't the time.

"Nothing comes to mind at the moment."

Marcelo drove home to make telephone calls to find Barry before going back for the evening shift. He went to the restaurant section in the St. Pete Yellow Pages and picked up the phone. He figured Barry wasn't using his real name. Most likely, he was using his brother's name. And Barry wouldn't be working as a waiter—he'd be exposed to the public and be easy to find. Marcelo called just about every place in town, from Fisherman's Inn on the north side of town to Seaman's Cove in the south with no luck.

Carlos drove up, and Marcelo filled him in on his lack of investigative success.

"I just drove around Woodlawn," Carlos said. "I thought I might spot his car."

"That's what I did last night—drove around the Old Northeast with no luck."

"I'll call hospitals." Carlos grabbed the phone book. "But I hope he's not hurt."

The search widened, and the mystery deepened. Marcelo took a drive before heading to work. The sign on the luncheonette he'd had his eyes on still read "For Rent." Fate continued with its parade of opportunities. Through the storefront windows, he spotted a guy in overalls vacuuming the floor. The machine expelled more dust than it absorbed. Marcelo went in.

"Sorry, we're closed for business." He kept stroking the carpeting.

"When did the place close?"

"Three weeks ago." He shut off the machine.

According to the guy, the story had repeated itself, and Marcelo knew it: someone had taken the place over, and it had closed in two months. Marcelo knew it wasn't the location. It was near the telephone company and the county building.

"You want to talk business, you talk to me. I'm the owner," he said.

"Let's talk, then."

The guy stood the vacuum cleaner against the lunch counter, and they took one of the eight tables in the place.

"If you're interested, it's a year lease," he said. "You pay first and last month and an extra month's deposit, and it's yours."

"I can't do twelve months; might not be a decent location," Marcelo said. "Everyone who opens here closes in a couple of months."

"It's a gold mine, and you know it." He looked in his eyes. "That's why you're here."

Marcelo had learned to remain quiet. Two businessmen in suits walked by; one looked in the window before they kept on. Their afternoon shadows stretched long and thin.

"Well, I'm listening." The owner raised an eyebrow.

"What if I rent the place for three months? After that, I might be in a better position to sign a longer lease."

Marcelo had Tyrone ready to take the leap of faith and help him open the place, and he was a monster of a cook. Barry would wait on customers at the lunch counter after he cleared his name, and Marcelo could take care of the tables. And they could switch places. They would need a hostess/cashier and a dishwasher/kitchen helper. Heavy traffic rolled north and south outside.

"Three months?" he asked. "I can't go on not knowing where I'll be in three months."

Marcelo knew exactly where the owner would be in three months: sweeping and cleaning the place again after another person had failed to make it go, and he told him so.

"That's my offer, a three-month lease." Marcelo rose.

"Hold on. When you planning going into business?"

"Ready when you are."

"You got the cash?"

He nodded. He had over $4,800, thanks to the generosity of others. That money was the gateway to countless possibilities.

"Three months could work for me, then." The owner handed him a business card. "Call me, and we can draw up the papers."

Marcelo exited the parking lot and drove to the Vineyard. He was ready to make the deal he'd wanted, but he never imagined he'd be going it alone. Barry hadn't met his part of the bargain and had disappeared. Maybe he had never been a good choice for a partner. He recalled how Roger had once said that Barry would bet on two cockroaches crawling on the kitchen floor. Marcelo smiled. Still, he wished Barry would turn up and help him open the business.

Marcelo and Sherry took inventory of the glassware in the lounge. Glasses of all shapes and sizes blanketed the horseshoe bar: highball, rocks, Collins, wine, and champagne glasses, brandy snifters, and pony glasses. He tried to keep his mind on his work. Earlier, Carlos had told him he'd called every hospital in the county but hadn't found Barry.

Monica and Angie stepped into the lounge.

"Guess what?" Monica beamed. "Angie got an interview with Eastern Airlines."

"Congratulations," Marcelo said. "This could be the catapult that launches your future in another direction."

"Good for you," Sherry said. "When's the interview?"

"In a couple of weeks," Angie said. "I need time off to do some shopping and get ready. I've got to get a new dress, shoes, do my nails and hair—"

"And I'm helping her prepare for the big day," Monica said. "Everything will come out lollypops. You'll see. But first you've got to get the time off."

"Carmine's working tonight," Marcelo said. "He's in the office."

"Imagine me getting lucky in Rome and Paris," Angie said. "I'll get some discount tickets for you guys, too."

The two went away, deciding where they'd fly off to and who'd go with them.

"I finally heard from Tallahassee on my cosmetologist license." Sherry sighed.

"You don't sound like you have good news."

"They turned down my application," she said. "In Florida you need twelve hundred hours of training, and I only needed nine hundred to be licensed up north."

"That's a bummer," he said. "If you need time off for class, let me know."

"Thanks, but I'll let it ride for now."

They counted each of the different types of glasses on the bar, and Marcelo wrote the count on a clipboard. Highballs, Collins, and wine glasses were in short supply. They were the most used, and the most likely to break or grow legs and walk out. Marcelo brought replacements from storage. The next day, he'd place an order to keep them in stock.

"Everybody's happy with the job you're doing," Sherry said. "What's your secret?"

"Not everybody's happy," he said. "And there's no secret."

"Well, he doesn't count," she said.

"I treat others the way I want to be treated. It's simple and old as time, but it works."

With the clipboard under his arm, Marcelo crossed the service area into the kitchen. He'd write up the glass order that night and call it in to the vendor in the morning. Then he could—

Angie stormed out of the office and slammed the door, enraged and trembling.

"What's up?" Marcelo asked.

"Carmine said I could have the time off, then dropped his pants and said I had to get him off first." She hyperventilated. "He pulled me down, but I clawed his ugly face. Let him explain that to his unfortunate-looking wife."

"Get a drink of water and relax before you do anything you might regret."

"Oh, I won't," she said. "I'm not quitting because of that bastard."

Marcelo waited for a moment. A position of authority brought with it a set of unavoidable responsibilities. He opened the door. Carmine stood in front of the wall mirror. When he turned around, Marcelo noticed three bloody scratches across his face.

"Shouldn't you be up front?" Carmine asked.

"I need to be where I need to be." He shut the door behind him. "What happened?"

"It's called foreplay, that's all." Carmine faced the mirror. "I didn't take her for one that played hard to get." He examined the scratches. "Of all people, Angie and me should've been messing around a long time ago. But that's none of your business."

"Employees are my business. You should apologize."

Carmine eyed him through the mirror.

"You're taking this job too serious." Carmine turned. "Everybody knows she's easier than fishing in a barrel, and I didn't ask for nothing she hasn't done a hundred times before."

"She's no prude," Marcelo said. "But she decides who she messes with, not you."

Carmine shortened the distance between them.

"Are you a smart guy, Marcelo? I bet you're a smart guy." Carmine pinned his eyes on him. "Don't mess with me or you'll regret it."

"You don't scare me." If he didn't stand for something, he'd fall for anything. "You apologize to her." Marcelo shut the door and returned to his duties.

What a trip! He knew Carmine wouldn't say "I'm sorry." Why would Carmine care? His life was littered with trashy memories. What was one more? It was Carmine who wasn't taking his job seriously. He was dumb as dirt and damaging to the Vineyard.

XXXVII

Emily

Grandma held her chest and panted. She could barely breathe. Emily felt her forehead. The fever had shot up. Sweat soaked her brow. Grandma shivered and coughed up thick green phlegm. It hurt her chest to take a breath. She was fading in and out. Emily didn't want to wait.

"I'm taking you to the hospital."

Emily helped her into her robe and sat her up on the bed until she was oriented. She put Grandma's slippers on her and led her down the front steps to the car. During the ride, Grandma closed her eyes and labored to breathe, and Emily prayed for the first time in years.

"You'll be fine in no time," she said at a stop sign. "You'll see."

Her mind raced. She could see herself pulling up to the emergency entrance, alerting the desk of Grandma's arrival, demanding immediate medical attention.

Emily sat by Grandma's side in the emergency room. A mask on Grandma's face delivered oxygen to her lungs from tanks on the floor. Her breathing had relaxed, and she'd fallen asleep. She'd had a thorough medical examination and diagnostic tests. Having her recent medical history at the hospital saved time in the evaluation and diagnosis.

This time, the emergency doctor was a gentleman with graying hair at the temples. Emily didn't want to hear what he had to say. The diagnosis was acute respiratory distress syndrome.

"When pneumonia involves most areas of both lungs, breathing is difficult, and the body doesn't get enough oxygen," the doctor explained. "She'll need to stay here until it is safe for her to go home. She'll need oxygen therapy, fluids, and treatment for her pneumonia. We have to be very careful because of her age. She's in a very delicate condition."

"Whatever needs to be done, of course," Emily said, and he left the room.

She squeezed Grandma's hand lightly. The morning had begun differently. Emily had awoken to sparrows chirping in the trees outside her bedroom window as the sun sent beams of light through her blinds. Then her morning darkened.

"I'm sorry about this," she said. "Sorry about everything."

Tears welled up in her eyes, but she had to regain her composure. She wanted to go home, slip into something comfortable, and return to keep her company. For Grandma, she'd bring her makeup bag for when she felt better, another nightgown, toiletries, and anything else she could think of. Emily wasn't ready to drive yet, and she wanted to get some fresh air.

"I'm going to Roser Park." Emily kissed her hand. "I'll be back soon."

Emily walked the lengthy hallway leading to the front of the hospital. Doctors in white coats and with stethoscopes around their necks rushed in both directions, entering countless rooms on each side of the hall. Nurses wearing caps carried patients' charts. Orderlies in white uniforms pushed patients in wheelchairs. Out the front entrance and down the steps she went.

The park sloped down for a block until it reached Roser Park Creek, a stream enclosed by cement walls that made it possible for her to step up to the rim and peek into the water five feet below. She took one of the benches in the ample grassy real estate. Moss hung like icicles from trees dotting the landscape. Across the creek and the road running alongside it, homes with sloped roofs soared three and four stories into the sky on land slanting toward the creek. Garages occupied the lower levels of those houses. Emily had been inside one of those homes.

"I need to collect a down payment on an insurance policy I sold," her father had told her.

The owner of the house had a daughter her age. They drank cherry Kool-Aid and played while the adults drank coffee and talked policy coverage. The house was four stories tall, counting the garage on the ground floor and the attic.

An older lady about her grandmother's age took the other side of the bench. She wore a black dress, bone-white gloves, and a pearl necklace. The black hat had a veil that hid her face.

"It's a beautiful neighborhood," the woman said. "Isn't it?"

Through the elderly woman's veil, Emily could see the excessive rouge on her cheeks.

"It's got its charm," Emily said.

"When I married, my husband brought me to that house." She pointed to one with broad windows on the second floor. "You should've seen it then."

She recounted how the immaculate homes with well-manicured lawns had been replaced by dilapidated ones with peeling paint, missing roof shingles, and overgrown brush. Roser Park, once the pride of St. Pete, had faded into history.

"I can imagine it was something else then, but it doesn't look like much now."

"It's still beautiful." She scowled. "When we married, he promised he'd never leave, and he never did. We were so happy in our home, we never moved. He passed on recently."

Life was cruel. "I'm sorry for your loss."

"This was our favorite bench," the lady said. "It's been replaced several times, but I come here to be with him. Oh, he's with me at home too. We have a hundred memories in that house. Every nook and cranny reminds me of him. I could never move. I could never leave him."

They sat a while, and she enjoyed the fresh air and the conversation.

The veiled lady said good-bye and started on her way, a black patent leather purse hung from her arm. The lady crossed the short bridge over the creek and hiked up the redbrick road.

Emily had attended Roser Park Elementary when she lived in St. Pete. Could it be recess time? She climbed the grassy slope to the brick road and followed it to the school. She'd left the school in the fourth grade, when her family moved after her dad got a job in Ft. Lauderdale.

She neared the school but didn't hear or see children play-ing four square, hanging from the monkey bars, or swaying on swings. "This can't be." The school had closed down. A chain-link fence encircled the grounds, including the passageway leading to the main entrance. A sign on the wall read, "All Children's Hospital Storage Unit."

Emily had cried when her father announced they were leaving St. Pete, the school, and her friends. Memories buried ages ago surfaced in her mind. Back then, she aspired to join the school patrol, to wear the orange belt and yellow helmet and to direct students across the street before and after school. There would never be children chasing one another or skipping around the playground as she once did. Her history, part of her life, had been erased.

XXXVIII

Barry

Barry paid the guy at the pawnshop ten dollars for the bicycle, hopped on it, and pedaled to work. It was a girl's bike, baby blue with a straw basket in front, but it was getting him where he needed to go. His open shirt flapped behind him, and sweat ran down his face and chest as he baked under a punishing sun. The mercury had climbed into the high nineties, but it was payday and that was refreshing. His paycheck wouldn't be much, just chicken feed. But he could ask his Eve out—*stop it! You have to keep your distance from her. From everyone.*

With his check, he could pay a week's rent and buy a few days of groceries. He'd eaten so much fried chicken lately that he felt baby feathers sprouting through his skin. He could see them if he looked hard enough. He locked up his bike on the pipes holding up the store sign and went in. The chill of the air conditioner entered his humid lungs.

"How's it hanging, baby?" Eve said, and then covered her mouth as if she'd said something she shouldn't have.

With his hand, he combed his hair back and stood straight. A dumpy girl carried a massive metal tray of coleslaw portions from the kitchen and stuck them in the fridge. The poor girl was no match for his Eve. She hadn't pushed away many leftovers at the supper table.

"You ready to give me what I want?" Eve had said to him the other night.

Man, he was more than ready, and that orangutan of a boyfriend of hers had better not come after him. He'd kung fu him in the groin and watch him moan and roll around on the ground. Then he'd step over him, with Eve on his arm for a night of passion in his penthouse in the sky. They could have children, dress them up on Sunday, and show them off like monkeys. He could do all that, be her hero, or he could just go home and crawl into his cage.

The manager stretched his chicken head in from the kitchen.

"You giving the girls trouble?" The manager frowned. "Do me a solid and let them be."

What's this all about? This clown wants to be separated from his teeth!

"He's not bothering us," Eve said, but the plump one kept her trap shut.

"Just joking," the dork said. "Had you going there for a second, didn't I."

Barry followed him into the clammy kitchen. The comedian couldn't make a hyena laugh, and his life wasn't about jokes. It was a voyage aboard the Hindenburg, on a collision with disaster. Pimples stirred and browned chicken at the stove. Barry could hear their splatter and their cries of horror but ignored them.

In the office, an old man in a Panama hat sat across the desk from the manager, with his hands on his bloated belly. He raised an eyebrow and gave Barry the hairy eyeball. *What's this guy here for?* The boss flipped through a bunch of envelopes. Barry's heart started to beat faster.

"Here we go, Mister Gregory."

He snatched the check, went outside, and unlocked his bike from the store sign.

"Wait a minute." The old coot from the office stood at the door. "Is your name Barry?"

His heart sputtered like a badly tuned diesel engine. He went light headed.

"You…you got me mixed up with someone else." Barry straddled the bike for balance.

Pops fanned himself with the straw hat. "The radio said the guy who ran over the girl in Saint Pete was Barry Gregory, and that he had a chewed-up ear like yours."

Barry threw the bike down and tapped the guy's chest. "You've been watching too much *Hawaii Five-O*, old man. Don't mess with my life!"

The guy stepped back. "I'm going to have you checked out just in case."

The guy's eyes told him he wasn't yanking his chain.

When the old guy went inside, Barry pushed his bike behind the dumpster and waited. The old man could see through him like an x-ray machine. He couldn't let him turn him in. He'd follow him home—*and crack him over the head so you have nothing to worry about.*

Minutes later, the old geezer came out, got into a car, and drove off. There was no way he could keep up with him, even if he drove a Chevy Vega.

Barry pushed his ride across the atrium to the elevator at the Georgian. He'd been jittery and had walked home. The seeds of anxiety had begun to take root. Two guys who looked like they'd had unprivileged lives sat in worn wingback chairs. One slept slumped in one. The other wore a fedora and eyed him with curiosity and dislike. The desk clerk filed mail into square boxes.

"Got any mail for me today?" Barry didn't expect any.

"Not today." He didn't bother to turn around.

Barry pushed the UP button at the elevator. Two guys from nowhere rushed inside with him, one at each side of him. The elevator climbed. Barry pressed the button for his floor. The others didn't move a finger. *Where they with the Soviet KGB?* The walls closed in. He could hear his heart thumping. Barry pushed the button for the next floor and turned to face both guys.

"Who are you?" He looked across their faces. "What do you want from me?"

The doors opened. Barry backed into the hallway pulling his bike out by the handlebars. The guys glanced at each other. The doors closed, and they continued up. Barry took his bike up the stairs. His anxiety lessened, and he could suck air again. Maybe they hadn't found him.

In his room, he sat by the window. He spied on the world that spied on him. Flashes of lightning lit up the horizon like gigantic flashbulbs on a camera. The gods were taking his picture.

The I-75 and I-4 interchange came to life with streams of car grills and taillights flowing in opposite directions. *Why don't you run out in front of that traffic and see what it's like?* It would only hurt until a second car finished him off, and then his agony would end. He found himself in a sea of tormenting pain and was sinking fast. The concrete sidewalk fifteen floors below had no disease-ridden soles walking on it. What a plunge and a half that would be. *I know you could fly.*

He turned on the radio. The Legionnaires' disease bacteria had been isolated in Atlanta. The radio guy told him the disease got its name in July 1976 when it broke out at an American Legion convention in Philadelphia, killing some. They were sending him a direct message.

That's what had been going on with him. *They've planted the bacteria in my brain!* He was on to them: the government had contaminated the poor legionnaires during their convention, working on the bacteria to implant in his brain! The government wanted to test how resourceful he was: could he go underground and avoid detection from the police and sheriff with a parasite in the brain? For that, the young girl had been run over and old soldiers had died, but the few must be sacrificed for the larger good. He was hip with that. He'd figured out the plan!

You have to contact them and let them know you know. The CIA had been watching him for a long time. They needed his physical abilities and intelligence for the national good. And why wouldn't they? He was bright and sharp as a brand-new butcher's knife. The geezer at work had to be his contact. That's how he knew his real identity. He'd look for him the next day and tell him what he knew. The government would be double-impressed with him. Not only had he shown he could go underground and vanish with a parasite in the brain, but he'd figured out their plan! Man, he was ready to begin his secret assignment ASAP. But for that, he had to make it through another night.

Barry crawled into bed and shuddered, scared to fall asleep. Afraid villagers would come for him in the dead of the night with pitchforks and torches, to take him away and burn him at the stake. Objects in the darkness came to life, and he welcomed the alliance. He wasn't alone, and there was strength in numbers.

Barry woke up in a sweat and sat up, shaking and gasping. The nightmare had him and his father locked away, sharing a cell at Raiford State Prison. A place with a hundred rules to follow and toes too dangerous to step on. The bad dream dug up memories buried deep. *You're no good and will never be.* Could he call Marcelo? He knew he could count on him to come and help, and that was the reason why he couldn't reach out—he didn't deserve anybody's help.

Sunlight filtered through the window and announced the birth of a new day. He threw the bedcovers off, sprang to his feet, and turned on the radio. The Allman Brothers' song "Ramblin' Man" was playing. He wrung his hands. The early morning stillness made him uneasy, and he had to be the one who broke the silence. He greeted the infant yellow sun at the window.

What am I thinking? The fuddy-duddy at the chicken coop wasn't a CIA contact. Only someone who'd lost his mind would think that—*I'm not crazy!* The old coot had probably called the fuzz on him already. And they hadn't knocked on his door because he'd given a fake address.

When it came time to go to work, he took his wheels and rode the elevator downstairs.

Puffy white clouds hung from denim blue skies like cotton balls on construction paper. He stopped at the Midnight Diner for a bite. The breakfast sandwich wasn't half bad, and the coffee was hot and strong. A cop cruiser pulled up outside his window, and two pigs strutted in with their annoying walkie-talkies on. They walked around not caring whom they aggravated. The flabby one eyed him up and down. Barry shifted his view, hoping they couldn't read his face.

"Can I see some ID?" the cop asked.

Their noisy walkie-talkies continued. The pigs eyeballed each other, and that gave him a split second—he dashed out the door and took off around the building. Climbing over a concrete wall, he heard two shots whizz above his head.

"Stop! Police!"

He jumped into a backyard full of grapefruit trees. *They want you dead now!* He ran out the front gate, crossed the street, and dove into palmetto bushes. His heart raced. He had a clear view of the threat. The cops came through the gate across the road. The portly one bent over, put his hands on his knees, and struggled to catch his breath. The other looked both ways down the road, threw his cap on the ground, and stomped his feet like a big freaking baby.

What a trip! Barry had to stay put for a while before making his next move. His life was a chess match, and he was in check. One bad move and he wouldn't have another. No, he wasn't crazy enough to go back for his ride. That'd be a definite checkmate!

He took the back roads until he came to the alley behind work and hid behind the dumpster. It gave him a decent view of the parking lot and anyone coming in. His Eve pulled into the lot in a hot-red Pinto. *We're not going anywhere until we take care of that.* The fuzz pulled in right behind her and snapped him out of his passion. It was the same two cops. One went to her car and talked to her. She nodded her head, and then both followed her inside through the back door. It was time to split. He came out from behind the dumpster and backed away for a few feet before he turned and ran for home.

Come back to me! she called for him. He stopped and turned. *Don't be a fool, forget about her!* He took off, and his heart escaped the meat grinder that was love.

XXXIX

Marcelo

At ten in the morning Marcelo rolled up his sleeves in the garage. Car parts waited on the concrete floor in bright, colorful cardboard boxes that looked like Christmas presents. Inside the packages, a four-barrel carburetor, a high-rise manifold, headers, and Thrush mufflers waited to be installed in the Mustang. Carlos joined him, stretched out his arms, and yawned.

"Let's get going," Marcelo said. "I want to stop at Emily's later."

"Too bad; I work by the hour."

They lifted the hood, and Marcelo disconnected the linkage to the stock two-barrel carburetor with a screwdriver, along with the fuel line and filter. Then with open socket wrenches they unscrewed the nuts on the four studs fastening it to the manifold. Carlos tapped the carburetor with a rubber mallet to loosen it. He slipped it off the studs and removed the old gasket and the carburetor spacer.

"I called hospitals in Tampa too. Barry wasn't in any of them either," Carlos said.

"That's good news, I guess."

Carlos placed the carburetor and the spacer on the workbench.

"He's not working anywhere, he's not in the hospital," Carlos said. "What now?"

"We keep looking, that's what. He'd do the same for us."

It had been two weeks since the night of the fight. He'd never gone that long without hearing from Barry, and he'd always known how to get in touch with him. Barry was in big trouble, but he didn't want to worry his brother.

"Changing the subject," Carlos said, "I can't believe Curtis and Connie are together."

"You couldn't see that coming?"

"I'm glad she gave up on that jerk of a boyfriend," Carlos said.

"He's a punk. Curtis might not be Mister Account Executive, but he's twice the man that coward will ever be."

"Still, I didn't think she'd get rid of him that easy," Carlos said.

Loosening the bolts on the intake manifold sitting on top of the engine block was more of a struggle. They hadn't been removed since the factory installed them in 1967. After they got them off, Carlos pried the manifold off the block with a screwdriver. Marcelo placed it on the workbench next to the carburetor. The gasket came off without breaking apart.

"Can you open a restaurant here and keep dating Emily?" Carlos asked.

"Hope so," he said. "She'll visit here to see her grandma, and I'll go down there, too."

"How long would that last? She's bound to meet another guy."

Nothing was for certain. If she met someone, he didn't know what he'd do. When people wanted to go their own way, there was nothing anyone could do to stop them.

"Mom called," Carlos said. "She wants to know when we're coming down."

"I'll be down there soon enough. You can tag along."

Could Emily lose interest in him? He didn't want his decision to boomerang and bite him in the rear. Their relationship was a gem that could appreciate greatly in time.

They cleaned the engine block where the manifold had rested with rags soaked in gasoline until it was shiny and smooth. Marcelo tore the packaging and pulled out the rectangular gasket. It was metallic, with dimples like soda crackers. He coated it with anti-seize compound and put it on the manifold and lined it up. Then they placed the hi-rise manifold over it and inserted the bolts, fastening them first with their hands and then with wrenches.

"How did your tennis game with Jim go?" Marcelo asked.

"He didn't even show up, the athlete that he is."

Marcelo put the carburetor spacer and coated gasket on the manifold and placed the four-barrel carburetor on it. Again they inserted the bolts manually and then tightened them with open wrenches. Carlos hooked up the linkages to the gas pedal and the gas supply.

"Getting twice the gas, this car will fly when you floor it," Marcelo said.

"And cost that much more to drive it."

"True," Marcelo said. "Break time."

They wiped the grease off their hands and went inside. Carlos took out a plastic pitcher from the refrigerator and poured two tumblers of iced tea. Marcelo added ice cubes.

"Since Barry isn't here, I can help you open the business and start school later," Carlos said. "Let's grab that place before someone else does."

"You have a deal with Mom and Dad." Marcelo took a sip. "We can't break it."

"Why don't you go to State with the scholarship then? I would," Carlos said. "At least let the thought marinate in your brain overnight and then see where you are."

Marcelo knew where he stood. He had concrete and defined dreams. His business wouldn't be much to begin with, but in time it would be all he'd ever wanted.

"I'm staying put." Marcelo put the tumbler in the sink.

"You don't have to stay here because of me. I'll live with Mom and Dad and go to community college down there, and we'll all be together again."

"Break's over," Marcelo said.

They took off the old exhaust system. The pipes that were attached to each side of the engine block converged into a Y and a single exhaust leading to the muffler. Brand-new headers went in its place, wider and with a dual exhaust system with individual Thrush mufflers.

"The neighbors are going to hear you coming from two blocks away."

"We'll find out how much they love me."

After calibrating the carburetor, Marcelo cranked it up. The Mustang roared to life from a deep slumber. The four-barrel carburetor provided greater combustion and horsepower. The dual exhaust system rid the emissions more effectively without choking the engine in its fumes. The roar of the engine made the hair on Marcelo's arms stand up.

"Looo-king goood," Carlos said. "This car's banging."

That evening the beast rumbled down the road and let the neighbors know of its arrival. Beast and human readied for the undiscovered challenges that lay ahead.

"Alaskan king crab legs would be a nice dinner special, too," Tyrone told Marcelo. "We can offer it the same evening as the Maine lobster so people can choose one or the other."

"The crab legs are split," Marcelo said, "It'll be easier to eat for those who don't want to go through the hassle of cracking a lobster."

"Marcelo, everybody!" Monica yelled into the kitchen. "Up front, quick!"

Everyone stampeded to the lobby, where cautious customers had backed up to the walls, leaving the center area open. Some were walking out, but others stayed on with curious eyes. Connie, Curtis, and a guy in a three-piece suit stood in center stage.

"This bum is Curtis?" The man turned to Connie. "You replaced me with this loser?"

Marcelo stepped up. "It's time for you to go."

"Leave, now," Connie said. "You're making a fool of yourself."

"You heard the lady," Curtis said. "She's not telling you twice."

Marcelo grabbed the guy's arm, but he shook it off.

"If you don't leave," Tyrone stepped up, "we'll throw you out."

"Curtis is a nobody in a monkey suit," the troublemaker said to Connie, backing away, "slinging hash for the change in my pocket." He laughed. "Did he give you a sob story about why he never made anything out of his pathetic life?" He pointed at Curtis. "You're nothing!"

Curtis jumped at him, but Carlos and Roger pulled him back. Marcelo and Tyrone shoved the agitator toward the door. When he resisted, each grabbed an arm and leg and rammed him through the door, head first. He crash-landed on the concrete walk. The crowd applauded.

"This is not over, Connie!" he yelled from outside. "When I catch you, I'm going to beat you like a Grand Canyon mule, and you know that's a promise! And you bunch of stupid trained monkeys can't do anything! Yeah, you heard me! You won't recognize her when I'm through!"

"Are those Halloween masks still in the office?" Roger asked Marcelo.

"Yep, in the closet."

Roger sprinted toward the back, followed by Tyrone and Carlos.

"We're sorry for the inconvenience, ladies and gentlemen," Marcelo said. "Please have a complimentary drink or dessert with your entrée tonight."

"That mister got what he deserved." The child held her mother's hand.

Marcelo went to Connie. "Take the rest of the night off and relax."

"I can't relax. Not with him running loose."

"Curtis, stay with her," Marcelo said, and rushed through the freshly mopped kitchen and out the back door. A troop of gorillas in rubber masks was going bananas on the coward in the parking lot, their twelve extremities striking sensitive areas. To his credit, the chicken swung aimlessly before his wobbly knees dropped and his face kissed the tarred lot. Marcelo returned inside, followed by the troop.

"Ooohhh ooohhh aahhh aahhh!" They pounded their chests in jubilation.

Jim and Harry hurried out and stuffed the abuser in his car. An hour later, Marcelo watched the car crawl off the lot.

"How's your grandma?" Marcelo leaned back in the office chair, talking on the phone.

"She came home yesterday," Emily said. "She's much better. She's been out of bed since she got here. I'm so glad. I haven't been that scared in my life."

"I'm happy both of you are OK." He didn't tell her about what had happened. It wasn't necessary. "That was a scary thing you both went through."

"But now she wants me to get out of her hair," Emily said. "She wants me back to work."

"Great." He put his elbows on the desk. "I'll tell Connie and Sergio. I'm sure it'll be OK."

Carlos stopped by the office as he hung up the telephone. "You think we'll hear from that coward again?"

XL

Barry

Barry bought another bike from the pawnshop and pedaled away. This time it was a boy's bike: metallic red with a banana seat and twenty-inch wheels. Man, Kennedy Boulevard was busier than the Florida Turnpike on Labor Day weekend. The sweltering heat roasted him without mercy, but he rode on, checking out restaurants on both sides of the road. Above, the sun and rainclouds wrestled for air supremacy. It wouldn't be long before the sun cried uncle to dismal rain.

The Granada Restaurant came into view. The building was Mediterranean style with white stucco walls and red terracotta roof tiles. It offered Spanish cuisine and had been at that location for a hundred years. It was as fine a place as any to stop. Inside, the dining room was half full, the lunch rush minutes away. He washed up in the restroom and went back to the lobby. A chick with large eyes and chestnut hair checked him out. *Could she be the one for me?* She was more beautiful than a bouquet of fresh spring flowers.

"One for lunch?" she asked.

He looked down and stuck his hands in his pockets. "You need a prep cook?"

"No, but the kitchen might. I'll be right back." She smiled with unholy intentions.

He hadn't been with a chick in so long; his manhood was on the endangered species list.

A dark wooden bench rested against the whitewashed wall, and he took a seat. Two lions faced and snarled at each other in a family crest across from him. He picked up a magazine beside him and leafed through it. "Arron Marshall completed a world record shower of 336 hours," he read. *Man, what did that guy do to feel so dirty and so guilty?* He knew how the sap felt, but Barry wasn't that bad. More often than not, Barry only washed and scrubbed his hands for five minutes after going to the toilet, just to make sure he had exterminated all the germs from his hands. On a filthy, dirty day, it might be ten minutes.

A stubby dude in a spotted kitchen uniform came into view and walked up to him. He had a bald spot that had taken up the crown of his head and had pushed the hair to the temples. The battle continued on the dome, with the follicles in eternal retreat.

"I'm Armando. You're an experienced prep cook?"

He got up, scratched an arm. "Yes, in a steak and seafood and in an Italian place, that kind of stuff."

"Come in at eleven a.m. tomorrow and see what I have."

After what he'd just been through, he'd be ready at sunrise like a sundial if need be.

On the ride home, he bought a *Tampa Times* to look for a decent place to live. He rolled his bike past the front desk to the elevator at home. There was no need to ask for his mail. Eyes crawled all over him like roaches while he waited for his lift. *What in creation are they looking at?* He turned around, but the reception area was empty. The doors clanked open. Upstairs, he spread the newspaper on the dinette table and found the Apartments for

Rent section. He had to move out of the rat hole. One of the doors in the hallway slammed shut.

"Let me in, or I'll break the door down!" a guy shouted.

"Break it and I'll break your face!" Barry yelled.

What's wrong with me? His ear wasn't the only hard and callous part of him.

In bed, he traveled back to a not-too-distant past, to Carlos, Marcelo, and the Vineyard, when barrels of laughter flowed as easily as pitchers of beer at the Bull Pen. Carlos and Marcelo were the only family he had. A moment of peace came over him when he remembered all the stunts they'd pulled. What were that horndog Roger, Tyrone, and of the rest of the guys doing? Winter must be cold for those with no warm memories, he thought....

Barry lugged a greasy bus pan full of plates, cups, glasses, and silverware from the dining room. *Damn!* He almost lost his grip pushing through the swinging doors into the kitchen. The first bus pan, and he'd already messed up his kitchen whites. Why didn't the night dishwasher run the tubs through the machine at closing? He had to suck it up and wash dishes until a prep cook job opened—a waste of his talents. At least the job wasn't as repetitious as the one at the chicken coop. Still, it didn't challenge him much, and that was good. He lined the saucers in the rack like Boy Scouts in formation.

"Take your battle positions." He saluted the cooks and got ready for the lunch rush.

The guys behind the line didn't seem bad, but he'd just met them, and people never failed to disappoint him. The dark-haired girl said hello to them and headed his way. *Does she know that love is a fruit in season at all times?*

"Just hang in there," she said.

Could she see the confusion and loneliness in his soul? He'd do anything to connect with her in the biblical sense. He could use the company and some kind words. Was the feeling in his heart real or imagined, like the ghost pain of an amputated arm no longer there?

Armando called him to the office. The guy had a worn shoe-lace begging to be replaced.

"Fill out the W-2 form." He scratched his baldness. "Don't worry about the job application, but write down your phone number."

Armando looked at the W-2 Barry had completed. "Tom Jones," he read. "I like your music." He laughed.

Barry had no idea why he'd picked that name, but he'd have to get a fake ID to hide his identity and cash his check. He was glad he wouldn't attract attention from the heat by the uniform he wore. He didn't have to wear his kitchen whites out in the world, like the black-and-whites from the Vineyard, which he'd worn as often as the habit of a monk.

"What's that phone number?" Armando took a pen.

"Don't have one. But I'll make it here, no problem."

Armando studied him with a question mark on his face. "Get back to work."

Three bus pans full of grimy dishes waited for him, but he was in no hurry. He checked out the lobby. It buzzed with customers, like mosquitoes flying around the trailer park. He got back to the machine and broke down the bus pans. On the radio, the Commodores sang "Brick House." Barry was scraping the crud off bowls when late-breaking news came on.

"The young man wanted for questioning in the hit-and-run accident of a runaway girl in Saint Petersburg is Barry Gregory. It is known that Mister Gregory works in the restaurant industry and may be working under an alias and possibly in the kitchen, out of the public eye. He is described as five ten with a stocky build and sandy brown hair. He is driving a sixty-nine Pontiac Catalina and has a callous ear from his time on the high-school wrestling team."

I'm dead meat!

"That sounds like you, my man," the fry cook said. "That messed-up ear."

"Leave him be," Armando told him from behind the line.

"Everybody in wrestling has a cauliflower ear," Barry said. "That don't mean nothing."

You're safe. Don't let Fry-boy see you sweat.

Barry slid the dish rack into the machine and pushed the ON button. The water pumped and sprayed the plates inside from the top and bottom. He leaned back on the wall, and wished he were waiting on customers in the dining room, on the floor. It was his stage and his public. There, he was the Star, the main attraction. Everyone anticipated and welcomed his appearance. Everyone craved his presence. Everyone applauded each award-winning performance.

It is what it is.

There wasn't even one waitresses there to gawk at from time to time. Only waiters and—

"I'm watching you." The fry cook pointed two fingers at his eyes and then at Barry.

If eternity is your destination, I'm the travel agent, you SOB!

Granada Restaurant wasn't a huge place—not like the Vineyard anyway. It sat about one hundred people at most. The whole place looked as if the Count of Monte Cristo lived there, with iron chandeliers and iron lamps mounted on the walls. The buzzer told him the wash cycle had ended, so he pulled out the rack of dishes. He'd let the steamy dishes cool off until dry.

"Where do you live, man?" the ponytailed fry cook asked.

The jerk was looking for the lunch special—knuckle sandwich, two for the price of one.

"Why don't you come here and find out?" Barry said and watched the plates cool.

"OK, cut it out!" Armando said and put up lunches under the heat lamps.

Barry stared the troublemaker down. If he kept it up, he'd be spitting out bloody teeth like cherry gumdrops. He'd win that fight by KO in the first round. *Go ahead ring the bell.*

The lunch rush began and everyone got busier, and that gave Barry a chance to be alone in his head. Sometimes his thoughts were monkeys, swinging from one subject to another without rest. They landed on a familiar topic. What was happening at the Vineyard? He recalled the nightly concerts of chatter and clatter in the dining room, ones that stimulated his senses and lifted his spirit. Marcelo was probably ordering silverware or dishes; Tyrone wouldn't be in until later. It'd been ages since he'd seen any of the guys. Could he ever show his face around there again and go back to things as they were? His life had become a crown of thorns, and there was no salvation. And what little existence he had left, ponytail wanted to ruin.

"You better get your ID soon," Armando told him at the end of his shift. "I got this cook saying you're some psycho killer."

The instigator wanted him exposed to the world like the frog he dissected in eighth-grade biology class: left wide open with nothing to hide. *You could grab a couple of beers with him and shut him up for good—I can't do that!* He was only sure of two things in life anymore: his name and the day he was born. Fear and paranoia had invaded and conquered his soul without his knowing.

XLI

Emily

A flood of activity inundated the dining room on Emily's first day back to the daily grind of work. Connie and Jim had pushed two of her tables together for a party of six, a family of three generations it seemed. She greeted them as the mother led the grandmother to the restroom. The granddad and dad smoked awful-smelling, unfiltered cigarettes. A teen boy in a baseball cap ogled her while the infant girl couldn't keep her hands off the sugar packets. Nothing had changed in her absence.

"What happened to Barry?" the father asked.

"Barry's no longer here," she said. "I can come back to take the drink order."

"What about Roger? He still here?" the granddad asked.

"Let's start over," she said. "I'm Emily, and I'll be your waitress tonight."

"Ain't she a looker?" The dad elbowed the teen boy, who blushed.

"I'll come back later."

"Yes, come back later," the mother said on her return.

The guys reduced their world to the space between the menus and their eyes.

She came back and took their order, which required as much effort as extracting impacted molars. At the bread warmer, Monica and Angie waited for the rolls to heat up. Somebody hadn't replenished the drawer. Emily got two breadbaskets and leaned back on the counter.

"Emily should've come with me to the Gallery Lounge last night," Angie said.

"Angie met a real nice guy, it sounds like," Monica said.

"I'm sure he's a first-rate guy," Emily said.

Angie filled her basket. "My new guy will be there tonight. You're all welcome."

"You want to go with?" Monica asked Emily.

"I'll pass, but if you want to go to Club 29 for a quick beer, I'm game."

"Cool."

Emily delivered the rolls to the table. The grandfather was back from the salad bar with a plate as colorful as a box of Crayolas. On the board, her number lit up, calling her to the kitchen. She brought their iced teas before picking up. She turned in her order and waited behind Roger. His crew cut needed a trim. Still, his hair was in no danger of being declared a fire hazard.

"I heard you almost got lucky when you went out with Angie." Roger raised his eyebrows and put a crab claw appetizer on his oval tray.

"I wouldn't have called that lucky," she said.

Curtis was picking up a broiled fisherman's platter ahead of Roger. "Don't talk to Emily that way," he said. "She's a nice lady."

"Who made you the moral authority at the Vineyard?" Roger sneered.

"I'm just saying." Curtis shouldered the tray and went to his people.

"Then say it to somebody who cares!" Roger yelled.

Emily walked over to the dessert cooler and got a carrot cake for one of her ladies. One who didn't need it; she was two desserts away from a massive coronary. Emily rejoined the line.

"You rejects remember nobody shouts in this kitchen but me," Tyrone said.

"Lay off Curtis," Emily told Roger. "He's a nice guy."

"No, he isn't." Tyrone's grill sizzled when he placed a porterhouse on it. "He loves a piece of tail as much as the next guy."

"And that makes him a bad guy?" she asked.

"Not as long as it's not mine he's after." Tyrone laughed.

It was part of the deal working here, having to put up with mindless diatribe. Still, it was difficult to imagine that in a few weeks she'd be gone.

When her turn arrived she called her table, and two surf and turfs went up under the lamps. The meat in the lobster tails was white, lightly sprinkled with paprika to give them that golden touch. Plump, medium-rare filet mignons steamed on their plates. She added a couple of lemon wedges to accompany the cups of hot drawn butter. She shouldered the tray and met Monica in the corridor.

"I told Curtis we're going to Club 29 tonight," Monica said.

In the dining room, she stood a tray stand next to her deuce and lowered the tray. The young couple looked with anticipation, empty salad plates set aside. Jim halted his efforts at the next table and removed them. The meals released their aroma in front of them.

"This smells great," the guy said.

"You're a first-rate cook," the girl said.

"I'm an even better bartender," Emily said. "You should try my after-dinner drinks."

Emily walked to the congested foyer to call Grandma. She let Connie know she'd have a four-top available in minutes. At the register, Jackie flipped through the credit card booklet, looking to see if the credit card Roger had presented to her was valid. One of the two pay phones in the restroom area was available.

"What are you up to, Grandma?"

"About five foot, three inches last time I checked."

"You'll catch up to me soon." Emily laughed. "I'm going out for a bit after work, so don't wait up for me."

"I'm already in bed, but thanks for the thought. Say hi to Marcelo for me."

She wasn't going to see Marcelo. In a few weeks, she'd be back in south Florida. She didn't want to, but it was time for her to wean off him.

"Hey," Jackie said when Emily passed the register.

Jackie stuck her chin in the air and handed her the telephone over the counter. It was Marcelo calling. He told her he had good news, and she could always use good news.

"I'm going to State," he declared.

"What?" Did she hear him right?

"I can register as a non-degree-seeking student and then apply for admission in January."

He'd given it plenty of thought and had found out what he needed to know. All he had to do was call Sally, and his housing, tuition, and books would be paid.

"Are you sure you want to do this?" Her excitement was difficult to contain.

"More than anything in the world," he said. "It's what I've always wanted."

It was a fabulous note on which to end the month of July. She couldn't have scripted a better ending. After work, she met Monica and Curtis at Club 29 for a nightcap. Roger wasn't there to paw at Monica. He'd been hot on her trail since Emily had been there, and it was getting old. Monica could be trusting as a lamb at times, and from what she heard, Roger had a taste for lamb. After a couple of beers, Emily headed home before the strike of midnight.

Emily drove back from the A&P to find her mother's car in the driveway. Not cool! She hadn't returned her mother's calls, and ignoring them apparently had backfired on her. She took a deep breath, opened the door, and borrowed a smile.

"Look who came for a surprise visit," Grandma said. "I had no idea she was coming."

"Mother, you should've called, really," Emily said.

"Then it wouldn't have been a surprise," Mom said. "I've missed you, too."

Emily excused herself and went to the kitchen, unpacked the groceries, and put them up on the cupboard. The milk and OJ went in the refrigerator. She folded and put the paper bags away and returned to the living room.

"Saint Pete is the only home I've known," Grandma said. "I was born here."

"It was for me, too," Mom said. "But we moved. Right, Emily?"

"They are two different situations, Mother." Emily took the armchair.

"You're not helping me here," Mom said.

If Emily helped her, she'd be a hypocrite. And she wasn't willing to carry that heavy anchor. She didn't even want to be in the middle. She supported Grandma on her decision.

"You had a husband and children," Grandma said. "I'm eighty, and I want to die here."

"Don't talk that way, silly," Mom said. "You're not going to die."

Emily cleared her throat. "Grandma belongs here, Mom."

Mother scowled at her. The tension was as thick as lentil soup. Emily didn't want to add to the friction, but love meant allowing others the right to make choices for their lives.

"Home's where your family is," Mom said. "I've brought brochures. These are all senior communities where you'll be with people your age."

The brochures on the coffee table described the amenities at the retirement communities as if they were vacation resorts, from tennis courts to swimming pools to spas. But their names sounded more like cemeteries: Centennial Gardens and Serenity Valley.

"You said, 'home is where your family is,' Mom. I don't see *Family* in the booklets."

"Emily, whose side are you on?" Mom said. "Help me out here."

"I didn't know there were sides to take," Grandma said. "I've been thinking about where I could live when I can no longer manage on my own. There are places in town I'd consider first. Walter's buried here."

Emily had discovered that home was where loved ones were buried and where memories lived. It would be horribly sad to live out the last days in a place void of memories.

"That's out of the question," Mom said. "It's too far for us to come and visit regularly. And we do want to see you often."

"I can tell," Emily said. "It's all about Grandma's convenience. Your peace of mind shouldn't come at Grandma's expense."

It was apparent Mother didn't know how to love without being selfish. She didn't have the yearning to nurture or the empathy to care. Emily didn't want to be that way.

"Enough," Grandma said. "I don't want to talk about this anymore."

"We have to talk about it," Mom said. "Emily, you were supposed to talk to your grandma about this. What have you been doing all this time?"

"Is that why you came this summer, Emily—to persuade me?" Grandma asked.

"That's not the reason I stayed," Emily said.

"Somebody's got to talk some sense into you," Mom said.

"I have plenty of sense. Why would you two manipulate me that way?" Grandma held up her hand, silencing all rebuttals, and went to her room.

Emily was glad she'd taken a stand: inaction had meant complicity.

"Are you happy now?" Emily asked. "You've ruined everything."

"If you'd done what you came here for, we wouldn't be in this mess."

She wasn't going to do her mom's dirty work and told her so. She hadn't wanted to come to St. Pete at first but was glad she did. She didn't want to debate the issue any longer: the more she struggled to free herself of it, the more she became entangled in her mother's web.

"Don't play the martyr here," Mom said. "You only care about yourself."

"I'm my mother's daughter," she said. "I had the best teacher."

Mom stood up. "How long did you have that one in the holster?"

"We're done talking." Emily showed her the door. "It's time for you to leave."

"You're an ingrate." Mom glared at her. "Since you like it here so much, don't bother coming home. You're an adult and not my responsibility anymore."

Hardly another word was spoken. Her mother gathered the brochures, stuffed them into her purse, and walked out. After she drove away, Emily landed on the couch and sobbed.

The relationship with her mother was a tapestry of dysfunction with no end in sight. She wouldn't go home; she didn't want to end up alone and bitter like her mother. She blew and dried her nose with a tissue. Above all, she was glad she hadn't backed down; loving someone carried certain undeniable responsibilities.

XLII

Marcelo

"**K**iss my grits!" Curtis told Roger and received fifty dollars for winning July's wine-selling contest.

"You'll meet your Waterloo in August." Roger got thirty-five dollars for second place.

Marcelo returned to the office to collect the Vineyard utility expenses to turn in to the accountant by the fifth of August. He loosened his tie and unbuttoned the collar of his shirt at the desk. He went through the bills in the IN basket. It amazed him how much it cost just to light and air-condition a place that size. The electric bill would easily eat one day's lunch sales and drink the happy hour's profits. Something weighed heavily on his mind. His decision wouldn't be met with a rousing chorus of approval. Sergio walked in, and Marcelo rose.

"You wanted to see me?" Sergio asked.

Marcello's throat got tight as a knot. "I'm leaving at the end of the month. Carlos and I are moving to Miami. I'm going to State."

"You're not going anywhere." Sergio raised an eyebrow. "You're jiving, right?"

He didn't say anything, and Sergio got the message.

"That sucks. Terrible for me, but I guess great for you."

The twenty-fifth of August would be his last day. That gave Sergio three weeks' notice to find a replacement. He was leaving the Vineyard and giving notice as he'd always planned.

"Are you sure about this?"

He nodded. "It's the right time."

"Before you leave," Sergio said, "help find someone to take your place."

"You don't have to look far," Marcelo said. "Curtis's been in the business for years and knows what he's doing."

"I'll look into it." They shook hands. "All right then."

After totaling expenses, he planned to place the order for fruits and vegetables along with dry goods—mainly flour, pasta, canned tomato sauce, and canned fruit. He had three weeks left and hadn't heard from Barry. It was as if the man had been swallowed alive by a sinkhole. He dialed the telephone and rubbed the tight muscles on the back of his neck.

"No, we haven't located him," the SSPD desk sergeant told him.

Marcelo took the Tampa Yellow Pages and flipped to the Restaurants section. He had to find out if Barry, under his brother's name, was working anywhere. After two dozen calls, he still hadn't found him. But there were hundreds of places, including new ones that weren't listed. Had Barry met with tragedy, or was he well guarded behind a shield of protection?

He headed to the liquor room to stock the cases of liquor and wine delivered that day. The room was long and narrow, with shelves of bottles stocked to the ceiling. At times, he thought the shelves would tumble down on him. He searched for the key on the ring. Curtis and Roger hung around the ice machine.

"Larry Holmes is going to be a great heavyweight champion," Curtis said.

"Man, you're out to lunch," Roger said. "He got lucky beating Ken Norton. Holmes is a sparring partner at best. He'll lose his title the first time he defends it. He's no Ali."

"Why talk about boxing?" Angie joined them. "It's stupid, two guys beating each other up. You don't see women doing that, do you?"

"Anyway, Ali couldn't punch a time clock." Curtis waved Roger off and then turned to Marcelo. "What do you think?"

Marcelo fumbled with the keys. "I didn't see the fight."

"What boxer do you like?" Roger asked him.

"Roberto Duran. But there isn't anybody for him to fight."

"Take my word," Roger said. "That Holmes better make the best of his fifteen minutes of fame because when his first defense comes, he's toast."

Marcelo unlocked the liquor room and pulled the string to the light bulb above. Shelves of bottles rose up all around as they did the last time he was in there. Vodka, rum, whiskey, and gin bottles waited for their call to duty. He left the door ajar. Cases crowded the floor, and he stepped around them. He opened the first box and, one by one, lined the bottles of scotch with similar company. Yes, he would miss his job.

The warm glow of a summer afternoon sun shone over Sunken Gardens. A collection of more than five hundred species of tropical and subtropical plants, surrounded by pools and cascading waterfalls, called the gardens home. Emily and Marcelo reached the flamingo exhibit.

"The first day of school," she said, "we'll go to the Student Union after class and toast the future."

Just about everyone on campus could enjoy a nip anytime, since the legal drinking age was eighteen. She told him that one night a week, students gathered on the main lawn to watch movies in the open air. That wasn't all: a bowling alley tested students' averages of another kind at the Student Union. The campus even had its own post office and police force.

"I heard about some of that from students I've waited on."

"Now you'll do the telling." Emily leaned over the rail of the Flamingo exhibit.

One flamingo strolled around the pond, and another rested on the bank. They were masses of pink cotton candy with black stick legs. The bird planted each foot with care, as if walking on a mine field. Strangely, their knees folded toward the back instead of toward the front, as with people.

"Have you been to plays in the drama department?" Marcelo asked.

"Oh yes…the arts. How did you know about that?"

"You hear everything on the job." He strolled with hands in his pockets.

Live performances were available to the student body at low cost once they went public in the school theater. But before that, students could attend rehearsals at no cost. The music department also offered performances of all kinds, from orchestral classical music to two-piece sonatas. She enjoyed the piano and cello sonatas most, and so did he.

"You never cease to amaze me." She held his arm, not wanting the conversation to end.

The souvenir shop was a classic example of a 1930s Florida roadside commercial attraction, and Sunken Gardens was one of the oldest commercial tourist attractions on Florida's west coast. It was full of tacky items only a tourist would buy: T-shirts with maps of Florida and palm trees, snow globes with a tiny chair and parasol, conch shells replaying the eternal sound of the ocean, foot-long rubber replicas of alligators, coffee mugs with tropical scenes, and other items.

"Take one of these so you don't get homesick." Emily showed him a T-shirt with pelicans resting on a wooden wharf and St. Petersburg, FL written underneath.

He laughed. "It'll take me a while to get that homesick."

In the lounge, Sherry showed Marcelo the two unsteady barstools reported by her customers. Marcelo got on one and swiveled around. They'd been right on that one.

"Marcelo, you're wanted in the office." Jackie stood at the entrance.

"Can't it wait?" Marcelo asked, but Jackie had left.

"They'll be here when you get back," Sherry said.

In the office, Carmine and Sergio waited for him. Not again. Sergio wore the same vacant expression he'd had when he told Marcelo he didn't get the promotion on his birthday. He didn't like the vibes. He took a chair and sat on the edge.

"We got a serious problem," Carmine said. "The guy you had beat up the other day had his attorney call. He wants to sue us. We didn't know anything about the beating until he called."

He'd suspected that afternoon might boomerang and bite him, and it had. Carmine had picked up the scent of blood and was circling for the kill.

"I didn't have anyone beat up."

"What happened that day?" Sergio asked.

Marcelo explained the sequence of events, about the threats the coward made to Connie, and how the confrontation developed suddenly and without planning.

"Why didn't you tell me?" Sergio asked.

"He got what he deserved," Marcelo said. "And I thought we'd never hear from him."

Sergio paced the room. "If we fire the three guys who beat him up and apologize, maybe the guy won't go through with it," Sergio said. "Who were they?"

"Come on," Marcelo said. "He has no case. He can't finger anyone involved."

Sergio locked his arms and looked him in the eye.

"And if they find out who we fire," Marcelo said, "what prevents him from pressing charges against them, felony assault and battery or who knows what?"

"It's all going to come out in court," Carmine said. "We're not taking the rap for this."

"We don't need the legal expense or the bad press," Sergio said. "Just tell me who the three guys are, and you'll be off the hook."

No, he couldn't give up his brother or the other guys. His throat went dry. He couldn't and he wouldn't be a snitch. His principles wouldn't change, even if his brother wasn't involved.

"We'll find out who they were," Carmine said. "And they're going to jail."

Marcelo swept across their faces. "I don't know who was involved."

Sergio looked away. "You know what this means."

"I want to have a chance to say good-bye to everyone," Marcelo said.

"Tomorrow can be your last day," Sergio said. "Why are you so hardheaded?"

"And don't go too far," Carmine said. "You'll be called to point fingers in court."

Marcelo was ready for his brother's reaction when he told him he'd been fired. They faced each other in the service area. Others had given them space and privacy.

"Why shouldn't I walk out?" Carlos asked. "Barry always said that bastard wanted to get rid of you and him. Carmine knew you wouldn't give us up."

"Don't give him the satisfaction of walking out," Marcelo said. "I'd rather have it this way."

"I'm not giving that jerk anything," Carlos said. "It'll be my pleasure."

"You only have a few days here. Finish them out."

Marcelo went out the back door to get a breath of fresh air and walk around the lot. The next day would be his last night at the Vineyard. He'd talked Carlos out of walking out and following his pattern. It felt weird. Barry and he were both gone from the Vineyard.

He was a failure. He had failed as a friend, and as a manager, and he had failed looking after his brother. What would Carlos be charged with, assault and battery? And what could he be charged with if he didn't tell, obstruction of justice, accessory to the crime? He took a deep breath to keep his eyes from welling up in tears. What pained him more was that he had failed his parents, and he didn't know what to do.

Thunder cracked at a distance and lit the sky with fireworks. Menacing storm clouds formed over Tampa across the bay.

XLIII

Barry

Two cop cars were parked in front of the Georgian when Barry rode up. In the atrium, four pigs were hassling the clerk at the front desk. One of them was long overdue for slaughter. Luckily, they squealed good-byes and went to their pens. Barry asked about the visit.

"They're looking for some guy named Carmichael, but there's no one here by that name."

Hell, Carmichael was his mother's maiden name. *That's the signal to contact them!* TPD was cooperating with the CIA and—*don't be such a fool. TPD just made a routine stop.*

"You OK?" the clerk asked.

"Barry?" He turned around, but nobody was there.

Upstairs, he lay in bed and stared at the stars out the window. He felt safe in up the clouds. Cops searched for him on the ground below, but they had to see him to find him. He had just about disappeared from the world. Who would care if he died? The duffel bag on the floor took the shape of a dog and wagged its tail. He wasn't alone. The cups and glasses on the table multiplied in number, turned to chess pieces, and began a game. *No, not tonight.*

He got up to turn on the radio, but it was gone. His hands palmed the dresser in the dark but couldn't find it. He'd been ripped off.

"Damn it!" He smacked his palm. "Which son of a bitch stole my radio?"

He stormed into the hallway and went banging from door to door. When pain was the game, he came ready to play....

Barry gritted his teeth and pumped the pedals riding to work. His unbuttoned shirt flapped behind him. A box truck beside him screamed like a tortured animal when shifting gears.

Man, he had to get out of that rat-infested dump of a hotel sooner rather than later. The night before was the last straw: a toothless neighbor told him he was calling the heat, just because Barry was choking his yellow-eyed alcoholic roommate against the hallway wall, the grip on his windpipe strong as a pit bull's clenched jaws. Just tell me who's got my radio, was all that he'd wanted to know. Another ten seconds under his grasp and yellow eyes would've told him anything he wanted to hear. To make matters worse, the insect desk clerk was no help.

"I didn't see you bring no radio when you moved in," the clerk said.

And the losers on his floor said they'd never heard any music from his room. He was on to them: the riffraff covered one another's hairy backs.

He locked his bike to a pole by the kitchen door to the Granada. Above, rumbling clouds rolled in and chased out the blue skies. They threatened to rain and cleanse him of his sins—*Impossible!* Barry crossed the tiled kitchen floor to his washing machine.

"That's an ugly deformed ear, freak."

What the hell? Barry turned around, but the fry cook acted innocent.

"You're overcooking my grits, dirtbag," Barry said.

The guy looked at him and shook his head. Didn't that dirtbag care if he saw the sun rise the next day? Barry swept and mopped around the machine, dirty from the night before. Why did he always have to clean up after the night dishwasher? He leaned the mop against the wall.

"I need these five minutes ago." The fry cook walked carefully on the wet floor, carrying a load of dirty pots and pans. They fell from his arms into the sink like rocks down a hill.

"Those are from last night!" Barry said to his back.

"Just do them, freak!"

Blood rushed through his veins and throbbed at the temples. *You're dead meat!* Barry grabbed him by the collar, banged his head against the machine, and threw him down. The sad sack looked as if he didn't know what hit him. He slipped on the wet floor trying to find his footing to get up.

"You're freaking crazy!" The punk rushed out and marked up his floor.

Armando came his way, and he could read his future on his face. He was about to be canned from a dishwasher job, the lowest rung in the restaurant ladder. Oh yes, he felt special, all right...as a bastard on Father's Day.

"Punch out!" Armando told him. "You're done here."

"I knew that when I bashed his head against the machine."

"I'm calling the law!" Fry-boy went into the office.

Barry pushed Armando aside and burst out of there like a bull through a corral fence. He pedaled home like a demon. There was nothing cops liked better than the free meal of an open-and-shut case. It wasn't raining yet, but it would be soon—a storm by the smell of it. Dark clouds thickened and decided to burst and pour down on him. Thunderclouds clapped their giant hands. Thunder cracked and cracked up…and laughed at him all the way home.

At the hotel, Barry made wet tracks to the elevator.

"Murderer!" he heard. *Ignore it!*

He pressed the cold metal button. The old lift came quickly. As it climbed, the walls closed in on him. He pounded the doors, fearing he'd be crushed. It opened on his floor, and he stumbled out gasping for air. In his room, he crawled into bed and dozed off.

Loud country music from the hallway penetrated the walls. He awoke in a damp darkness. Man, he wanted some nap time, but somebody was looking for scrap time.

"Turn down that radio!" he yelled.

"Sure, I'll turn it down!"

Instead, the volume went up. And a bunch of laughing hyenas invaded the corridor.

Barry sprang to his feet and swung the door open. Scraggly faces looked up from Boone's Farm wine bottles. The radio on the floor still blared. *That's your radio!*

"Where you get that radio?" Barry glared at the bum sitting next to it.

"Get back to your hole before you regret it." He took a drag off his cig.

"You heard him, sideshow freak," a derelict leaning on the wall said.

Barry picked up the radio, yanked the cord out from where it was plugged in around the door, and smashed it on the floor. The guy pushed off the wall and came at him. Barry grabbed the guy's wrist and dropped to his knees, shoved his other arm under the guy's crotch, and flipped him over his head. The derelict landed on his back and groaned with a wrinkled face.

"Call the police!" someone yelled and shut the door.

The bum sitting on the floor threw the cig down and rushed him. Barry took a knee, grabbed him around the thighs, and lifted him off the floor. Then he swung the guy's legs from under, dropped him to the floor, and landed on him. The loser just lay there like a popped water balloon. Everyone else had scattered. Faint police sirens grew in his ears. *Were they real or imagined?* From the sound of it, half-a-dozen cruisers raced toward him.

"I told the cops you got a gun!" A voice shouted from a room.

The sirens are real! Barry retreated to his apartment and looked out the window. A handful of police cars pulled up to the entrance fifteen stories below. He panted for air, like a hiker who'd climbed Mount Everest. *They know I killed that girl.* The CIA didn't want him anymore. And they couldn't afford to have him walking around free, living and breathing, for the Soviets to recruit him. In spite of his skills, they wanted him taken out, and TPD had been chosen for the honors.

There were three exits to the building. But the police had the elevator and the stairwell covered. Only seconds kept the law from his floor and bullets from his body. The third exit wasn't his first or even second choice, but the only one left. At the window, he looked at the concrete sidewalk below and took a deep breath. He'd definitely go to hell for taking his life, but then he'd be rescued from eternal damnation by an armada of trumpeting angels. Who could blame him? The elevator bell rang and the doors clanked open. Footsteps and two-way radios rushed toward him.

His knees wobbled, but he climbed on the window ledge. The sidewalk below called his name.

He was sure he'd win one day because even he couldn't be perfect at losing, because he couldn't be perfect at anything.

They'll have to scrape me off the freaking pavement like armadillo road-kill to get me.

Two cops burst through his doorway with guns drawn, and he jumped...

XLIV

Emily

Emily and Grandma arrived at Crescent Lake at midmorning, decades after their last visit. Back then, Emily had loved riding her bicycle around the concrete walk encircling the kidney-shaped lake. If her memory wasn't failing her, her father had said the path was slightly under one mile.

They took a bench facing the lake. The surface was smooth as polished marble. Across the pond, a young woman in a white uniform pushed an older lady in a wheelchair. The old woman's spine was so bent; she could only see the concrete at her feet. Ahead of them, two teen lovers strolled hand in hand. Ducks dove and splashed into the lake. The morning sun warmed up for its matinee performance.

"Forgive me, Grandma," Emily said. "I didn't come to persuade you to move."

"If anyone has to apologize, it's your mom. Children want aging parents to give up their homes and go to a retirement home. They say it's for our own good, but it's really so they can sleep better at night." She sighed. "Enough said on this topic."

Brown ducks waddled out of the lake and shook the water off their tail feathers.

"What kind of ducks are those?" Emily pointed.

"Florida mottled ducks. They're non-migratory ducks that only live in Florida."

Molten-brown-colored feathers covered both birds. Iridescent green-and-purple patches adorned the wings. The male watching them had a yellowish bill, the female, an orange one.

"You've been living here too long if you know that much," Emily said.

Grandma laughed. "Your grandpa was the nature buff. He'd talk my ear off. Sometimes when I close my eyes, I can hear his voice. Silly of me, isn't it?"

"No...not at all."

Grandpa had loved the outdoors. Emily and he had camped at Fort Desoto Park, had hiked Boyd Hill's Nature Trail, and had gone clamming at Boca Ciega Bay. She loved plucking the clams from the wet sand after the receding waves revealed their burrows.

"Marcelo likes fishing," Emily said. "But I don't have the patience for it yet."

"Grandpa did too, but he wouldn't hunt. That, he wouldn't do."

When she was a little girl, Emily didn't see any difference between hunting and fishing: both killed living animals. Even as an adult, she still had difficulty understanding the difference between the two. She smiled whenever she saw a *Field & Stream* magazine and remembered how her Grandpa labored to explain his rationale for differentiating between the two.

A girl about four years old with reddened cheeks rode her bicycle with training wheels past them. She looked back at her long-stepping mother close behind and pedaled faster.

"Let's walk a bit," Grandma said.

They continued around the lake and looked out for two-wheeled speeding youngsters. They came to the thickest tree she'd seen in her life.

"The Great Banyan Tree," Emily said.

"Your mom loved this park when she was little, too."

Emily had imagined herself living in a tree house on top of the banyan when she tried to climb it in her childhood. It was a jungle gym to her then, and it still was.

"Let's have lunch before I go to work. You pick the place."

"Oh dear, let me think." Grandma brightened up. "How about the Owl Restaurant?"

"Do they still have hundreds of owl figures all over the place?"

"Yes. You wouldn't know it, but they make the best Peking duck in town."

Before she went on the floor, Emily cooled off with a glass of iced tea in the break room. She was happy she'd come to St. Pete for the summer after all. Her relationship with Grandma was an unexpected gift, and one she wanted to fertilize and grow. She wouldn't have to see her mom for a while because Emily lived on campus, which worked out fine for her. She was flipping through the newspaper when Marcelo walked in. She'd never seen him so serious.

"Can I see you in the office?" he asked.

As she followed him, he didn't say another word on the way. The commotion from the kitchen still filtered through the closed office door.

"This is my last day at work." He gave her a quick grin.

"Get real." It wasn't true. *Was it?* "What's going on?"

He dropped the mother lode of news on her. He told her about the impending lawsuit. She was at a loss for words. It wasn't the festive summer ending she had envisioned. But Marcelo wasn't sorry about the thrashing the abuser got: the vampire had been bleeding the life out of Connie long enough.

"Why didn't you tell me this had happened?" She grabbed the doorknob. "I can quit now and spend the last few days with you and Grandma."

"Don't quit. I didn't want you to worry, and I can use the time to try to find Barry before we leave." He sighed. "I always thought we'd be in each other's weddings and see our children grow up together. I guess things never work out the way we expect them."

Fate had smiled on Marcelo, and he'd risen to the unexpected challenge, only for fate to turn on him as fast. Life was fickle. She couldn't quite read him. Was his psyche fractured, broken like an umbrella after a strong wind? But unlike umbrellas, humans mended.

Emily completed her sidework and looked over her section. It was ready to go. Angie and Roger inserted the Tonight's Specials flyer into menus at a booth. They worked in an unusual silence, with Angie in the mix. In the service area Emily ran into Curtis. Each grabbed a bundle of napkins to fold. They took a table next to Angie and Roger and began to crease and fold, crease and fold. Folding napkins always needed to be done when nothing needed to be done.

"Roger told me he leaves in December after he graduates," Angie said.

"You're so close to graduation," Emily said. "That's fab."

"Cool City, man," Roger said. "You and Marcelo aren't the only ones flying the coop."

Angie told them she wasn't flying anywhere. She'd be there, at the Vineyard, anytime anyone wanted to visit. Angie's biggest regret was losing the people she'd gotten to know. For once, Emily identified with her. Emily anticipated the emptiness leaving would bring.

"I'm staying put," Curtis said. "Now I feel guilty for taking Marcelo's job."

"Don't worry," Carlos said. "He wanted you to take his place."

"You've earned it," Emily said. Others echoed the sentiment.

"I'm just a small-town cowboy trying to stay on the saddle," Curtis said.

They returned to their stations, ready for the dinner rush. Behind the register, Jackie supplied the fishbowl on the counter with after-dinner mints. Connie began writing Tonight's Special's on the board. Marcelo made his last solitary trip to the foyer and opened the doors for the early bird flock perched outside.

XLV

Marcelo

Connie drew heart-shaped leaves on a vine around the border of the Tonight's Specials board; green chalk dust covered her fingers. Marcelo had his coat on and his tie loosely knotted around his neck. Curtis walked up and ran a pick through his 'fro.

"Don't be doing that up here." Jackie stared Curtis down.

"How stupid of me, Your Highness." Curtis turned to Marcelo. "Thanks for hooking me up with this gig, man. I'm sorry the way things turned out."

Connie tore her eyes away from the board. "It's my fault. I brought both of you into this."

"Neither one of you had anything to do with what happened," Marcelo said. "I was leaving anyway."

"That still doesn't make me feel better." Connie went back to her work.

Marcelo went into the lounge, where Sherry was washing glasses behind the bar. Sergio entertained a handful of boastful drinkers in suits at the bar. Marcelo greeted Sherry and straightened his tie.

"Is everyone on the floor ready?" Sergio asked.

"Roger got stuck in traffic after class," Marcelo said. "But he made it in."

Sergio pulled Marcelo to the side. "What happened that day doesn't erase all you've done here, OK? Let's get to work."

Marcelo followed him to the lobby, where Carmine leaned on the counter at the register. The smell of Hai Karate cologne hung in the air. Jackie handed Carmine a pack of Dentyne gum.

"Check this out." Carmine showed Sergio and Marcelo a dollar bill before he paid. "Should I call this number?"

The bill had a drawn heart and a telephone number written in red ink across George Washington's face. It was the same bill Marcelo had gotten the night of the robbery and had shown Sergio. The one he bought a pack of gum with—the one that only the thief could have. Sergio glanced at Marcelo, then turned and left. Marcelo followed him to the office.

"My brother's a thief," Sergio said. "Carmine knew the insurance would cover the theft. Jackie had to be in it, too. She left the deposit on the counter on purpose."

"That's why Carmine didn't lock the door." Marcelo rubbed his chin. "And Jackie was the only one who saw Barry earlier that night. How convenient was that?"

Sergio massaged the back of his neck and picked up the telephone.

"Have Carmine come to the office," he said.

Tyrone cleaned the grill with a wire brush while Marcelo wiped the eighty-six board.

"You got any news from Barry?" Tyrone asked.

"No. I'm afraid something happened to him."

"This place is a soap opera." Tyrone sat the brush down and wiped his hands. "I don't know if I'm writing a Greek tragedy or *Animal House*."

"I'm sure you'll figure that out. And be kind to my character when you write."

"I hope I can hold on to my failing sanity long enough to finish this book."

Loud yelling from the office grabbed Marcelo and Tyrone's attention. The brothers were getting into it hot and heavy. Then Carmine stormed out of the office and slammed the door. On his way out, he punched out the time clock and pushed his way through the double back doors, like an outlaw in a western saloon. Glass shards from the clock's face littered the red tile. Sergio came out of the office and looked at the mess.

"What did this freaking clock ever do to anybody?" he asked.

Marcelo and Tyrone found out that Sergio had fired Carmine, even though his brother had denied the theft. And when Sergio asked Carmine how he could get in touch with the attorney regarding the lawsuit, he couldn't give him a straight answer and said he didn't know the lawyer's name.

"I bet nobody called," Marcelo told Sergio. "Jackie must've told Carmine about the butt whipping. That's how he knew."

"I guess Carmine had it in for you," Sergio told Marcelo. "And he wanted to ruin your reputation here."

Carmine was a man enamored with the idea of revenge.

"This is insane," Tyrone said. "*One Flew Over the Cuckoo's Nest* stuff."

Marcelo agreed to stay on as he'd planned, until he was ready to leave. That would give him the chance to get Curtis situated in his new position.

"Check this out," Sergio said. "I bet Connie's ex won't be watching any *Planet of the Apes* movie marathons anytime soon." The three of them broke out in heavy laughter.

Marcelo let out a big sigh of relief. He would leave as he'd always intended, on his own terms. His battery had been recharged and he was ready for the few laps left. He went looking for Curtis to tell him the news and found him talking to Roger in the service area.

"How long did you live in New York City?" Roger asked.

"A couple of months," Curtis said. "I was in an off-Broadway production near Times Square." Curtis always cheered up when he spoke of his acting days.

"When I was in Times Square," Roger said, "all I saw was nothing but porn shops, massage parlors, adult theatres, and prostitutes. The smut capital of America—I loved it."

"You're twisted," Curtis said. "New York is the cultural and economic capital of the planet, you pinhead. It'll come around."

"Curtis, can I talk to you?" Marcelo said.

That evening cars streamed into the Vineyard lot from the river of traffic on Thirty-Fourth Street. The live Maine lobster special had gotten the interest of passing motorists. A one-hundred-gallon tank in the lobby allowed diners to choose their lobster for dinner. Crustaceans waited in the tank with thick rubber bands of different colors keeping their claws clamped. In the dining room, customers wearing bibs cracked claws and dipped the sweet meat in melted butter before savoring its spongy texture.

"What's shaking?" Marcelo asked Tyrone in the calm kitchen.

"It's busy up front, but not so much here," Tyrone said. "All we do is drop and boil them in the lobster mix. That's about it."

"Beaucoup bucks from minimal effort," Marcelo said. "That's what it's all about."

"Marcelo, you have an important call from Tampa." Jim carried in a full bus pan.

After the day he'd had, anything else would pale in comparison.

XLVI

Barry

With his head murkier than the waters in Lake Maggiore, Barry drifted in and out in the doctor's office. The medication had slowed down his brain activity. His mind no longer bombarded him with all kinds of half-baked thoughts or ideas. Objects no longer came to life in front of his eyes. Delusions and hallucinations, Dr. Kimball called them. And he no longer ached from the fall he'd taken several days earlier, though his skin was still marked with cuts and scrapes.

"I called your friend Marcelo," Dr. Kimball said. "He'll be here within the hour."

"Thanks, Doc," Barry said. "I didn't know how he might take it."

"What do you mean? He's been waiting for news from you for weeks."

The doctor took the black leather chair behind his desk. Diplomas and certificates on different frames hung on the walls behind him, many with gold seals and blue-and-red ribbons.

From what Barry was told, paramedics had brought him to the Tampa Medical Center Psychiatric Unit after he jumped from his second-floor apartment hoping to end his life. Luckily for him, gardenia bushes below his window broke his fall.

"My apartment wasn't on the fifteenth floor?" Barry asked.

"You had several hallucinations. That was one of your imaginary perceptions."

The hospital intake records indicated that Barry was out of control, acting out in a full psychotic episode the night he took the jump. The police report stated he'd started a fight over a radio that wasn't his. And when police tried to help him on the lawn after his plunge, he'd fought with them, and they had to subdue him. He'd been rambling about wrestling with Satan himself during the scuffle. Barry tried to make sense of what the doc was telling him.

"Hold on," Barry said. "It wasn't my radio?"

"Nobody heard you play a radio the whole time you were at the Georgian, based on the police report. And the desk clerk didn't see you with one when you checked in."

"I had it. I played it. I heard it," Barry said.

"They might have been hallucinations, too."

"And I didn't run over that chick?" Barry asked.

Barry remembered the traffic news had come on the radio that night after he left the Bull Pen. And when he'd taken his eyes off the road to search in his glove compartment for a number to calm his nerves—THUMP! He'd hit her.

"Maybe you heard about the accident on the radio and the similarity of the suspect's car to yours and imagined hitting the girl."

"I thought I hit a dog." Barry wrung his hands. "But when my face turned into hers in the mirror, I thought I'd done it."

"Maybe you hit a dog or imagined the whole episode. But there was only one hit-and-run that night, and the guilty driver turned himself in days ago. It's been all over the news."

"Then why was that cop looking over my car at the salvage yard after I sold it? That cop was looking for me."

The doctor leaned forward on his desk. "The cop at the salvage yard could've been real. Cops stop in at yards in case they find a car they're looking for."

"What about the cops that chased and shot at me and the old coot that was going to turn me in?"

"To my knowledge there are no reports of any chase and shots fired when and where you said it happened. And no one turned you in for anything." Dr. Kimball leaned back. "We looked into it to put the pieces together. Except for the CIA bit, we didn't think it was necessary. Delusions and hallucinations are symptoms of schizophrenia."

"What about what I heard?" Barry asked. "Like when one of the bosses at the Vineyard said, 'This jerk's got to go'?"

"It could have been an auditory hallucination. That's when you hear noises, sounds, or voices that aren't there. When you heard him say that, did anyone else hear him?"

"No, I just happened to overhear him, and he tried to act innocent."

"You were fragile then, feeling pretty lousy about yourself. Maybe nothing was said."

He'd been fragile as a child's sand castle for a very long time.

"That ponytailed cook never called me freak?"

"Did you feel like a freak? Think about it."

He remembered he'd walked into the kitchen after riding his bike to work, angry about having his radio stolen and not too happy about living at the Georgian with losers. That place was a circus and the tenants a bunch of clowns and animals, but he was no better.

"Fry-boy probably didn't say anything," Barry said. "I was looking at his back when I heard him, the poor bastard."

"Empathy is good," Dr. Kimball said. "You'll get better by following treatment."

It was beginning to make sense in an insane kind of way. He'd heard water running, his name being called, and even taps on the shoulder, but no one was there and none of it had been real, especially Roger's head catching on fire.

Barry had started on psychotropic medication after he arrived. His body was still adjusting to them. He'd have to take medicine for a long time. Maybe forever.

"Why don't you wait in the day area until Marcelo gets here?"

He'd been told he needed rehabilitation, psychotherapy, and psychotropic medication. Pills he could take, but he'd need heavy machinery to unearth his feelings. Was he sturdy enough to sustain the pressure that life would soon throw upon him? Dr. Kimball had told him that with time, Barry could design a world custom made for him, one that would fit him comfortably.

He strolled into the main living area of the locked adult unit. Patients watched a western movie on the tube while others read newspapers or magazines. Behind the TV area, two speedy patients played a competitive game of ping pong. A lady with messy hair completed her call and hung up the patients' pay phone when he walked by.

With clearer vision, reality was inescapable. The world was starting to reveal itself, and he didn't like it. Fantasy had been a lifesaver in troubled seas. Man, Eve and that chick at the Bull Pen probably hadn't been interested in him, and he'd imagined the whole thing. Meeting chicks was the farthest thing from his mind at that moment. How could he have found harmony with a chick when he was seriously out of tune?

His heart sank. Would Marcelo be happy to see him? What did Barry have to offer? Not much, but he was no longer caged in, locked up behind bars he couldn't see. Maybe Yogi Berra was right.

"It ain't over till it's over."

XLVII

Emily punched in and crossed the quiet kitchen heading up front. Tyrone stocked his refrigerator with filet mignons. Harry stacked a rack of clean coffee cups in the service area. Jim poured buckets of ice into the salad bar. The red-and-black carpet of the dining room muffled her steps before she stepped on the tiled lobby. Why was Monica working the register?

"You look like you've seen a snowman in Florida," Monica said. "Jackie got canned for being in cahoots with Carmine, and I'm filling in tonight. Everyone's happy she's gone, but nobody wanted to work the register."

"Everybody wanted a parade but no one wanted to sweep the street." Emily giggled. "But I heard Carmine never admitted it, and that Jackie denied being involved."

"Jackie wouldn't rat on Carmine and stuck to her guns. Until this afternoon when Angie told her how Carmine had gotten the scratches on his face. The ones he'd lied to her about. That's all it took, and she puked her guts out to Sergio: Carmine told her to leave the money on the counter."

"Looks like there's trouble in paradise," Emily said, and they laughed.

Could Emily rejoice in someone else's demise? Of course she could. They'd hung themselves. Carmine's presence in the restaurant had been nothing more than a patchwork of deception. He was fortunate Sergio hadn't turned him in to the police.

"Carmine wasn't an owner, just an employee," Monica said. "Like the rest of us."

Emily was going to miss the dramatic comedy that was the Vineyard. She picked up her checks, initialed the sheet on the counter, and went to check her station. Next to her, Angie was straightening her chairs. She congratulated Angie on getting Jackie to turn on Carmine. It was the least Angie could do to pay back Carmine for the disgusting office episode.

"I almost forgot," Emily said. "How did your job interview with Eastern go?"

"It was all of five minutes," Angie said. "The bastard said I wasn't what they were looking for. You imagine that?"

"That's a real bummer," Emily said. "The guy made a mistake. Maybe Pan Am will—"

Angie interrupted her with a rude wave of dismissal. "He was the sorry one when I told him to shove the application where the moon don't shine."

Angie always docked with a boatload of pleasantries. She dropped the subject and wiped the chairs and wine lists in her section, and then poured herself a Coke at the service bar. Sherry was refilling drinking straws and cocktail napkins.

"I hope your grandmother's better," Sherry said.

"We're doing well, thanks." Emily twirled the ice in her glass with the straw. "My mother hates me, though."

"Now, I know you're exaggerating," Sherry said. "She doesn't *hate* you."

"Well, I did call and apologize for throwing her out of Grandma's house."

"You did *what?*" Sherry asked. "That may take a while to smooth over."

Emily strolled into the kitchen, which hummed with preparations. Carlos placed ice on the endive and sliced lemons at the pickup line. Tyrone continued to stock his refrigerator, this time with freshly cut New York strips. Harry mopped the floor around them.

"You heard the news?" Carlos smiled. "Marcelo is on his way to see Barry."

"When did he find out?" Emily asked. "I'm super glad."

"Me, too," Carlos said. "We found out an hour ago. Marcelo didn't tell me where he was going. Don't say anything to anyone until he knows what's going on."

Marcelo followed the directions to the adult psychiatric unit at the hospital. When the heavy metal door buzzed open, he stepped in. An attendant led him down the long corridor to the patients' activity room. It was a colossal room with three long couches angled around a large projection TV and two ping pong tables behind the sofas. Shelves of books lined one wall. Marcelo noticed Barry flipping through a magazine. He was a shadow of his former self. Thinner but rested as if he'd awoken from a period of hibernation. Barry noticed him.

"I'm glad you came." Barry stuck his hands in his pockets.

"Why wouldn't I? Don't disappear like that again."

They shook hands and then pulled each other for a hug. Barry choked up. Marcelo's legs got rubbery. They took a seat.

Barry told him he'd believed he'd killed that girl and panicked. He'd felt his life was a train wreck, and that he wasn't worth the oxygen he breathed. But in the last few days he'd realized he could start over, at any moment, and rebuild his life.

"We looked but couldn't find you," Marcelo said. "We didn't know you were sick."

"I didn't either, but I'm glad I know."

Barry had been searching for answers to questions he didn't even know.

Schizophrenia, the doctor had called it earlier when he spoke with Marcelo on the phone. He'd said Barry had a mild case and that diseases varied in degree of severity. Marcelo had only heard of schizophrenia and knew less about it. Dr. Kimball had told him that Barry had experienced his first psychotic breakdown, though symptoms had been there all along. Marcelo hadn't known that Barry's forgetfulness, lack of direction, paranoia, and hypersensitivity were possibly related to the illness.

"Tell me," Barry said. "What's going on with you and Carlos?"

Marcelo told him about work and about how well they were getting along as roommates. He didn't say anything about his leaving in days. It wasn't the right time.

"Tell me about you," Marcelo said. "I get bored talking about myself."

"I'm trying to figure out where to plant my next footstep. The doctor wants to meet you. He can explain what's been going on."

They waited outside the doctor's office until a patient finished his session.

"As his condition worsened," Dr. Kimball said, "thoughts and perceptions became distorted and led to delusions and hallucinations. Barry's improved considerably in a short time."

Dr. Kimball explained that Barry would need psychiatric care regularly. But all was not as bad as it sounded. If he followed medical treatment, he would continue to improve.

"I'm popping more pills than Elvis did," Barry said.

It had to be that way for him to have a normal life, or one as close to normal as possible. The long-range goal was for Barry to go back to work and support himself as before.

"When can I wait on tables?" Barry asked. "That's what I do."

He couldn't work in what he knew best because he couldn't work with the public yet, Doc said. That was stressful, and he didn't need that when he first went back. The first step was to find a group home in St. Pete where he could live and work before he got a place of his own. But Barry needed cash. He didn't have toothpaste or shampoo.

"You say I'm getting better," Barry said, "but I have more headaches than before."

"Can your mother help?" Dr. Kimball asked. "How about other family?"

"I'm the only other family he has," Marcelo said. "I can help out."

Marcelo and Barry left the office and took seats in the main room. Patients' rooms lined three walls, all with doors open and two twin beds. Two workers in uniforms white as Antarctic ice read magazines behind a counter and supervised the hall. Marcelo listened while Barry told him where he'd worked and where he'd lived while on his unnecessary flight.

"Do you need me to get anything from the Georgian?" Marcelo asked.

"My Italian suits and Kashmir coat," Barry said. "My stuff is gone by now. Most of my stuff is at my mom's garage. Can you ask her to bring me clothes?"

"Sure. And I'll get you toothpaste and shampoo. Anything else?"

"Five bucks for the candy and Coke machine. It's the only vice they allow here."

"Sure. Call me if you need anything else. I'll be back in a day or so."

"What you want me to do?" Barry's mother asked.

Marcelo stood on the front porch with her on the other side of the screen door. On the TV in the living room, Richard Dawson kissed contestants on the *Family Feud* game show.

"He's better off locked up like his father probably is, if you're telling the truth."

"He wants you to come see him and bring him some clothes."

"I can't go to Tampa." She kept her eyes on the tube. "Don't have bus money. They cut the phone off, now they're cutting the lights if I don't pay." She turned to him. "He got cash?"

"Yes. He told me to give you this." He gave her ten dollars. "He'll be happy to see you."

"When's he getting out?" She put the bill in her bosom. "You sure he's locked up?"

"He could get out soon. They're looking for a place for him here in town."

"Hell, he can wait then. No use wasting my good money making the trip to Tampa."

Reality hit Marcelo like a brick to the teeth.

"And don't be coming around here all the time," she said.

She returned to the couch and lit a cigarette without even asking for a telephone number to get in touch with her son. Barry didn't need anything from her: half the money Marcelo had gotten was his. In the garage, he looked through Barry's belongings and clothes. He moved Barry's transistor radio and opened a cardboard box.

Barry was grateful to Dr. Kimball and the hospital for making him feel human again. The fight was over, but the battle had just begun. It wouldn't be an easy road back to sanity: he'd never been where he was headed. Man, he was in the right place. Still, there were patients in that place who scared him, like his roommate. The bearded guy didn't say a word or move an inch. But his overgrown green toenails could make Barry's ankles bleed if he ever got in a scrape with him.

Marcelo came to visit carrying Barry's backpack.

"I better go change before this T-shirt and jeans fall off me," Barry said.

In a flash, Barry returned from his room in a clean shirt and jeans.

"What's been going on in the world since I left?" Barry asked.

He was pleased to hear that Tyrone, Roger, and the rest still worked at the Vineyard. And he was even interested in what was going on with Angie. Man, that chick had mowed down more guys than John Deere had mowed lawns, but Carmine was no better. Marcelo filled him in on his relationship with Emily, about the scholarship, and about the money he'd received in the mail.

"The business will have to wait until I finish school."

"You waited this long," Barry said. "You'll be done with JC in no time."

Marcelo lowered his eyes. Barry didn't know if he wanted to hear what came next.

"I'm leaving in a few days," Marcelo said. "I'm going to State with Emily."

What could Barry expect? He was wrong to think he could go back to his former life as it was when he left it. But going to State was the ultimate for his friend, so he put his arm around Marcelo and shook him. If anybody deserved to go, it was him.

"I made these plans before I knew what had happened to you, and—"

"I'll be in town when you get back," he said. "You'll know where to find me."

Yep, he'd be hoofing it at the newest restaurant in town, much as they'd done since high school. That was OK, because when school was the game, he was no Rhodes Scholar. But he told Marcelo it would be different this time. He was learning that the quality of his life depended on the choices he made, and that one single incident could change a life for better or for worse. It was a simple bit of information, but one that he'd never been taught or learned.

"I can go out on pass Saturday," he said. "That is, if you want to get together before you leave." He cracked his knuckles. "When's my mom coming to see me?"

"That'll work out fine. We don't leave until Sunday," Marcelo said. "We can go see your mom then if you'd like."

"I see…"

Marcelo left, and Barry lay down in bed. The dream of a restaurant with Marcelo was shattered: the only bridge to his future had collapsed on him. There was much work to be done to build another one. Earlier, he'd seen the news. The *Double Eagle II* had completed the first transatlantic helium-filled balloon flight when it landed in France after lifting off from Maine six days before. Anything was possible. But first he needed to tend to his life, plant and fertilize healthy habits. Dazed, he fell asleep and began to dream. He was in a lush garden, watering seedlings reaching toward the light….

XLVIII

Wearing a coat and tie, Curtis met Marcelo in the lounge. He was timely as a parking meter and eager to assume his new role of assistant manager. They grabbed a cup of coffee in the lounge. Sherry wiped the dust off the liquor bottles on the shelves above the bar. They reviewed the assigned server stations for that night, with steamy cups beside them.

"Has Sergio found anyone to take Carmine's place?" Curtis sipped his coffee.

"That won't happen," Marcelo said. "After I got promoted, he realized Carmine needed help because he didn't do anything."

"He not only didn't carry his weight," Curtis said, "he dragged others down with him."

"Right on. You're better off without him." Marcelo blew on his cup.

"I managed a restaurant five years back," Curtis said. "The business was smaller, but the operation was similar. Here we buy in larger quantities and have bigger bills to pay."

"That's about it," Marcelo said. "The figures here have a couple more zeroes at the end."

Sherry stopped dusting. "You'll do fine, as long as you treat everyone right."

Minutes later, Marcelo led Curtis through the lobby and opened the front door for the Friday dinner crowd. They took their places at the podium. Behind the counter, Monica put a fresh roll of receipt paper into the register. The new cashier was set to start the next day.

"This is your last shift, and then you'll be forever free," Monica said.

"I can't believe I'm leaving this place."

Most of all he couldn't believe he was leaving town. He was following his rainbow. Ever since Emily entered his life, his destiny had changed. She was his amulet. His lucky charm.

"My brother went to State," Monica said. "He had a blast going to class, living on campus and going to football games. He wouldn't trade those memories for anything."

"I catch your drift," Marcelo said.

"You deserve it," Curtis said. "Carlos is so happy for you."

Of course he was...that was all Marcelo, Barry, and Carlos had talked about when they were kids. But they never imagined things would turn out as they had, with none of them having a chance to go until now. It had been Carlos's dream to attend State, too, but he wouldn't get the chance. What was he thinking?

"Excuse me," Marcelo said. "I have to make a phone call."

He rushed to the back of the restaurant and fumbled in his pockets for the office key. How could he have been so blind? He turned the key in the lock, pushed the door open, and freaked out! Sergio and Angie lay on the desk, absorbed in erotic passion.

"I'm...I'm sorry." Marcelo stepped outside and shut the door.

Moments later, Angie came out fixing her hair. "Don't you know how the hell to knock?"

"I don't need to knock. I've got a key."

Marcelo took a deep breath and walked into the office. Sergio was buttoning his shirt in front of the wall mirror. He turned, pasted on a smile, and tucked in his shirt.

"I have to make a telephone call," Marcelo said. "It's private."

"See you up front when you get done." Sergio ran a hand over his hair, grabbed his coat, and shut the door behind him.

Marcelo found the business card in his wallet, crossed his fingers, and dialed the number. After the call, he returned to the lobby. There was more that required his attention. He found Sergio at the bar in the lounge handing bottles of rum from a case to Sherry.

"I need to leave for a couple of hours," Marcelo said. "There's something I have to do."

"But I need you here," Sergio said. "It's your last night."

"I'll come back when I'm done. Curtis can take care of business in the meantime."

Sergio pushed the case away and took a barstool. "Whatever you've got to do must be important. Go on. Thanks for all you've done. Curtis will take it from here."

Marcelo jumped in his car and pulled into traffic. What was he thinking? His biggest regret was not going to State as a freshman, and he didn't want that for his brother. He could never recapture the last three years, but he could make sure Carlos had his.

The telephone call had convinced him that it was the right thing to do, and the outcome was more than he'd imagined. He pulled into his driveway and rushed inside the house. Carlos was resting in bed with headphones on, listening to a Deep Purple LP rotating on the turntable.

"I can't go to State." Carlos put the headphones down. "You're the one with the scholarship."

"You have a scholarship, tuition, housing, and books. All paid. It's all set."

Marcelo told him Sally had agreed to give the scholarship to him when he called her. Carlos sat up. The night she offered it to Marcelo, she'd said it was his unless he knew of someone more deserving than he. Destiny had not yet been written for either one of them.

"But it was given to *you*, not me," Carlos said. "What are you going to do now?"

"Well," Marcelo said. "Rather than transfer the offer to you, she gave both of us one."

"For real?" Carlos broke into a smile of disbelief. "But I'm not registered, and—"

Marcelo sat next to him and commanded total attention. Carlos could stay with Mom and Dad, and sign up and take classes as a non-degree-seeking student this term. Then he could apply for acceptance in January and move into the dorms. "I've written down the scholarship information you'll need."

"Looks like you've done your homework." Carlos's spirits flew into soaring winds. "We'll both be at State like we always wanted."

"I'm not going yet. I'm staying put."

"Why? Curtis has your job," Carlos said. "It has to do with Barry."

He couldn't leave a fallen brother behind. That he could never live with. He'd find a job as he'd done a hundred times before. Somehow, he didn't think that would be a problem.

"But what about Emily?" Carlos asked. "I'll stay behind for Barry instead."

There was nothing to discuss. Marcelo had made up his mind. He went to his closet and brought back the gray-and-gold Dolphins football jersey he'd bought to wear at games.

"This is yours." Marcelo tossed him the jersey.

Carlos stroked the gold letters on the jersey. His eyes widened, and he looked up. "I'm leaving tomorrow. I'm not waiting until Sunday."

Marcelo jumped in his car and drove to Emily's home. He didn't know what she'd do or say when he told her of his decision. He hoped she'd understand. She was a treasure he'd stumbled upon when he wasn't looking, and he wasn't about to let her go. He pulled into her driveway, shut off the engine, and took a deep breath.

Emily sensed her face blush when she saw Marcelo pull into her driveway and get out of his car. She stepped down from the porch and threw her arms around him. Apprehension seized her when she noticed the look on his face. She hoped all was well with Barry. No! She was floored when he told her he'd decided to stay. Her prince had turned into a toad.

"After the plans we made?" Her voice trembled, and she stepped back.

"Forgive me." His sincerity was evident for her to see. "I can't go. Barry doesn't have anybody. That's why I have to stay for now."

She sat down at the porch steps. "You mean you *want* to stay." She buried her face in her arms. "I should've known you'd never leave."

"I don't want to stay, but I have to." He knelt beside her. "He'd do the same for me."

He explained he couldn't abandon Barry, not when he needed him most. He couldn't dispose of a lifelong friend like a used-up razor blade.

"But I love you." There. She'd said it, and at the worst possible time. That left her heart open, raw and vulnerable.

"I love you, too." He held her hands. "Our plans don't have to change. I'll move down there in a few months. We can see each other on weekends and holidays until then. When I go to see my parents, and when you come to see your grandma. We can make it work."

She had never intended to start anything that summer that she'd regret. It was a whirlwind romance that had spun out of control. The sparks she'd felt had ignited into flames.

"But you work weekends and holidays," Emily said. "When will I see you? And what are you going to do here? You gave up your job."

"I'll find work," Marcelo said. "And I can go to JC full-time. It's paid for."

"Can you go back to the Vineyard?"

"I might want to start fresh someplace else," he said. "School starts in a few days. I'll worry about work later."

"It won't work." She sobbed and got up, and so did he. "I don't see how, Marcelo."

He told her they could make it work if they wanted to make it work. He'd move there next summer to continue with school after he graduated from JC.

"That's almost a year from now." She shook her head. "I need time to let this sink in." She walked up the steps and then turned. "You can't change the rules in the middle of the game. That's not right."

He grabbed her hand and pulled her to him. Her eyes had reddened. "I'm sorry, but my place is here, for now." He kissed her, and she buried her head in his chest and cried. "I'm not going to let you go." He sighed. "I'm going to make sure we work out. I'll be down there for good next June after school ends."

"It's a long time from now." She looked into his eyes. "I…I might as well leave for school. I'm just about packed, and there's no reason to wait until Sunday. I'll call you before I leave." She rushed up the stairs and into the house.

Marcelo held back the tears as he drove away but choked up. It wasn't his intention to hurt anyone, most of all Emily. One thing he was certain about was that he loved her and wouldn't let her go, not as long as she wanted to be with him. He'd go to south Florida on a regular basis to visit her, to visit his family. He hoped their love was true and rock solid and that it would sustain the test of the next few months.

The next morning Marcelo helped Carlos pack and load his car before sitting down for breakfast. It could be the last meal they'd have together in that house, in St. Pete. When he sent Carlos off to Miami, he couldn't remember when he'd seen his brother as happy. Marcelo was torn with extremes of emotions. He hoped that in time, fate would be kind.

Marcelo put the top down on the Mustang that afternoon, hoping the wind would lift his spirits. In minutes, he was rumbling across Howard Frankland Bridge on the way to Tampa. The emerald-green waters of the bay sparkled under a late summer sun. Marcelo sighed and looked into the distance—the road was clear and there wasn't a cloud in the sky.

The End